T0199100

Make Your Move

Laura Heffernan is the author of:

The Reality Star Series

America's Next Reality Star
Sweet Reality
Reality Wedding

The Oceanic Dreams Series

Time of My Life

The Gamer Girls Series

She's Got Game
Against the Rules
Make Your Move

Make Your Move

Laura Heffernan

LYRICAL PRESS
Kensington Publishing Corp.
www.kensingtonbooks.com

LYRICAL PRESS BOOKS are published by

Kensington Publishing Corp.
119 West 40th Street
New York, NY 10018

All Kensington titles, imprints, and distributed lines are available at special quantity discounts for bulk purchases for sales promotion, premiums, fund-raising, educational, or institutional use.

Special book excerpts or customized printings can also be created to fit specific needs. For details, write or phone the office of the Kensington Sales Manager: Kensington Publishing Corp., 119 West 40th Street, New York, NY 10018. Attn. Sales Department. Phone: 1-800-221-2647.

Lyrical Press and Lyrical Press logo Reg. U.S. Pat. & TM Off.

First Electronic Edition: December 2019
ISBN-13: 978-1-5161- 0850-3 (ebook)
ISBN-10: 1-5161-0850-7 (ebook)

First Print Edition: December 2019
ISBN-13: 978-1-5161-0853-4
ISBN-10: 1-5161-0853-1

Printed in the United States of America

To Michelle and John
Someone needs to hurry up and invent teleporters,
because we don't see each other nearly often enough.

And to Hilary K.
I still won't play Instructures *without you.*

Chapter 1

"It costs nothing to be kind to someone in need." —Nana

Boston was a hotbed for crime lords and tax evaders. According to my mother, at least. She went on and on, driving my near-frantic pace as I walked toward Game On!, the local game store where my friends and I played after hours. Finally, the store appeared ahead of me like a beacon, a sign that this conversation, too, would pass.

While opening the door, I shoved my phone between my ear and shoulder, careful not to put the speaker too close. Hearing the words coming from the other end would do absolutely nothing to improve my mood. "Yes, Mom, I parked as close to the store as possible. Boston is perfectly safe. It won't even be dark by the time I head home. Would you prefer I took the T?… Well, moving back to Florida is not an option… I'll have one of the guys walk me to my car later."

I would do no such thing, but being my mother, she grasped at the straw unwittingly dangled before her. "Boys? What boys will be there? Tell me more."

"It's not a high school party, Mom." A deep breath masked my heavy sigh. "It's Gwen's husband and Holly's fiancé. You've heard me mention them a million times."

"What a shame."

"Actually, it's great. I'm happy for them." It wasn't worth telling her that our group did also include a single male. No reason to get her hopes up.

Holly smiled and waved at me in greeting. Not for the first time, I marveled at how her belly swallowed her average-sized frame. The pregnancy also made her thick honey blonde hair even more lustrous and shiny. Throw in her dancing hazel eyes and massive smile, and pregnancy truly made my friend glow.

In response to her wave, I rolled my eyes and pointed to the phone. She came over and took the cookies out of my hand, which let me shift everything into a better position.

"Shannon, we really need to talk about your love life," Mom said in my ear.

No, we didn't. My last boyfriend was a couple of years ago. I'd repeatedly explained why I didn't date much. Sometimes I wished I hadn't bothered. She still seemed to think I chose a life of solitude rather than it being difficult to get to know someone in this age of swiping right and immediate gratification.

When I didn't reply, she sighed. "I just want you to be happy."

"I am happy."

"Why can't you settle down like your brother?"

"Sorry, Mom, I'm about to go through a tunnel. Gotta go!" Before she could say anything else, I hung up and shut off my phone.

"Tunnels in the store, huh?" Nathan asked as I walked into the back room where we played board games after the store closed for the night. Holly's fiancé looked every bit as excited about the baby as she did, with the same eager gleam in his blue eyes. Their happiness radiated out of them, making it impossible not to share their joy.

"A convenient tunnel is an excellent way to get off the phone," I said. "That woman would spend all night lecturing me on the importance of finding a nice man if I let her."

"She's your mother. She means well," he said gently. At forty-three, Nathan was the oldest of our group and also Gwen's father. "We want the best for our children, even when we don't understand what it is."

"I know. I get it. And I appreciate her interest." I flashed a sympathetic smile toward my friend, who sat in the corner already munching on a cookie. "But I wish we could strike the right balance between not caring at all and being obnoxious."

"It exists," Gwen said with a nod toward her dad. "Trust me."

"Well, we're unfortunately not going to become BFFs, either."

"She still bugging you to have babies?" Holly asked.

"That's the end game, I'm sure. For now, she's settled on insisting I find someone and—air quote—settle down. Sometimes, when I think of how much money my parents dropped on Chris's wedding, I want to tell her I'm getting married and take the cash. Thirty grand would certainly fund a lot of game-making." During the day, I worked for a small local toy and game manufacturer, focusing on board games for children. At night, I made games for adults. The intent was to someday branch out on my own, which required start-up capital.

"She might want to attend the wedding," Cody pointed out.

"No problem. I'm sure someone would meet me at City Hall for a percentage. I'd probably only have to pay a few thousand dollars."

"As someone recently accused of fraud," Holly said, "I'm going to recommend against that course of action. Let's start the game before this baby's born."

She wasn't due for a couple of months, but point taken. I stopped complaining.

Gwen said, "Thanks for the cookies. Did you bring your new game?"

A guilty twinge hit me, not because I hadn't brought the game, but because at the moment, there *was* no new game. I should be at home, figuring stuff out, instead of here playing. "Um, well, I sort of hit a wall."

The bell over the front door jingled, and the final member of our group appeared in the doorway, carrying a bottle of whiskey. Tyler had close-cropped dark hair, a friendly smile with perfectly straight teeth, and such smooth brown skin Gwen said he belonged in a skin care commercial. "What did I miss?"

"Shannon was about to tell us about her new game," Nathan said.

My intent had been to create a social deduction game, which technically wasn't a board game because it lacked a physical board. Social deduction meant most of the players shared a specific goal, such as finding a werewolf. They used visual cues and other clues to determine which of their friends secretly worked against them. One of the more popular varieties was a murder mystery dinner party game. Personally, I preferred purely cooperative games, but lots of people liked the thrill of outsmarting their friends and family. People like Gwen and Cody, but also a ton of others. The key to success in social deduction games was largely in its theme: We'd played versions where we worked to find cannibals, Nazis, traitors, evil cultists, werewolves, and more.

"I'm afraid there's not much to tell. It's going nowhere."

"Uh-oh," Tyler said. "What happened?"

"I found another game with the exact same theme," I said. "Same name and everything. I don't want to be accused of copying."

Holly made a face. "That sucks. What is it?"

Quickly, I gave an overview. My game was set in the 1920s, inside a speakeasy. Players/mob members sought to determine which of their friends was secretly an undercover police officer, working to unmask that person before they turned everyone in for illegally drinking. Larger groups could assign additional secret roles such as the mob leader and the hit man. Each secret role had their own goals, which could affect the other players' strategies, whether they knew it or not. As the game developed, I found myself adding some surprisingly subversive elements.

Surprising because normally I didn't go for lying and being sneaky, but in this game those elements added depth lacking in some of the other, similar games we played. Overall, I'd been proud of what I'd accomplished before discovering the need to shelve the project indefinitely.

"Hold on," Tyler said. "Has anyone here heard of that game?"

Everyone shook their heads.

"Do they sell it here so we can look at it?"

"No," I said.

"Then maybe it doesn't matter," Gwen said. "Sounds like the other game isn't terribly popular. Or maybe you could design a better version."

"It's only got a handful of reviews on BoardGameNerd.com," I admitted. "And I thought of it on my own. I just hate the idea that someone might see it and think I took their game."

"Not to be that guy, but it's not *that* original," Cody said. "There are dozens of social deduction games."

"Yeah. The twist with this one—which I really like—is that the players working together are the 'bad' guys, and they're trying to unmask the 'good' guys to win. Most social deduction games are the other way around."

"It sounds like fun," Tyler said. "See what you can do to make your game stand out. I'm happy to help, if you want to brainstorm or play-test. Or, um… even if you want some artwork for the prototype."

I cocked my head at him. "You draw?"

He looked away, grinning sheepishly. "A little. I took a graphics design course in college. It wouldn't be great, but it might help you put some life in the concept."

"He's just being modest," Cody said. "He's really talented. Won a bunch of contests."

"Wow. That would be awesome, thanks," I said. My phone beeped, drawing my attention to a text from someone responding to my Craigslist ad listing my spare room. Since they opened with "I'm 420-friendly," I deleted the message. I tended to be pretty live-and-let-live, but not when sharing an entry hall with my grandmother.

Seeing the look on my face, Gwen asked, "How goes the roommate search?"

"Boy, do I need a drink before answering that question."

"That good?" Cody reached for a cookie, pushing a lock of curly brown hair out of his eyes. It always cracked me up that Gwen, whose pale skin and red hair got many Anne of Green Gables comments over the years, wound up with a guy who resembled the original Gilbert Blythe.

"Umm... No." I nodded at the bottle in Tyler's hand. "Thank goodness someone brought something other than wine and beer."

"Your other friends are all lightweights." He poured me a shot.

Accepting the glass, I sniffed it. Smoky, dark. A sipping whiskey. Gratefully, I tasted it, letting the warm alcohol roll over my tongue. A purr escaped me. "Thanks. I needed that."

"You're welcome. So, what's the problem with the roommate search?"

"Well, apparently everyone in Boston who needs a place to live is awful," I said. "One guy actually asked me if he had to wear clothes in the common areas."

Gwen laughed, and Holly shuddered.

"You know, Shannon," Cody said. "Tyler might have a solution for you."

"Oh, yeah? Do you know someone who's looking?"

"I do." Tyler hesitated for a second, glancing away before meeting my gaze squarely. "Me."

Huh. That gave me pause. I liked Tyler, always had. But he'd had a crush on me for quite a while, and living together could create an awkward situation. It didn't help that he'd kissed me last winter, while we were all in Mexico for Gwen and Cody's wedding. I'd had to explain that I didn't feel sexual attraction for people before I formed a deeper connection with them. He claimed to understand, but something in his expression when I caught him looking at me from time to time made me suspect that, even though he respected my rejection, he'd change the situation if possible. The whole thing left me feeling terrible, even though it wasn't my fault.

Speaking of awkward, this wasn't a conversation to have in front of our friends, even though they knew our history. "I'd love to talk about it, but I'm starving. Come with me to the kitchen?"

He must have sensed my hesitation. When we got to the other room, he said, "I know what you're thinking. I'm over you."

I wanted to believe him, but his request made no sense. "You've never even been to my apartment. You live in Harvard Square. I'm way out on the blue line. Why would you want to move so far away from everything?"

"Well, obviously, I need to see the inside before signing a lease," he said. "But my company opened a new office in Revere, and they put me in charge."

"That's great! Congratulations!"

"Thanks. It's a huge opportunity. But commuting on the T is a pain now, and I don't want to deal with Cambridge traffic in the mornings."

"You make good money. Why don't you get your own place?" A bit nosy to be sure, but sometimes curiosity made us ask rude questions.

"That's the plan. But you know how ridiculous Boston housing is, especially when I work such long hours. Why pay fifteen hundred dollars a month to rent five hundred square feet I'm only sleeping in?"

He had me there. I lived on the top floor of my nana's two-family unit. In exchange for doing her grocery shopping and running other errands—which I'd have done anyway—she gave me low rent on a three-bedroom apartment I could otherwise never afford. Even with a roommate.

"Yeah, I get it." The kindest thing would be to tell him no, but we would be sitting in a room together for the next three or four hours, and I didn't have the heart to shut him down. Again. A possible out occurred to me. "I've got a couple of people lined up to see the place already. I'll text you later this week?"

"Sounds good. Thanks."

"Sure."

What I didn't tell him was that I absolutely, positively had no intention of letting a guy who used to have a crush on me anywhere near my spare room. Not when his actions sometimes suggested that it lingered. Tyler was a nice guy, and I wished him well, but we couldn't live in the same apartment.

* * * *

The next evening after a long day at work, I couldn't wait to get home, make a pot of the tea normally saved for special occasions, and unwind in the bath with a good book before working on my latest project. Unfortunately, I had an appointment to show my apartment.

In college, like everyone else, I got assigned to a dorm room with three random strangers. I'm easygoing and try to be considerate, but not all my roommates were the same. We argued over things like whether all the towels needed to be hung up so the edges formed a straight line and if it was acceptable for one girl to have sex in everyone else's beds because she hadn't washed her own sheets. (For the record: no, and absolutely not!)

In grad school, I found Gwen and Holly, who turned out to be a gold mine. We'd hit it off better than I ever dreamed. When we graduated, Holly moved in with her then-fiancé Lucas, and Gwen put all her stuff in storage, ready to live the life of a travel-blogging nomad. Nana offered me the upper floor of her two-family unit, and another friend of ours moved into my spare room. Ellen was such an introvert, we didn't see each other much, which worked out well.

But now I feared I'd used up my good roommate karma over the years, even hesitating to list the place when Ellen gave her notice. There were so many roommate horror stories on the net (which Gwen and Holly helpfully sent me when I first mentioned posting on Craigslist). But I couldn't let fear stop me. I didn't need the perfect roommate, only someone reasonably respectful. Between work, my friends, and making games on the side, I led a full life. As long as my roommate wasn't incredibly loud, overly sloppy, and didn't mess with my stuff, we'd get along fine. Oh, and they couldn't want a romantic relationship with me.

The first candidate showed up fifteen minutes late. Not the best start, but traffic sucked, and the T was wicked unreliable. In Boston, if you gave up on everyone who showed up late once in a while, you'd never make any friends. Not to mention, no one could hold a job if our bosses insisted on a firm start time in a city where the trains ran late more often than not. She could have texted, but maybe she got stuck underground or something.

After my third *Are you still coming?* text, I started to reconsider that bath. Or at least curling up with a good book. I'd just settled into my chair when something scratched against the front door, so faint I might have imagined it. It sounded like a kitten had gotten into the hallway by mistake, an impossibility since the only other person who lived in the building, my Nana, was also allergic.

Upon opening the door, I found a small, dark-haired girl, utterly swallowed by the enormous beat-up old jacket she wore, staring at the mat. "Hi! You must be Kimberly. I'm Shannon."

"Hi. Was I supposed to wait downstairs at the outside door? I couldn't decide."

"I would've come down if you'd rung the bell, but it's fine. I left the main door unlocked."

She jumped, and for a second, I thought she was going to turn and run. But finally, she nodded. "Okay. Sorry I'm late. I wanted to make sure I had the address right, so I checked and then I checked again, and then I went through all your texts and emails, but I thought maybe I had the wrong street, so I walked back to the T and started over. Twice."

"It's not a problem," I said. "You could've texted, and I'd have sent it to you again."

"I worried I might have the wrong number."

I didn't know what to say. At least she was thorough? Odd that she didn't respond to our existing message thread, but I understood not thinking clearly when stressed. "Well, I'm glad you're here now. Let me show you the place."

She stepped in, too close, peering into my eyes intently. Her pupils were huge, so big I wondered if she'd been taking something. I took a step back, all the way to the wall to give her room to pass. She remained where she was, peering at me like she wanted to see my soul.

"You're very pretty," she said. "Not conventionally attractive, maybe, because you're so big, but there's something about you."

I swallowed my surprise. Not to mention my sudden desire to send this woman back out the door. Something didn't seem right. But I was almost twice her size, and my cell phone lay in a pocket of my cardigan, within easy reach. "Thank you."

"Am I pretty, too?"

Truthfully, I had no idea, but this didn't seem the time for honesty. "Yes, very pretty."

"You're just saying that to make me feel better." Yes, I was. I didn't answer, and she said, "I'm sorry. You think I'm weird."

Once again, I lied. "No, not at all. You seem lovely. Just a little nervous."

She nodded emphatically. "Definitely nervous. So anyway, tell me about this place."

I took Kimberly around the apartment, pointing out the features, showing her the kitchen, the screened-in back porch, and finally the room that would be hers. She squealed, clapping her hands together. "Awesome! Oh, this is so great! I love it! And I'd be sleeping right next to you?"

"Well, I'd be in my room." With a lock on the door, at this rate. Kimberly had been a bit reserved in our emails, and she seemed nervous when she arrived, but I was starting to wonder if something was off about her. At first, I'd thought she was dealing with anxiety, but her demeanor made me uneasy.

She nodded several times, eyes darting around the room. "I love it. Don't have any furniture, though."

"That's not a problem. There's plenty of furniture in the common areas. All you need is whatever you want for the bedroom."

"Good news. I can find a bed anywhere." Her tone suggested she was thinking about looking in dumpsters or, say, the neighbor's house. She held out one hand. "Do we have a deal?"

"Well… I have a few other people to interview first," I said, not wanting to get into a discussion about my reservations. Maybe she was the kind of person who had to meet someone a few times before relaxing. I knew all about that. "It would be rude to cancel on them at the last minute. But we can talk at the end of this week."

"Sure thing. I like you. You like me, right?"

"Absolutely." My hand inched toward the phone in my pocket.

"Hey, do you always get your mail delivered this late?"

"Late? I don't know. It's usually here when I get home from work. Why?"

"Your mailman was coming up the walk when I was debating whether to ring the doorbell."

I shrugged. "He must've been running late."

"Okay. Can I use the bathroom before I go? It's a long ride."

"No problem." I pointed her to the door, then went into the kitchen, not wanting to be creepily lurking in the hallway when she came out. I'd hear the door open. Besides, at this rate, I needed a fortifying drink before my next interview arrived.

Kimberly took an inordinately long time in the bathroom, so long I started to wonder if something was wrong. Finally, when five minutes ticked by after I'd started to worry, I tapped on the door. "Everything okay in there?"

"Rooty-tooty-absolutely!" came the immediate response.

I was still deciding what to do when a text came in from Tyler. *Hey. Have you given any more thought to the roommate thing?*

Well, you're looking way better than the woman here now, I replied. *She asked to use the bathroom before leaving, and she's been in there forever. I'm starting to worry. Am also mildly concerned that she might be on drugs. If you never hear from me again, tell police to start with Kimberly from Craigslist.*

Tyler: *Do you need me to call with an emergency so you can ask her to leave?*

Me: *That might not help, if she's stuck on my toilet.*

He replied immediately. *I can come over. Seriously. I want you to be safe.*

I'm fine, I typed. *Just concerned that she might need medical attention.*

The lock on the bathroom door cracked open, making me jump. Kimberly appeared in the doorway, face flushed. She'd slicked her hair back, and it took me a minute to realize it looked different because she'd wet it thoroughly. "Sorry about that. I feel much better now."

"No problem." I went to the front door and opened it. "It was great to meet you. I'll be in touch."

Once the door shut behind her, I checked to make sure she'd gone through the landing out the main door, then double-locked everything.

After a quick text to Tyler to let him know Kimberly had left me alive, I went to turn on the fan in the bathroom or light a candle.

At the entrance to the room, I stopped dead. Water covered the floor and counter. Not droplets, puddles. The cabinet doors stood open, with a box of feminine products hanging haphazardly out the front. Okay, that explained some things, although she could've asked me for a tampon. But when I went to put the box back, it was empty. I could've sworn it had been about half full last time I used it.

A drip called my attention to the shower. Leaning in to tighten the knob, I noticed two things: first, my razor, sitting on the edge of the tub rather than in the hook on the wall where I always left it. Second, a wet towel lay on the floor of the bathtub. I never left wet towels in the tub. My mind didn't want to accept the evidence, but it seemed obvious that Kimberly had used my shower while I waited in the kitchen to see her out. My shower, my tampons, my razor, and my towels.

With a shudder, I shut off the taps, tossed the towel in the hamper by the door, threw my razor in the trash, and put everything back in the cupboards. As I was washing my hands, something drew my attention to the cup next to the sink. The empty cup.

She'd stolen my toothbrush.

Chapter 2

"Grandparents and grandchildren get along so well because they have a common enemy." —Nana

The next morning, I got up to eat breakfast with Nana before work as usual. Nana's apartment was a no-cell-phone zone. Seriously, she put it in my lease. When I visited, the phone stayed upstairs at my place. She didn't realize that, with my "young ears," as she called them, a loud ringtone carried down to her kitchen. For important calls, I'd just turn the volume up, come visit, and excuse myself as necessary.

Today, I hoped for no important calls. Nana's apartment also served as an excellent place to unplug, which was my goal after waking up to twenty more messages about my room for rent, many of which grew increasingly disturbing. No, I didn't want to live with someone who said they'd rent from me as long as I wasn't fat. (Boy, would they have been disappointed if we'd actually met. I'm by no means svelte.) Might as well give myself some peace, grab some delicious waffles, and spend time with my favorite person in the world.

To my surprise, when I tried to open the door after knocking twice, which I did every morning, the chain lock stopped me in my tracks. Nana always unlocked her door as soon as she got up, and I'd never known the chain to be engaged. I had a key for emergencies, of course, but that didn't do me any good against a chain.

A tremor went through me as I tried not to imagine her lying passed out on the floor of the bathroom or having banged her head on the kitchen stove. She'd been sick about six months ago, sure, but she was fine now. The likelihood of her injuring herself or getting sick on the one day she happened to lock me out must be incredibly low. But still, the barrier worried me. What if she'd locked it in her sleep or something?

"Nana?" I called through the two-inch gap in the door. "Is everything okay?"

Her reply came instantly. "Yes, dear! Sorry, I didn't see the time."

What did that mean? Was she in the habit of setting the chain at night and then opening it in the morning? That seemed dangerous. Even with her improved health, relapses happened. Illnesses came back, and falls occurred. I worried about her, down here all alone. Maybe I should get a small saw, in case she needed me to take the chain off one day.

The door swung shut in my face, sending me flinching back off the cupcake-covered "Stressed is just desserts spelled backwards!" welcome mat. On the other side, a chain clinked, and then the barrier swung open. Nana stood in her entryway, her face flushed like she'd run to let me in. She wore a housecoat and slippers, unusual for her even at seven o'clock in the morning. Nana tended to wake up early, get dressed, and put on full makeup before leaving her bedroom. A trait I'd inherited from her, much to the dismay of my all-natural, cruelty-free mother.

As usual, when I entered Nana's apartment, I inhaled deeply. On an ordinary day, the scents of freshly percolating coffee mingled with the sweet smell of Nana's cinnamon vanilla waffles or chocolate chip pancakes, punctuated with a hint of maple syrup. This morning, I smelled nothing but her lilac-scented plug-in air fresheners. Maybe I'd been right to be concerned.

"Nana? Is everything okay?"

"Fine. Why?"

"Well, you're not dressed yet. There's no coffee, no waffles, nothing on the stove. And I'm actually a few minutes later than usual. Are you coming down with something?"

She laughed, a small tinkling sound that never failed to bring a smile to my face. "Don't be ridiculous, dear. Everything is fine. I overslept. It happens."

In the entire three and a half years I'd lived upstairs, Nana never overslept. I'd used her as my backup alarm more than once. "You're sure you're not sick?"

"Of course not! I'll just put on the coffee and pop into my room. As soon as I get my face on, I can whip up something for us."

"Don't worry about it. Let me make you breakfast this morning."

She smoothed back her short golden hair, the first time I'd ever seen it out of place. Not blonde, but tinted gold in that way only women over sixty can pull off. Sharp blue eyes darted toward the back of the apartment. "Are you sure?"

"How will we ever know whether I've mastered your recipes when you do all the cooking?"

She vanished into her bedroom, leaving me to fill the percolator's lower chamber with water and add coffee grounds to the top. As a child, I loved watching the liquid pop up and down in the small indicator on the top of the device, going from clear to dark brown. These days, I usually arrived after Nana was on at least her second cup, so I didn't get to watch much anymore.

Soon, the butter on the griddle sizzled, letting me know it reached the right temperature. I poured a quarter cupful of batter onto the hot surface, thinking about how Nana always used to make me funny shapes as a kid. Nana's house was a haven, especially for a girl whose mother shunned carbs and sweets. Mom wouldn't allow anything she deemed unhealthy near the house, and what she found unhealthy constantly changed with the latest fad diet. But pancakes were permanently banned, along with cupcakes, cookies, and pretty much anything else Nana made. No wonder I loved this place so much.

A thump jarred me out of these memories, followed by a grunt of pain. A *male* grunt of pain. I whirled around, spatula raised as if it might make an effective weapon against an intruder.

A short, white-haired man stood in the dining room, picking a chair up off the floor. That explained the thump. His eyes caught the look on my face as he straightened, and his face turned red. "Why, hello there."

I blinked several times, my mind unwilling to put together the picture in front of me. Nana, oversleeping for the first time in probably fifty years. A door locked against me, of all people. A grown man, sneaking out of my grandmother's bedroom. Not to mention the sheepish looks worn by both of them.

It took a moment, but finally I regained my composure. "Good morning. It's nice to meet you…?"

Before he could reply, Nana scurried out of her room, patting her hair with one hand. She still looked flustered, but far more put together than when she'd opened the door. When she saw the two of us talking, she stopped dead, and her face flushed. Out of the corner of her mouth, she said, "You were supposed to sneak out quietly while she was cooking."

"Nana! Are you trying to hide your friend from me?" I moved closer, and with a start, I realized I knew this man. Hadn't recognized him without the uniform and cap, but once I got a good look at his face, it didn't take long. "And Michael! You were going to leave without saying hello?"

At that, his flush turned an even deeper shade of red, making his white eyebrows stand out almost comically. "I didn't think you'd know me without the mail bag."

"I almost didn't." Behind me, the skillet sizzled a reminder that I'd been in the middle of something before they distracted me. A row of bubbles formed on the surface of each pancake. I flipped the globes one at a time, finding a perfect shade of golden brown on the other side. Delicious. And now I knew why my toothbrush-stealing potential roommate saw our mail carrier arriving at the apartment so late in the day. "Won't you join us for breakfast?"

"Oh, no, I can't. I'm running late already."

Nana walked him to the door, speaking quietly. I moved closer to the stove and the percolator to give them some privacy. While I waited, I put a small pot of water to boil on the back of the stove, adding the maple syrup container. An old trick to warm the syrup without cracking the glass bottle.

A moment later, Nana returned, standing sheepishly at the edge of the counter while I focused on making breakfast. "You weren't supposed to see that."

"Obviously," I said. "Why not? Are you ashamed of him? Ashamed of me?"

"Don't be ridiculous! It's just that, well, I figured you'd be grossed out by the idea of an old lady having a sex life."

"Sex is a healthy part of growing up, right? You taught me that." Sliding two pancakes onto a plate, I handed it to her while leaning over and kissing her cheek. "I've known Michael for years, just like you have. I've always liked him."

"He did mention that you chastise him for carrying heavy packages up the stairs."

"Every time. He refuses to leave them on the porch for me to do it," I said. "He's a dear. I'm delighted for you. And you're not *that* old."

My grandfather had died when I was a kid, close to twenty years ago. Nana met him back when people married young, and my parents had been college sweethearts. It hadn't been terribly long since Nana and I went on a cruise to celebrate her sixtieth birthday. She was relatively young and in good health ever since her last round of scans came back clear. Why shouldn't she have someone to spend private time with?

She poured herself a cup of coffee slowly, as if the lengthy gesture allowed her to measure her words. "I guess I figured that, since you never talk about your love life, you wouldn't want to hear about mine."

Warning bells sounded in my head. Any time someone brought up dating these days, it triggered my fight-or-flight instinct. No, I didn't date much. I was very tired of so many people giving unsolicited advice on my personal life. Why did people even care whether I was in a relationship? After all, I didn't go around telling couples to break up because I wouldn't have been happy in their shoes.

But this was Nana, and she never judged me. I took a deep breath to settle my pulse, then added another two pancakes to a plate, grabbed the now-warm maple syrup from the stove, and set both on the table. A moment later, Nana set the percolator down, and I helped myself to a steaming cup of coffee. In any other location, I preferred tea. But here, at Nana's, coffee was king. No cream or sugar required.

Carefully considering my words, I took a long sip to delay the inevitable. "Nana, I don't talk about my love life because I don't *have* a love life. I'm happy that way."

"No one is happy alone, dear."

Oh, this conversation. We hadn't had it in a while, but I knew the lines. I could recite the words in my sleep, even doing voices for Nana and Mom. If game-making didn't pan out, I could write a one-woman show and take it on the road.

"I'm not alone." I took a large bite before I continued. "I have you and my wonderful friends and a good job and a burgeoning business that needs a lot of tending. Even if I wanted to go on dates with strangers—which I very much do not—I wouldn't have the time. Anyway, I hate to eat and run, but I have to be at work early this morning."

"Uh-huh. You're avoiding the conversation. I didn't just fall off the turnip truck, you know."

After wolfing down a few more bites, I said, "I would never imply that you're anything less than brilliant. We've got an all-staff meeting first thing this morning. Sounds like a big announcement coming."

Instantly, she grew serious. "A big raise for everyone?"

"I doubt it. That's done on a case-by-case basis, not at an office-wide party."

"I figured, but it was the best news I could think of," she said. "My only other guess is layoffs."

"Let's hope not." As I rose, I stuffed the last few bites of pancake into my mouth before carrying my dishes into the kitchen.

"I'll send you positive thoughts," Nana said. "Best of luck."

Chapter 3

"People say never to discuss religion or politics. I say that's hogwash. If I meet someone with the poor sense to dislike Justin Trudeau, I want to know right away." —Nana

Although I'd spent more time than intended at Nana's after encountering Michael, I made it to work with a couple of minutes to spare. I still had no idea why this meeting in particular was mandatory, but it made me worry that Nana was right. Maybe layoffs loomed on the horizon. Mandatory meetings usually affected everyone. Losing my paycheck wasn't what I needed to be worrying about when I didn't have any rental income and I needed my savings to launch my own business.

At least Nana's early morning surprise gave me something else to think about while waiting for the meeting to start. About half of my coworkers sat inside the conference room. On my way to snag a seat, my phone chimed with a text from my "work husband."

Ryan: *Stopping at Dunkin's. You need anything?*

Me: *You're going to be late.*

Ryan: *They can't fire me. I'm the only non-white employee. For that matter, they can't fire you, either, Token Female.*

Me: *I'm not the only female. What about Megan?*

Ryan: *Boss's daughter doesn't count. Want to skip the meeting and gossip?*

I'd love to, but avoiding unpleasant work events wasn't my style. If I only attended stuff I enjoyed, I'd miss out on all the networking and half the staff meetings. Besides, if my boss wanted everyone at the meeting, he must be announcing something big. No one's job was safe. Not even the almost–Token Girl or the Asian, despite the fact that we also comprised the entire LGBT+ section of the workforce. Not that we were dumb enough to talk about our personal lives to the alpha males prowling around. Our silence and friendship led to much speculation about the two of us, but that beat letting them know the truth.

Speaking of, the worst of the pack bumped into me right when I finished texting my order back to Ryan and putting my phone away. No way it was an accident.

"Sorry, Shannon," Dennis said with zero sincerity. "I didn't see you standing there blocking the door so no one else could get to the meeting."

"Then maybe you should get your eyes checked." At nearly six feet tall, wearing my trademark high heels, I was hard to miss. Not to mention my ample curves and full lavender skirt. "The other door is open."

Still not moving, I pulled out my lipstick and reapplied it, my eyes never leaving Dennis's face. He could walk to the other entrance five feet away if he needed to get to the meeting so badly. Once upon a time, I'd have apologized and moved out of the way. After all, that was common courtesy. But Dennis used to walk all over me when I started, shoving me out of the way, brushing just a little too close. Nothing I could prove was harassment, but uncomfortable all the same. I quickly learned to stand up for myself.

A high-pitched voice invaded our standoff. "Shannon! Was that you I saw on my way out of Game On! last night?"

Ugh. Megan. She'd gotten the job by being Daddy's Little Sweetheart and not through actual creativity, qualifications, or even team spirit. She pretended to be sweet as pie, but her smile didn't meet her eyes. Ever since we met, she rubbed me the wrong way. On top of that, I didn't have a clue what she did for the company.

Warily, I said, "Yeah. It's a great store. I didn't know you were familiar with it."

"Sometimes I stop in at the local stores to see how our stock looks on our shelves," she said. Maybe she did something related to marketing? "I'm glad to see you walking so far from home. It's good to exercise whenever you can."

There it was. Not even an original insult this time. Commenting on my weight was so easy. You'd think she'd use a bit of imagination, as someone who made children's games. But again, creativity wasn't her strong suit.

I knew better than to exchange barbs with her. Instead, I took a page from her book. "Yes, I love getting out to walk. Unfortunately, since I actually work around here, I don't have much free time."

Before she could respond, I entered the conference room, hoping to snag two empty chairs for me and Ryan.

No such luck. There *were* two empty seats together when I walked through the doorway, as well as a couple of others scattered around the table. But as I stopped to survey the room and say good morning to some of the guys who worked in the toys division, Dennis swept by me, plopping into the left seat of the empty pair. Megan went to the front as usual, sitting at Daddy's right hand. Meaning I got to choose between sitting next to my least favorite person on the staff or throw the man currently buying me tea and donuts to the wolves instead.

It was an easy decision. Dennis was the worst on so many levels. He was also a total brownnoser and wouldn't talk once the meeting started. A few more minutes hanging out by the door, and I could manage him.

A moment later, Jameson entered the room to start the meeting. We were largely an informal lot. We called everyone, including the boss, by first names. Most of the guys wore jeans or shorts to work. Even Jameson showed up in khakis and polo shirts, a couple of days' worth of scruff on his artificially tanned face, his long gray hair pulled back into a low ponytail. Our main office area was a vast open space, with the game makers on one side, the toy designers on the other, and the testing area in the middle. Jameson encouraged employees to bring their own kids in on Fridays to test the products. Most of the staff was fairly young and childless, but it was fun when someone showed up to play. I'd brought in my friends' kids before, and they always had a blast.

Unlike a lot of employers, my boss had no problem with us working on our own projects on the side, as long as we didn't use company time or resources or make competing products. No issue there. The company made toys and games for little kids. My games were designed with adults in mind, although anyone over twelve could play and enjoy. The two of us had virtually no overlap in our customer base.

At the front of the room, my boss cleared his throat, and I realized I'd been spacing out while everyone waited to start the meeting. Putting my head down, I scurried to my seat, unfortunately still beside Dennis.

"Too busy mooning over some guy to pay attention?" he whispered. "Who is he?"

"Your dad," I shot back, louder than intended.

"What was that?" Jameson asked from the front of the room. "Shannon, did you have something to say?"

The floor refused to open up and swallow me. This morning was a disaster, and it wasn't even 8:15 yet. I scrambled for something to say. "I was just telling Dennis that I think fathers especially will love this new game I'm working on."

"Excellent idea! So much marketing targets mothers these days. I can't wait to hear the details after the meeting."

Saved, for now. I just needed to come up with a new project to discuss before he asked for more information. Thankfully, he launched into the past month's numbers and current quarterly projections, taking the attention off me. Unfortunately, the data looked as bad as expected. When Toys "R" Us shut down, we'd hoped to open up a couple of local retail shops to keep our stock in the public eye. But we still couldn't compete with the big companies like Melissa & Doug. We made great toys, high-quality stuff... but quality didn't come cheap. In a society where people rented out their own homes while sleeping on a friend's couch to pay their mortgage, not a ton of people wanted to pay for premium toys anymore. Everyone wanted to buy cheap garbage from Amazon. The entire company was in more trouble than I thought.

By the time Ryan swept in, plopping my order in front of me on his way to his seat, the sight of the donut turned my stomach. Shoving it aside, I sipped my tea and let the warm liquid soothe me.

"So, I know what you're all thinking," Jameson said. "What does this mean for me?"

Around the table, heads bobbed.

"I'm an old man," he continued. "I've been in this business for a long time, but I'm ready to give up Boston winters and move south to work on my golf game. After a lot of consideration, I've accepted a buyout offer from Board Game Giants, Inc."

A buyout? Buyouts could be good or bad. It could mean severance packages or a new influx of cash, new management, new life. Maybe even a new, better working culture. My entire body perked up at the possibility. It would be amazing not to dread seeing my coworkers every day. I wasn't even hoping to become friends with most of them. Simply being able to make pleasant small talk while we worked together would be huge.

"This office will remain open. Sometime in the next month or so, you'll meet their head of Human Resources. When the merger is complete, we'll be hiring an executive game designer, someone to oversee everything within this office. This is a difficult decision for me. It's hard to admit that someone else can do your job as well as you can, but I know we've got the best person for the job right here."

Best *person* to do the job.... or best man? His eyes traveled around the table, lingering on each of us. Could he actually pick me? I worked harder than anyone, had been a loyal employee for more than four years now. Two of my projects won the coveted Mensa Select seal for games that placed in the top five at their annual competition. A third was named "Recommended by American Mensa," essentially a runner-up. No one else possessed my track record.

Unlike most of the other employees, I had a master's degree. Ryan and I were often the last two to leave the office at night. A lot of others used this company as a stepping-stone, a way of paying the bills until they springboarded to a place with more prestige, more pay. Not me. I loved the location, I loved the freedom to work on my own projects... and some of the bigger companies had even more toxic cultures. Sure, we had jerks like Dennis, but Jameson kept everyone in line most of the time. I'd never told him how obnoxious things could get.

My eyes met Ryan's. He looked as excited as I felt. Maybe things were starting to look up. Then Megan let out a little cough, and my spirits sank. She sat up straight, a smug smile on her lips. It couldn't be more clear who was going to replace my boss.

At the front of the room, Jameson raised his hands to get everyone's attention. "This is a hugely important decision, and one not to be taken lightly. We'll start interviewing at the end of the week. Meanwhile, I invite everyone who is interested to submit an application, along with their best new game idea. May the best game designer win."

Megan's smile faltered, but she recovered quickly. No one else seemed to notice.

On the other hand, I felt a rush of excitement. Applying for a promotion hadn't occurred to me because Jameson seemed the sort of ageless, full-of-energy type who would never retire, and we'd never had multiple levels of game makers here. But now, his offer was a brass ring dangling in front of me. More than anything, I wanted to grab it.

* * * *

After the meeting, Jameson swung by my desk. "Hey. What are you working on?"

My mouth went dry. In this open-office environment, I couldn't admit that I'd lied. Everyone would know in about ninety seconds. Hoping to stall, I reached for my tea. Out of the corner of my eye, I spotted Dennis smirking at me from his desk. No, I'd never admit the truth.

Pretending to misunderstand, I gave an update on my existing projects, all of which had placeholder names until the marketing department finalized the covers. "Project Match is close to done. My friend's nephew will be here on Friday to test it as part of a focus group."

"Sounds good. What else?"

Megan joined Dennis at his desk. Ignoring their scrutiny, I said, "I'll spend most of next week making tweaks based on their feedback. Then I've got the art department doing some preliminary sketches for Project Poop."

Jameson chuckled, shaking his head. "Love that name."

I resisted the urge to roll my eyes. "Well, it's a game about avoiding stepping in pig manure, so it applies. I'm working on the rules while I wait. Once you approve everything, we should be able to schedule a focus group for that, too. Hopefully early next month."

"Excellent," Jameson said. "So what's the new project you mentioned in the meeting? One for dads?"

Not a clue. My non-work time had been dedicated to finding a roommate and trying to resolve the problem of my speakeasy game, which I couldn't exactly pitch as appropriate for five-year-olds. Again, my tea bought me a couple of seconds.

Megan nudged Dennis, and a wave of loathing swept over me. I would tell Jameson literally anything to avoid letting those two see me embarrassed in front of him. Not when my worst idea was ten times better than anything either of them came up with. The last game Dennis suggested was essentially Old Maid with different pictures on the cards.

Their derision lit a fire under me. I sat up, ramrod-straight, and met Jameson's eyes squarely. When I spoke, my words projected across the room, as intended. "I'm really excited about this new game, but I have to get a few more ducks in a row before I go into detail. Why don't I tell you about it when I interview for the executive game designer position?"

He blinked at me, as if surprised to hear me contradict him. For the first time, I wondered if going out of my way to generally be nice to everyone was holding me back at work. Well, no more. "That sounds great. If you can get me your résumé by the end of the week, we'll talk."

"Perfect. I can't wait."

As Jameson returned to his office, I turned and glared straight at Megan and Dennis. They both looked a little shell-shocked. Never would it have occurred to anyone that the office mouse might one day wake up and grow a backbone.

My computer beeped with an internal message, breaking our staring contest.

Ryan: *Executive game designer? You go, girl! Just remember who brings you donuts when you're a bigwig.*

Me: *Haha. As long as it doesn't go to Dennis, I'm happy. He couldn't design his way out of a paper bag.*

A second message dinged, covering the first. I clicked it open, only mildly surprised to see the source. In the two years he'd been working here, I don't think Dennis had ever sent me a message. We rarely worked on the same projects, and when we did, our communication occurred in person or via email, not the messaging system.

Dennis: *You think you can steal my job?*

Me: *It's not your job yet.*

Dennis: *It will be when I tell Jameson you're lying about your new game idea.*

A chill went down my spine. He was, of course, exactly the type to sabotage his competitors rather than beat them fairly. But I had a couple dozen game ideas in various stages of readiness sitting in a doc on my computer. Any one of them should be good enough to pacify Jameson.

Me: *Whatever. Bring it.*

Chapter 4

"Never let them see you sweat, unless you're exercising. Then sweat all over them if they get too close." —Nana

During my lunch break, I found five more emails replying to my Craigslist ad. The first insisted on bringing her imported pet monkey, which I was pretty sure wasn't legal. Also, my ad clearly stated no pets because of my allergies. The second person used seven sexual innuendos in a one-paragraph email. Two scam artists wanted to send me a cashier's check for a thousand dollars over the security deposit, so I could cash it and wire them the difference. Something about my ad apparently labeled me a sucker. The first person got a polite reply; the other messages went straight to the trash.

I was about to give up when I read a message that sounded promising. A local female, twenty-five years old, no smoking, drugs, or pets. She had a good job, seemed nice enough, and didn't make any requests that scared me. Immediately, I replied to ask if she was free to view the place after work.

My roommate prospects seemed to be dwindling, so I crossed my fingers for a good match. I appreciated Tyler's offer, but preferred not to live with a cishet man. Ryan would be my ideal roommate, truthfully, if he didn't live with his extremely allergenic beagle, Zoe.

Speaking of Tyler, I found an email from him after I sent my reply about the apartment. I hesitated for a moment at seeing his name before moving to the subject line and realizing this message had nothing to do with the apartment.

Hey,

I've been thinking about the game you mentioned. I know you're trying to come up with another idea, but I wanted to give you an idea of the type of artwork I can do. Let me know what you think. I'm here if you want to brainstorm.

T

How thoughtful. Especially after I'd done my best to blow him off about the apartment. A lot of people would have changed their minds about helping me. Then I opened the attachment, curious to see the types of drawings he'd worked on in the past.

When the file loaded, I gasped, one hand covering my mouth to stifle the sound in our small office. Megan glanced up, but I ignored her.

This wasn't a picture of some old project he'd forwarded, like I'd expected. This was a drawing of a girl, clearly created after our conversation the other night. Tall, curvy, my naturally brown hair, with glasses, Tyler had drawn me as a flapper. I loved everything about it. It was so perfect, I saved it to my phone as my new wallpaper before responding to let Tyler know how much I adored it. Even if I couldn't find a way to use it in a new game, the gesture meant a lot.

Between anticipating my upcoming roommate appointment and squeeing over the picture of Flapper Shannon, the rest of my day flew by.

When I got home that night, I responded to a knock on the outer door to find a short blond girl about my age standing on the other side. She smiled broadly, revealing a small gap between her front teeth. It gave her character. "Hi, I'm Lana!"

"Nice to meet you," I said. "I'm Shannon."

"I. Love. Your. Dress. It's totes adorbs. Did you get it from Anthropologie?"

"Thanks. No, it's from my nana. She gave me a lot of vintage stuff she doesn't wear anymore."

She wrinkled her nose. "So, you're wearing an old dress?"

"Um, yeah." I wondered why it mattered. "Anyway, come on in, and I'll show you around."

We entered the shared hallway, and I gestured toward the stairs leading downward. "My nana lives there. She owns the building. I'm upstairs."

"I'm not getting the entire building?"

"Er, no. I'm just renting out the one bedroom. And the shared spaces in the upstairs apartment. Come see."

She followed me up the stairs and into the living room. "Oh, it's... cute!"

"Thanks! I like it."

"It seemed a lot bigger online."

My ad listed the square footage of the property, mentioned that it was the top unit of a two-family, and the pictures had been taken from basically the same place we stood. I didn't know what to say. "It's a good size for two people."

"Hmmmm." She wandered away toward the kitchen, so I followed, narrating the benefits of the apartment.

Before I turned the corner, a squeal split the air, so loud I feared she might've seen a cockroach. Which should never exist in my apartment.

"Lana? Are you okay?"

"Ermygorg! You got me cupcakes! You're absolutely the best potential roommate ever!"

I what? Was that initial sound even a word? What on earth...? A second later, I had my answers. Lana stood in the kitchen, holding a pink bakery box I'd left—closed—on the counter in one hand. In the other, she held a red velvet cupcake with a bite taken out of it. For a long moment, I just stared at her, completely at a loss for words. What kind of person walked into a stranger's apartment and started eating whatever they found?

"Are they vegan?" Lana asked.

An excellent question to put to someone *before* taking a bite of their food. Those cupcakes came from Nana's bakery, and she found the idea of vegan baked goods as appalling as if I'd suggested she quit work and move into a nursing home. "Um... no. Sorry?"

"Ew!" She spat a mouthful of crumbs into the box, coughing and gagging, still holding the rest of the offensive non-vegan cupcake. It didn't seem to bother her that she'd ruined everything else in the box. Maybe in her world non-vegan cupcakes deserved to be spit on.

I closed my eyes and counted to ten, determined not to snap at her. It took a lot to ruffle my feathers, and like Nana always said, kindness didn't cost anything. I could get more baked goods easily. Yelling at Lana wouldn't make either of us feel better.

On the other hand, I couldn't live with someone who exhibited so little respect for my stuff. "Okay, Lana, thanks for stopping by. I've got someone else coming to see the place in a few minutes, so I'm going to have to cut things short."

The remainder of the cupcake fell to the floor, sending an explosion of crumbs across the previously clean tile. Her face crumpled. "Oh, no. I just wanted you to like me, and now I've ruined everything."

A pang hit me. I did not, under any circumstances, want to live with this girl. Someone better had to see and respond to the ad, any day now. It was a matter of timing and luck. At the same time, I'd been raised to be polite, even to rude people. Throwing her out while she begged me to give her a chance seemed cruel.

"No, I'm sorry," I said. "You came all the way out here. When you're ready, let me show you the spare bedroom."

Before leaving the kitchen, I looked pointedly from the crumbs on the floor to the broom hanging in the corner to her face, but she made no move to clean up. Didn't even acknowledge the mess. Instead, she opened the fridge and put the now-contaminated bakery box inside. Why, I couldn't begin to guess.

Breathing deeply, I counted to ten for the second time. Then again. Lana stood there, blinking at me. Finally, I turned toward the rest of the apartment. The best way to get rid of her was to show her what she wanted to see as quickly as possible.

She wrinkled her nose when we got to the room vacated by my former roommate. "Is this the biggest room? How big is your room?"

"My room is roughly the same size," I said. "There's a third, smaller bedroom I use for my office."

"That doesn't seem fair! And we pay the same amount?"

She wouldn't be paying anything, but that was beside the point. "The market rent is over two thousand dollars. I'm asking for seven hundred fifty dollars for one room. That's fair."

"Maybe to you." She sniffed. "How often does the maid come? There's dust on that windowsill."

Maid service? What planet was this girl living on? I'd completely run out of words. It wasn't even worth arguing. "Tuesday mornings."

"You should speak to her, because she did a terrible job on this room."

The doorbell rang, a welcome savior. "Sorry, Lana, but my next appointment is here. It was nice to meet you."

With any luck, Interviewee #3 wouldn't insult my apartment, eat my food, make a mess in the kitchen, demand a discount on rent, and expect a cleaning service. At this point, anyone would be an improvement.

* * * *

Things with Interviewee #3, also known as Matt, went well enough, until he informed me that he would be bringing a service animal to help with his insomnia.

"I'm sorry, but I have severe allergies," I said.

"It's not a pet. It's a *service animal.* You can't turn me down."

I sent a silent thank-you to my brother Chris, a lawyer who had prepared me for this scenario. "Actually, I can. Because you would be living in the unit with me, and because the presence of any fur-covered animal would cause me severe respiratory distress, I don't have to allow your poodle into the apartment. The Fair Housing Act requires reasonable accommodation, and it's not reasonable for me to be unable to breathe in my own home."

"You're making that up."

"Thanks for stopping by, Matt," I said. "It was nice to meet you. Good luck with the apartment search."

Once he finally left, I texted my friends and begged them to hang out with me. I should have been working on my new game, but I was way too distracted. Besides, none of my ideas seemed to be panning out. Finding that other game so similar to mine had killed my mojo.

Holly and Nathan had childbirth class, but Cody and Gwen told me they'd already ordered takeout, paid for it online, and could I pick it up on the way? Immediately, I let them know they had a deal. After thinking a minute, I texted Tyler and asked him to be our fourth.

Sorry, I have plans, he replied a few minutes later. *Next time? I've got a new game I think you'll like.*

About forty-five minutes later, I showed up at Gwen and Cody's apartment with enough Chinese food to feed an army in one hand and a box of Nana's chocolate chip cookies in the other.

Gwen held out a whiskey and soda, which I gratefully exchanged for the food, downing about half of it in one gulp. When I paused for breath, I realized they were both staring at me.

"No new game?" Cody asked. "I hoped you were bringing something to test."

"Oh, I wish," I said. "My muse is still on vacation. Other than arranging for distribution and marketing for *The Haunted Place*, I haven't been working on my own projects at all."

"Want to talk about it?" Gwen asked as she carried the food into the kitchen.

We had very firm "no food around the games" rules ever since the time Gwen brought a date to Games Night who arrived with a Big Mac. Joan dripped special sauce all over one of Nathan's card games. He banned Gwen from ever inviting another date to play with us, even after she replaced the game. When she met Cody, he had to provide an affidavit of character before being allowed to join us.

Nathan was probably kidding when he asked for it, but Gwen didn't want to take any chances. Still, food and conversation first, then gaming.

We loaded up our plates with spring rolls, lo mein, and General Tso's chicken. As we ate, I shared the stories of Lana and Matt. By the time I finished, both my friends howled with laughter and I felt better. At the same time, I was starting to despair of finding anyone.

"Guys, they weren't even the worst. On Monday I spent half an hour with this girl who seemed great. Funny, smart, interesting... I was prepared to offer her the place on the spot. But then she made the most racist comment. Something I can't even repeat. By the time I finished explaining why I refuse to live with her, she must have been about three blocks away."

"Ew." Gwen wrinkled her nose. "In that case, I'm Team Lana."

"I'm Team None of Them," I said. "Nor do I want to live with the woman who stole my toothbrush. But I'm running out of options."

"Seriously, Shannon," Cody said. "What about Tyler?"

That was, of course, the million-dollar question. Tyler had presented me with a great solution. I knew we got along, and he'd definitely never steal my tampons. Rejecting his offer made me feel bad. But the memory of our kiss hung awkwardly at the edges of the conversation. He was a nice guy with a good job. He'd find another place soon enough.

"I like Tyler, but it's just too weird. He says he's over me, but..."

"I wouldn't worry about him," Cody said. "He's on a date right now."

For some reason, it surprised me to hear about Tyler dating. It made sense. He was an outgoing, social guy. My friends found him attractive, and his varied interests made him interesting. I enjoyed spending time with him because of his outgoing personality and great sense of humor. I considered him a friend. The idea that part of me expected him to be sitting home waiting for me to call made me shake my head at myself. How thoughtless.

"Having a roommate bringing home dates all the time creates another type of awkwardness, especially with Nana downstairs."

"You don't have any feelings for him, right?"

"I like Tyler. But if you're asking if I want to date him, no."

"Then I wouldn't worry about it," Cody said. "He met someone at the store, and he seems to like her. He's not dating lots of people, just one."

"Excellent!" I still wasn't a hundred percent sold on moving in with someone who had once kissed me, especially when his new girlfriend might have an issue with it. But at least I'd found one applicant for the apartment whom I'd get along with.

While I stood trying to decide, my phone beeped with a new email. I pulled it up to skim:

Hey. Saw the ad. Apartment looks sweet. Stopping global warming is very important to me. Are you up for showering together to save water?

He'd thoughtfully provided a picture of himself standing shirtless before the mirror. I wondered if he was naturally hairless or if he shaved his chest. Not that it made any difference. No thanks. You're so barking up the wrong tree. At least it wasn't a dick pic. I'd never done online dating, but Holly got a bunch when she first signed up.

Enough was enough. That message had to be a sign. As soon as Cody went back to the dining room, I pulled out my phone and texted Tyler. *Today's roommate meetings were a disaster. Do you want to come look at the place tomorrow?*

* * * *

The next day, my doorbell rang at 6:58, which made me happier than it should. People who were always late frustrated me to no end, even making allowances for public transit. So many people who asked to come see the place showed up half an hour late. One didn't show up at all, then texted three days later to ask if the place was still available. No apology, no excuses. Nope, sorry. And yet all of that rudeness was preferable to the person who showed up more than an hour early for a Saturday morning appointment last week. She smelled like she hadn't been home from the bar yet and didn't apologize for waking me up.

I opened the front door with a smile and led the way up the half flight of stairs to my place.

"Hey." Tyler held up several fresh tomatoes in a basket. "Nana asked me to bring this to you. Said she expects meatball marinara sauce tomorrow."

"Thanks! Glad to see she's putting you to work already. That means she likes you."

"She's great." After I took the tomatoes from him, Tyler held up his hands. "I was helping her for a few minutes. Can I use the bathroom to wash my hands? Oh, and also shower and shave and steal your toothbrush."

He made the request with such a deadpan expression that I tried not to laugh. But my lips twitched and soon I found myself doubled over in the hall. When I finished wiping my eyes, I said, "Oh, man. Thanks for that. Anyway, as you probably know, the downstairs apartment belongs to Nana. No wild parties, no smoking in the apartment, and never, ever visit her without turning your phone off first."

Tyler chuckled.

"I'm not joking."

"Right, sorry," he said. "So you want me to hang out with your nana if I move in?"

"What I want is irrelevant. You've known Nana for about ten minutes, and you're helping her garden."

"Touché." For the first time since he asked about moving into my spare room, Tyler looked like he might be starting to regret that decision. His eyes darted to the front door. If I really didn't want him as a roommate, this could be my moment.

But it wasn't my nature to take advantage of other people's discomfort. "Relax. Nana's amazing. I just meant that, once you taste her coffee and waffles, you'll be there all the time. I don't even like coffee."

"Oh, right." He loosened his tie a bit, the first time I noticed how fancy he looked.

At Game On! Tyler usually wore jeans and T-shirts, just like Cody and Gwen. Over the years, Holly had changed from the dressier clothes her former fiancé preferred to the opposite end of the spectrum and back. These days, she wore mostly leggings and geeky maternity T-shirts. After work, Nathan changed out of his mechanic's coveralls into worn jeans or khakis and a button-down cotton shirt or polo. My flowy vintage dresses usually stood out in the group as one of the dressier outfits. Until now.

"What's wrong?" Tyler asked.

I gestured at his gray slacks, crisp violet shirt, and patterned tie. "You didn't have to dress up for me. I mean, you look nice, but it's not necessary."

"I didn't," he said, giving me a quizzical look. "This is what I wear to work."

"Right." Mentally, I rolled my eyes at my own silliness. Of course he'd come straight from the office. Way to avoid making things awkward. "Well, I like the tie."

"Thanks. My uh…, a friend picked it out."

A friend, huh? Something in his tone made me suspect the tie came from the new girl Cody mentioned. They must have been seeing each other longer than I thought, but I didn't want to ask.

"Clearly, she has good taste," I said. He didn't correct my pronoun usage, essentially confirming my suspicion.

Tyler followed me as I started in the living room and gave my standard spiel about the place. Since Ellen gave me her notice, I'd honed my pitch perfectly, despite tailoring it to discourage some people after they'd shown up.

To help him visualize himself in the apartment better, I showed Tyler the empty shelves in the linen closet and the bathroom drawers that would become his if he moved in. When Ryan moved in with his last roommate, she'd left her stuff filling all the common areas: random toiletries scattered across all the shelves in the linen closet, both drawers in the vanity in the bathroom full of cosmetics, coats spilling out of the hall closet, etc. When he'd asked for a place to store his tampons in the bathroom, she acted like he burned her clothes. Not because he's trans, but because he wanted to share her space. It said a lot that Tyler was the first potential roommate I'd wanted to feel at home in my apartment.

When I finished going over the common areas, after a brief hesitation, I opened the door to my office. Unlike all the other rooms, it hadn't been cleaned recently, so I usually didn't show it to prospective roommates. No one needed to see it since the rental agreement didn't include this third bedroom. But Tyler was by far the most likely to move in, and he was a friend. I knew him well enough to understand that he wouldn't judge me for the mess.

"So this is where the magic happens?" he asked.

I chuckled. "Not exactly magic, but here's where I spend most of my time when I'm not at work. I tend to be a pretty quiet roommate, and I try to confine my mess to this room."

He looked around and shrugged. "I'll do the same with my room. I'm not a neat freak, but I'm no slob, either."

"Glad to hear it," I said. "Do you have any questions for me? The rent, utilities, or anything?"

"What are you working on now?"

"Pulling my hair out, mostly," I said. "I've been stuck ever since putting out *The Haunted Place.* I want to do a sequel, but I need to see how well the game is received before I pour the hours into it."

"That makes sense," he said. "You're on hold."

"I shouldn't be. I've got to keep moving forward so I can turn a profit and eventually make my own games full-time or even hire staff. But, for now... yeah, I'm basically on hold."

"Well, I'm here if you need anything. Someone to bounce ideas off or play-test or whatever."

I grinned. "You're literally here for me? Like, right down the hall?"

He shrugged. "Well, you know. If I get the place, I'm literally here, but if not, I'll still help you out. I liked your last game, and I'm happy to play more."

"Thanks, I appreciate it," I said.

My phone beeped in the pocket of my sweater. Tyler nodded toward the sound. "You need to take that?"

I glanced at my phone and quickly put it away. "It's nothing. My favorite streamer just went live on Twitch."

He laughed. "You're serious?"

The tone irked me. "I guess it's funny if you're not into streamers."

"It's funnier if you are," he said, reaching into his pocket. He pressed a button and turned the screen, showing me his most recent notification. A message from Twitch, with exactly the same wording as on my own device.

I wasn't much for signs or anything, but the fact that Tyler also watched my favorite streamer made me feel good about offering him the apartment. Not having to waste another second of my life looking for someone else to rent the spare room made me feel amazing. "Want to watch? I was planning to order takeout after you left."

"Thai?"

"Korean."

"I love Korean! The only place near me that delivers is wicked overpriced."

"Well, that's what you get for living in Harvard Square," I pointed out, taking his use of "wicked" as further evidence of our compatibility.

"One of several reasons I want to move," he said. "You know, if the food is any good, I plan to make you an offer you can't refuse."

A smile broke out across my face. "Works for me. If you're willing to call and place the order, this could be the beginning of a beautiful friendship."

"Deal."

In the kitchen, I pulled a menu from the drawer beside and handed it to Tyler, showing him that my usual order was already marked. Then I left him to place the call, going to pull up the stream we wanted to watch on the TV in the living room. With a happy sigh, I settled into my spot on the right side of the couch.

Tyler entered a moment later, surveying the room before sitting in the armchair to my right. His phone beeped again, and he pulled it out, typing away. Probably the girlfriend, judging from the way his face relaxed when he saw the display.

Despite my earlier reservations about bringing her up, if I was seriously considering living with Tyler, I wanted to address the fact that he'd started seeing someone. Especially when he was texting her while we hung out and she bought him clothes. "How are things going with the new girl?"

He looked surprised. "You know about her?"

"Gwen and Cody mentioned you were seeing someone. I was wondering if she's the type of girl who wouldn't be thrilled about the guy she's dating moving in with a female roommate." I didn't mention our history, not wanting to make things more awkward, but that absolutely created a valid objection to Tyler and me rooming together. Telling her would make things awkward; keeping it a secret would be worse. "You know, happy wife, happy life? Or, well, happy girlfriend, happy…"

"Whirlwind?"

"Something like that."

"We've only been out a few times," he said. "It's a little premature to call her a 'girlfriend.' She can complain, but unless she knows someone else looking for a roommate in this neighborhood who loves board games and Twitch and has a grandmother who makes cupcakes for a living, it's not going to matter."

"I don't want to cause problems for you two. Especially when you haven't been dating long."

"If she's right for me, she'll trust me," he said. "And if she's not…"

"I guess if she's not right for you, it won't matter who you're living with," I said.

"Exactly." He grinned at me. "See? We're already in sync."

"Only if I get to be Lance Bass."

He winced. "Okay, I promise to move in if you promise never make that joke again."

The fact that he even got the joke said a lot. Most people our age completely missed my not-so-veiled 'N Sync references. I held out one hand, which he clasped. It felt warm, smooth. Comforting. "You've got yourself a deal, roomie."

Chapter 5

"Never tell your friends how you really feel about their relationships. They won't appreciate your honesty." —Gwen

Now that I'd found out about Michael, he didn't feel the need to slink out the door the next morning before I arrived for breakfast. He'd also learned to make the coffee the way Nana and I liked it, which cemented my seal of approval. Too easy? Maybe. Percolators took time to master, though.

After he handed me a mug, I thanked him and asked if he planned to stay and eat with us.

"Not today," he said. "I've got to get to work early. Rain check?"

"You know it."

"I'll see you tonight," Nana said to Michael with a kiss as he left. Then she turned to me. "How's work going?"

Quickly, I filled her in on the merger news from yesterday's meeting. "If they make me executive game designer, that would be amazing. If Dennis gets it... ugh. I can't even."

"Maybe things won't be as bad as you think. It's possible whoever gets the job will turn out to be better at overseeing the department than interoffice communications. And don't count out the new owner. Who is it again?"

It was on the tip of my tongue to tell her that someone like Dennis didn't deserve a chance to prove that he'd be a better boss than coworker, but I wasn't in the mood to argue. Nana gave everyone the benefit of the doubt. "Yeah, Board Game Giants, Inc. BGG. I don't know much about the company dynamic, but they've made some great games. I'll try to stay open-minded."

"That's my girl," she said. "And if things go downhill, that's life. Making games for children was never your dream. Why are you still working there?" "Because I like to pay for luxuries like food and electricity," I retorted. I immediately felt bad. "I'm sorry, Nana. No, it's not my dream. I like my job, though. It's so much fun to see the excitement on a kid's face when holding a game and know that I made their joy possible. And it's nice to have something to pay the bills while I focus on making games for adults." "How's *The Haunted Place* doing?" "The Kickstarter orders have started to ship. We've got a couple dozen preorders to fill, largely thanks to John pushing it hard at Game On! I have to go over the numbers, but I should break even on it. I hope." "That's great!" Well, not really. Three years' work for zero profit? Some days, it felt like a waste of time, not "great." But building a game company was a marathon, not a sprint, and I'd get there eventually. Once the game got out into the world and more people started posting reviews, it could take off.

As long as I had some other way of paying the bills. It helped that Nana didn't charge me market rent, especially when I got monthly payments from a roommate. I saved every penny toward the day when I could open my own game business, but it would be a while before my safety net grew large enough. Most small business owners didn't draw a salary for several years. Another source of income was essential.

"Thanks, Nana. Your support means a lot." I gave her a wan smile. "But I'm not quite ready to give up the day job yet, so I may need to start looking around."

"You'll land on your feet. You always do," she said. "Anyway, tell me about that gorgeous man I saw headed up the stairs last night."

Darn. I had hoped to distract her with work talk until it was time to leave. "That was Tyler. He's moving into Ellen's old room next month."

"Well. If I were you, I'd invite him to share *my* room." She winked at me, and I repressed a shudder. "He looks like a young Idris Elba."

"Nana, you know I can't just jump into bed with people. I'm not going to date—or sleep with—anyone until I form a deeper connection. It takes time, and that's tough when most people are looking for a hookup."

"Oh, I know, dear. I'm just saying... Maybe you should get to know him. Give him a chance." She shrugged and fluttered her eyes innocently over the top of her coffee cup. "The man stopped to compliment my purple cone flowers on his way to the front door. Then he pulled some weeds and carried your tomatoes upstairs for me. That's a keeper."

Internally, I sighed. Yes, Tyler had good manners. Nana meant well. She was my biggest supporter when I told my family I was demisexual, and she truly wanted me to be happy. At the same time, sometimes she got carried away by her own ideas of what "happy" meant. "We're friends, and soon we'll be roommates. That's enough for me. Tell me more about Michael. How long has this been going on?"

My question seemed to be the invitation she needed, as she began to chatter excitedly about her new boyfriend. Apparently, he'd been sneaking out at daybreak for more than a month before I caught them. She hadn't wanted to say anything to avoid making me feel bad that my grandmother had a boyfriend when I didn't.

Sweet, but misguided. While demisexuality is on the asexual spectrum, I wasn't against romance or even love. I loved hearing about things that made other people happy. I loved flowers and poems and romantic comedies and Valentine's Day and all that stuff. It just took more than a pretty face for me to fall for someone. To be honest, if not for the media telling me, I wouldn't even know what made someone's face pretty or a person's butt "nice."

Contrary to what Nana—and all of society—seemed to think, I didn't need a partner to enrich my life.

* * * *

A few days later, after leaving Game On!, I stopped by the Harvard bookstore on my way to the T. Despite telling Mom that I drove when I'd be out at night, I much preferred to take public transit when I wasn't carrying a big, heavy game like *The Haunted Place.* She'd flip if she knew I planned to walk to the train, ride alone, and then walk the three blocks between the stop and my house at nine o'clock at night. In the middle of summer, it would barely be dark by the time I got there. Much easier to just lie.

The last time she brought it up, I read Boston's murder statistics to her (which were way lower than where she lived in Florida). It didn't help, but at least I amused myself.

Since school was currently between sessions, the bookstore wasn't quite as packed as it would get once the students returned. Still, in such a popular location, plenty of people filled the aisles, even fifteen minutes before closing. I wove in and out of the crowd, navigating toward the business section. Every few feet, I'd stop to page through one of the display books. Tempting, but I'd come with a purpose: Before dispersing *The Haunted Place* widely, I needed to set up an LLC, and I needed to do a lot of research about running my own business that probably should have already happened.

A deep laugh filled the air, a very familiar rumble. I spun around, then spotted Tyler about twenty feet away, paging through a new thriller. I shouldn't have been surprised to see him there. Tyler, Cody, and Gwen all lived within a mile of Harvard Square. Still, running into a gamer friend at the bookstore was like seeing your dentist at the sushi place.

On Tyler's right, a woman stepped closer to him, putting one hand on his back while she whispered in his ear. He leaned down, responding in an equally familiar manner. Their intimate aura made me feel like a Peeping Tom.

To my horror, when the woman turned, I recognized her. One hand flew to my mouth. What were the two of them doing together? How was this possible?

But the look on Tyler's face when he turned to Megan and replied to whatever she'd said told me everything I needed to know. This was the new girl he'd started dating. All of a sudden, I wanted to throw up.

It shouldn't have surprised me. After all, Megan had mentioned dropping by Game On! last week, when Tyler and my friends had been there. Even though I'd never seen her in the store, I knew she lived nearby. And yet, seeing the two of them together felt like getting doused with ice water.

It never occurred to me that she would know some of the other regulars at the store, especially the ones who lived in Cambridge. The local board gaming community wasn't that big; she just never seemed like someone who played games outside of work. Even if they'd met, I'd never have considered the possibility of Tyler and Megan being into each other. I wouldn't have thought she was his type. Not just because she was my physical opposite, but Megan was such a phony.

Maybe I was wrong. Maybe this wasn't a date; they could have just happened to run into each other. Or she was asking for help getting a book off one of the top shelves. Looking for directions. Anything other than the familiarity I witnessed through cringing eyes.

I'd been on the verge of going over to say hello to Tyler, but seeing him with her stopped me in my tracks. Instead I turned, seeking another path around the shelves.

Once arriving in the business section, it didn't take long to find the book Nathan had recommended. I appreciated any and all advice he gave me as someone who'd been running his own business for almost twenty years. Sure, a mechanic's shop and a game manufacturer weren't the same, but some ideas applied to any type of business.

I paged through the volume, more to give Tyler and Megan time to exit than to examine the contents. I'd be buying the book; I could read it at home or on the T. A voice came over the paging system, informing shoppers that we had ten minutes to proceed to the registers and make our purchases.

Keeping my head down, I counted to one hundred. I didn't fully understand my hesitation at letting Tyler see me. Under any other circumstances, I'd have walked up and said hello. But Megan.

"Are you avoiding me?" A voice in my ear made me jump. I looked up into Tyler's laughing brown eyes.

My face grew warm. "Hey."

"I know you saw me, so there's no point in lying."

"Busted," I said with a rueful grin. "It looked like you were here with someone. I didn't want to interrupt."

"Tyler! There you are!" Megan approached, grabbing his arm so tightly, her breasts might leave an imprint. She couldn't have been staking her claim more obviously if she'd planted a flag on him.

Of course, insecurity was Megan's middle name, so her reaction to seeing me talking to Tyler only surprised me because I still didn't understand why she was with my friend. My worlds were colliding, and my brain refused to make sense of any of it.

Apparently, she didn't get it either. Blinking at me several times, Megan asked, "Shannon? What are you doing here?"

"I was about to ask you the same thing," I said. "I just left Game On!. Hey, Tyler."

"But you live so far away." She wrinkled her nose when she said it, as if I lived somewhere dirty.

"Yeah, we're friends with the owners. I spend a lot of time up here."

"Oh. And how do you know Tyler?"

"We've known each other for years," I said. "Mutual friends." *And we're going to be living together, not that it's any of your business.*

"I got to play-test one of Shannon's games recently. Great game," Tyler said. "Also—"

She squealed and clutched Tyler's arm even more tightly. "You do play-testing, too? That's so cool! Next time you have to invite me."

In the several months I'd known Megan, never once had she displayed the slightest interest in playing a board game or spending time with me outside the office. Odd, given our line of work. Still, I didn't want to be rude. "That would be great. I'll keep you posted." To Tyler, I said, "I don't know if she mentioned this, but Megan and I work together."

"Really? Small world," Tyler said. "But it's cool that you're already friends, since I'm moving in with Shannon."

Calling us "friends" was quite a stretch, but I didn't correct him. I was too busy praying he hadn't known her long and it wasn't serious. The thought of Megan spending significant amounts of time in my apartment sent chills down my spine. I'd rather eat fingernails than spend an evening listening to her subtle digs and one-upmanship, especially when everyone else seemed to like her.

"You're going to live together? How fun!" A touch of annoyance flashed across her face, suggesting that she found the idea of Tyler living with a female roommate to be anything but "fun," but he didn't notice.

A voice came over the loudspeaker, saving me from this awkward conversation with the announcement that the store was now closing in two minutes.

Tyler ran one hand over his short curls. "We're just about to head out. Good to see you, Shannon."

"Yes, we're going *back to his place*," Megan said, so quietly only I could hear.

Her tone made me want to tell her that, if I'd had any interest in Tyler, we would have slept together months ago. That wouldn't make this encounter less weird, though. Or work tomorrow, now that I thought about it. The only thing I'd accomplish would be making Tyler even more uncomfortable and looking like a total jerk.

I forced a smile. "Have fun!"

"Oh, we will," she said.

Tyler shifted from one foot to the other, looking back and forth as if he wasn't quite sure what was happening. "Uh, I'll see you soon, Shannon."

Despite my better judgment, I couldn't resist having the smallest bit of fun with the two of them. "Yeah. Call me tomorrow so we can talk about move-in logistics. It's going to be great, us living together."

Megan's spine stiffened. She opened her mouth, but the loudspeaker cut her off.

"Attention, customers. The store will be closing in one minute. If you would like to make a purchase, please proceed to the registers immediately."

Thank goodness. An excuse to end the pain of this conversation. I held up the book still in my hand. "Gotta go. See you at work, Megan."

I didn't wait for her to reply. By the time I paid and left the store, they'd thankfully vanished. Still, something about the encounter stuck with me all the way down the stairs to the platform where I waited for my train.

Cody had said Tyler seemed to like this new girl. At the time I'd been excited for him, but upon seeing who he'd met, I found myself full of doubt.

Maybe she felt as weird running into me as I did seeing her outside the office. In private, she could be completely different. For Tyler's sake, I hoped so.

Then a thought struck me. What had I done? I'd been so concerned it would be awkward for Tyler to move in with me given our history, but him dating my coworker made it ten times worse. Things would only get weirder if Megan or I got the executive designer's job. It didn't even matter who. She'd be condescending if she got the promotion, and insufferably insubordinate if I took it. For a heartbeat, the situation almost made me hope Jameson gave the job to Dennis. Not quite, though.

Tyler and I had already agreed to live together, and he'd texted me back a signed basic agreement earlier that day. I couldn't tell him I changed my mind. But I couldn't let him move in without saying anything. Especially not if he thought Megan and I were friends.

After tossing and turning on the issue all night, I finally picked up the phone and texted Tyler. *Can you come over to the apartment tonight after work?*

Tyler: *No problem. Is 7 OK?*

Me: *Sure.*

* * * *

Once again, he showed up exactly on time. To show my appreciation, I didn't mince words. After making him a drink, I offered Tyler a seat on the couch, then said, "There's something we need to talk about."

"Yeah?" He met my eyes, then sighed. "Megan."

"Right. I'm sorry. Cody told me you were seeing someone, and that's great. Honestly, I'm happy for you."

"You have a problem with Megan?"

"Look, I don't want to tell you who to date, but..." *But she's absolutely horrible and you can do way better.* "When I leave work, I leave work. I don't want to come home and have my coworkers hanging around. At the same time, I hate the idea of telling you that you can't have guests."

"It's no big deal," Tyler said. "I can only imagine how awkward I'd feel getting out of the shower and running into one of the guys from work. Especially the boss's son or daughter."

"Exactly."

"Look, we've only been out a handful of times," Tyler said. "If things get serious, we'll go to her place. At least until you're more comfortable with the situation."

Honestly, I didn't think I'd ever get comfortable with the two of them as a couple. But if they weren't serious, they might not make it until Tyler's lease ran out at the end of the month. Maybe he would see how shallow and superficial Megan could be. Maybe she'd dump him for someone else. To listen to her talk, men lined up around the block to ask her out. A lot could happen in a couple of weeks.

The silence between us stretched, becoming thick. Finally, Tyler said, "Megan told me she's your superior at work. Does the idea of me dating your boss bother you?"

I wasn't even surprised she'd claimed to outrank me. Briefly, I considered asking Tyler if she'd mentioned what her job was. Instead, I said, "My boss is a sixty-seven-year-old man named Jameson. Also, he's married."

He chuckled. "Okay, the boss's daughter, then."

Under the surface, I sensed what he was really asking. He wanted to know if I was jealous. I didn't care whether Tyler dated; I cared that he find someone good enough for him, which Megan was absolutely not. But telling him that would make things even more uncomfortable if they fell in love. Especially when I couldn't quite articulate what bugged me about her. I offered a partial truth. "I want you to be happy."

"Thanks," he said. "You, too. How about this? Let's make a pact."

"A pact? Like, sealed in blood?"

"I think a handshake will do it."

"Okay... What kind of pact?" I asked.

"A lot of roommates don't share their personal lives. As long as I live here, we don't talk about Megan. I don't bring her over, don't tell you when I'm going out with her. You don't mention what it's like working with her. No complaints about her at the office, nothing. In this building, she doesn't exist."

That might help. "So the apartment would be a Megan-free zone?"

"Yes, but also, our entire friendship. No Megan talk, here or elsewhere."

I wasn't entirely convinced that would solve the underlying problem, but since I couldn't solidify why I felt like he shouldn't be with her, I didn't have any better ideas. It wasn't like I could complain that she disliked me for no reason. After a moment's thought, I held out one hand. "Deal."

* * * *

Two weeks later, Tyler showed up in the driveway with a moving pod, Cody, Nathan, and Gwen. No sign of Megan, thankfully. She'd avoided me at the office since we ran into each other in the bookstore, sticking to her usual nice-sounding-but-actually-snide comments when interaction became unavoidable. More than once I'd spotted her watching me from her desk across the room. I never engaged. Although I probably could diffuse the tension by telling her that I'd never had any interest in Tyler, I neither wanted to rehash our history nor lie. Knowing Megan, she'd ask a lot of prying questions it was easier to avoid.

I greeted my friends enthusiastically, still wondering if I'd made a mistake. Maybe I should have canceled the lease the second I found out about Megan, but I didn't see any way out of our agreement. A new girlfriend I could handle. His happiness made me happy. A horrible new girlfriend who I had to see at work every day did not. On top of that, for some reason I couldn't stop thinking about the day he kissed me.

My brain knew I was being silly. One kiss, before Tyler met Megan, that meant nothing. There was no reason to think he would ever repeat the gesture. It happened six months ago, at Gwen and Cody's wedding. At the time, I felt terrible.

Well, more to the point, I'd felt literally nothing at all. No reaction. No spark. Nothing. The total lack of emotion made me feel worse than if the kiss had been terrible or extra slobbery or if Tyler had acted rude or ghosted me after. Because I liked him. He was smart, funny, caring, and wicked sharp at strategy games. We enjoyed the same types of games, so we played well together. But our entire relationship was superficial. We barely knew each other.

The trip took place in February, and it had started off so well. Even though I delayed my flight when Nana had a minor medical episode, the doctors had given her a clean bill of health. I joined my friends in Mexico in plenty of time for the wedding festivities. Gwen, Holly, and I went to this "finding your inner diva" class. At dinner, Holly and I hung out with Cody's sister Tessa and Tyler. Holly was struggling to reenter the dating world after being royally screwed by her ex, but the two of us were having fun.

After the rehearsal dinner, everyone went to a nearby bar to continue the party. Since I'd arrived in Mexico nearly a full day later than planned and spent most of the flight worrying about Nana's health, my drinking game needed a serious boost. The mixed drinks at the resort were mostly water, so I wanted to break out of my comfort zone and try something a bit stronger.

Tyler had gone with me to the bar and helped me find the perfect whiskey. "Here, you'll like this. It's like drinking a campfire."

I racked my brain for a diplomatic response. "That's supposed to be a pleasurable experience?"

"Trust me."

With a suspicious sniff, I accepted the glass. To my surprise, it wasn't unpleasant. Strong and smoky. No one would accuse the resort of watering this down. I took a deep breath, then tilted the glass to my lips. Amber liquid flowed over my tongue, carrying not only what Tyler said was peat but a hint of caramel. Suddenly I got what he meant about the campfire. The whiskey went down smooth as glass, leaving a pleasant heat all the way from the tip of my tongue into my belly. I sighed with pleasure.

"This is the best shot I've ever had. Probably the first one I've enjoyed." Handing the glass back, I turned to the bartender. "I'll have a double."

"Neat," Tyler said over my shoulder.

"Awesome?" I asked him.

"Neat means no ice," he explained.

Right. The very reason I didn't order mixed drinks. "Thanks. Nice lookin' out."

"Any time," he said.

I sat on my stool, sipping from my glass and watching the crowd, thinking about tomorrow's festivities. People slowly piled into the bar, until the din started to give me a headache. At some point, Tyler left to go to the bathroom, then disappeared into the mass. Probably found someone else to talk to.

It wasn't terribly late, but I needed to get away. The air pressed in on me from all sides. I decided to walk on the beach instead of going back to our room right away, where Holly would want to chat and the television would likely be going. I loved my friend, but I needed a bit of alone time.

Where the sidewalk met the sand, I paused to pull off my shoes. My four-inch-high, bright red Mary Jane heels went fabulously with my black polka-dotted dress, but would be hell on the sand, especially with a couple of drinks in me. The beach technically didn't close until ten, but most people had already packed up and gone in. A couple sat on a blanket off to the right. Down by the shoreline, someone I couldn't quite make out threw a ball for a big black dog. And about fifty feet to my left, Tyler sat on the edge of a hammock, dangling his feet in the sand while swinging back and forth. I wondered what caused him to leave the bar, where he seemed to be enjoying himself, and wind up here.

I hesitated. Probably shouldn't have, but I did come out here for some solitude. Still, Tyler was a friend, and I couldn't bring myself to pretend not to see him when he appeared to be upset. If he wanted to be alone, he could tell me, and I'd go on my way.

"Hey." I spoke softly, not wanting to startle him.

He jerked, but then relaxed when his eyes met mine. "Hey, Shannon."

"Everything okay?"

"Yeah, you just startled me. Sorry," he said. "Did you follow me from the bar?"

His tone seemed almost hopeful, as if he wished I might have come looking for him. "No, I'm out for a walk before bed. It's been a busy couple of days, and tomorrow will be even more so. Thought it would be nice to take some time to relax and decompress."

"Me, too. Sometimes it's tough being an introvert in such a big group." I laughed. "Don't I know it. Anyway, I'll leave you on your own. Have a good night."

"Thanks." He hesitated, so I turned to walk away. Then he said my name, so quiet I almost missed it. I paused before turning back. "Do you mind some company?"

"You wouldn't prefer to be alone?"

"I can be alone with you." He smiled sheepishly. "You know what I mean."

"Yeah, I do." I held out a hand to help him out of the hammock. It was warm and smooth, soft.

Once he gained his footing, I dropped his hand. Something flashed across his face, and I wondered if I'd made a mistake allowing him to walk with me. Gwen and Holly both thought Tyler had feelings for me, but I'd never seen a hint of it. Unfortunately, I tended to be oblivious to things that allosexuals easily spotted. But this was Tyler, we were friendly, and it was too late to change my mind about the walk. Taking his hand, then running away would be beyond rude.

Side by side, we walked the beach in the moonlight, each lost in our own thoughts. The poets probably would have called the scene romantic, but I never understood poetry. Still, having a friend walk with me did turn out to be more comforting than walking alone. Especially a friend who appreciated the restorative nature of a good, long silence.

After a while, the bamboo torches set up by the beach resort ended, and a sign informed us that we were about to cross into a restricted area. Without a word, we turned and headed back. It was the most enjoyable walk I'd ever had with another person. I didn't know how long we'd been out there, and I didn't care. Sand beneath my feet, moonlight shining on the path, a light sea breeze, the smell of the ocean, and a good friend who could share space with me without feeling the need to talk. All the ingredients for a perfect Shannon evening.

We made it back to the sidewalk and stopped so I could put my shoes back on.

"That was exactly what I needed," Tyler said. "Thanks."

"Me, too. You may be the best walking partner I've ever found."

He grinned and ran one hand over his curly black hair. "Let me know if you want to go walking again sometime."

That sounded suspiciously like a date. For the first time, something awkward entered the silence between us. Not knowing how to respond, I instead put my shoes on the ground so I could step back into them.

"Here." Tyler offered me a hand, and I leaned into his shoulder for balance. Left foot, then the right. When I finished, he bent down and buckled each shoe for me. The tenderness of the gesture made me smile. "You didn't have to do that."

"I know." He stood, brushing sand off the knees of his pants.

Then our eyes met, and a sudden stab of dread hit me in the stomach. Uh-oh. Suddenly I knew, absolutely *knew*, that he was about to ruin our beautiful, friendly moment. And there wasn't anything I could say or do to stop it. I should have listened to my friends, but ignoring them had been easier than worrying about something I couldn't control.

On some level, I thought if I pretended Gwen and Holly were wrong, I'd never have to let Tyler down. The last thing I wanted was to hurt a nice guy. But as he stepped closer to me, I realized that it would have been much kinder to nip things in the bud early on, even if that might have made the play-testing sessions awkward. By pretending not to know, I'd made everything worse.

"I really like spending time with you, Shannon," he said.

One hand reached out to cup my face. Indecision froze me in place. What if I ran? That was a coward's way out, though, and cruel. I couldn't do it.

So I stood like a statue, giving him the opportunity to lean forward and place his lips against mine. As a teenager, every time I found myself in this position, some small part of me hoped it would work, that his kiss would unlock something in me. But in college, I'd finally come to terms with the fact that, if I didn't want someone to kiss me before they did it, their lips wouldn't serve as some magical elixir.

Feeling like the worst kind of asshole, I took a step back.

"Did I do something wrong?" he asked. "I thought—"

I shook my head. "It's not that. Tyler, I'm really sorry…"

"No, I'm sorry," he said. "I misread something. It seemed like maybe you liked me."

"I do! That's not it at all." His brow furrowed in confusion, so I held out one hand. "Come on. Let's walk back together, and I'll explain."

For a gut-wrenching moment, he considered my request. I thought he'd leave me standing there. But he put his hand in mine, and we turned toward the winding path that would eventually lead to our rooms.

As I tried to think of what to say, he broke the silence. "Cody said you weren't seeing anyone. Is it because I'm black?"

It broke my heart that he thought I rejected him because of his race. "No. My first boyfriend was black. My college boyfriend was Korean. I like you, as a friend. The thing is… I'm demisexual."

He chewed on his lip for a minute. "That's like being asexual?"

"It's on the spectrum," I said. "I don't feel sexual attraction for anyone until I get to know them."

"We've known each other for almost two years."

"I know. But it's not like a light switch. Sometimes, after a time, I feel attracted to a person. Sometimes I don't. There's a big difference between running into someone from time to time and forming a connection on a deeper level."

He nodded. "That makes sense. So you're saying, there's a chance, some day?"

"I don't want to do that to you. I don't know. I can't promise I'll ever feel anything. And it wouldn't be fair for you to wait, just in case." This was the point in the past where some men stormed off never to speak to me again. Still, I offered him the same truth I offered them. "I hope we can be friends."

"Of course we can. That was never a question," he said. "I like hanging out with you. If it could be more, cool. But it can't, and that's cool, too."

He'd taken the news so much better than expected, I wondered briefly if one of my friends had tipped him off. But asking would only make things more awkward. "I really am sorry."

"Don't be sorry. Be you." By this point, we'd reached the elevators. He pointed down the hall. "I'm over there. See you at the wedding."

He turned down the hall as if we'd been talking about nothing more serious than his favorite ice cream flavor. Fine with me. If he wasn't upset, that made everything so much easier.

And yet, part of me still felt disappointed that I couldn't turn physical attraction on and off as easily as some people seemed to think I could. Tyler was one of the good ones. He deserved someone special. It was too bad that person couldn't be me.

Chapter 6

"We spend too much of our lives working not to enjoy what we do." —Holly

Every job has its highs and lows. My lows largely came in the form of Megan, especially now that she shot me bizarrely hostile knowing looks each morning. As if I cared about her love life. At some point, if she was awful to everyone and not just me, Tyler would figure out who she really was and break up with her. Until then, a framed picture of the two of them went up on her desk, prominently displayed. She changed her text tone to "Boyfriend." Just when I thought she'd never find a more obnoxious song than "Diamonds Are a Girl's Best Friend," she proved me wrong.

The biggest high in my job was getting to host focus groups in the office. When a game was being tested, Friday mornings were by far the best part of each week. At eleven o'clock, the receptionist called to let me know that my focus group had arrived. I went down the hall to the elevator, where a group of kids and their parents met me. Tessa stood near the back with her two-year-old son, Preston. I gave them a small nod before addressing the group.

"Hello, everyone. My name is Shannon."

"Hi, Shannon!" the kids chorused back at me. Adorbs. I loved when they did that.

"How's everyone doing?"

The cacophony of responses made me want to laugh. "Do you guys like games?"

"Yes!"

"You do? Why, what a happy coincidence!" I let my mouth drop open and put my hands on my cheeks in a big display of surprise. "I've got a game for you!"

A couple of the kids cheered. Some groups were shy and barely interacted at all, so it was great to see so much enthusiasm. With the wicked little kids, you never knew what to expect. Some would think that you couldn't get useful feedback from two- to four-year-olds, but they never tried to spare my feelings. Their parents also provided a wealth of valuable information, both about the kids' demeanor and comments while playing and what they liked or disliked as the person with the actual purchasing power.

I continued, "In a minute, we're going to meet my friend Ryan. He's got a game set up for you. We're going to give you some time to play. After, we'll eat pizza and talk about what you liked and didn't like. How does that sound?"

"Pizza!" a little girl in the front said. Her pigtails and freckles reminded me of Gwen, and I grinned at her.

"That's right! Come on!" With a big wave, I turned and took the group into the main office area. On the small tables in the middle, Ryan had set up several copies of the nearly finished game.

The kids clustered around the tables, picking up pieces and chattering excitedly. This was part of the test: seeing how kids responded to the packaging and the pieces.

Tessa came up to stand beside me. "Preston is like a kid in a candy store today."

"So is Ryan," I said. "Kid focus groups are his favorite part of the job. Thank you so much for doing this."

"Oh, I should be thanking you. Today, I'm a hero."

I chuckled. "From what Cody tells me, you're a hero every day. Raising a toddler alone can't be easy."

She shrugged. "You do what you've got to do. Having family nearby helps a lot. Are you staying while we play?"

"I wish I could," I said, "but we don't want me to unintentionally influence their reactions. Ryan will explain the game, and then I'll go back to my desk. We've set up Wi-Fi-enabled cameras, so I can watch from over there."

Ryan started speaking to the kids, so Tessa lowered her voice to a whisper. "In that case, I'll let you get to it."

"Thanks! Have fun," I whispered back before I left.

Usually focus groups didn't faze me much, but Jameson raised the stakes with his retirement. I needed this to go well, especially since I didn't have another group planned before the executive game designer would be chosen. Making games was the only thing I'd ever wanted to do. I didn't even much care what type. I'd grown up playing stuff like Chutes and Ladders and Monopoly, like all kids. But I'd also loved Clue, Mario 64, Donkey Kong... basically anything available for my Nintendo at the local video rental place. My parents would check games out for a couple of weeks, and I'd beat them. At least until the video stores all went out of business. Then I went online to find new material.

But even more fun than playing video games alone (Chris never wanted to join me), I'd make up games for the kids in my neighborhood. I'd create scavenger hunts or elaborate games of make-believe. My parents had encouraged me to get good grades, come up with a plan for my future. They wanted me to become a doctor or a lawyer, insisting a person couldn't play games all their life.

They'd been wrong. Once I realized it was possible to make a living by creating the same games that enchanted me as a small child, I made my decision. Went to college, got the degree at their insistence, always with an end goal in mind.

I'd taken a few coding classes, just enough to figure out that I wasn't likely to make it in the world as a video game designer. Too bad, because I enjoyed play-testing and finding bugs, but ultimately video games weren't where my passions lay. This job had seemed the perfect fit. By creating games for kids, I could introduce them to the same wonderful world I'd experienced as a child, helping to nurture them into the type of adults who kept their local game stores in business.

If only people like Megan didn't exist in my glorious world. I did my best to put my head down, do the work, and ignore her, but that was easier said than done. My noise-canceling headphones didn't reduce the smug little smiles she sent my way.

Lost in my thoughts, I tripped over my desk chair. Behind me, Dennis snickered, and I shot him a dirty look. Sure, I shouldn't let him get to me, but I wouldn't put it past him to have pulled my chair out while I was gone to watch me trip when I returned. Usually, I pushed it in, especially when we had kids running around.

But I had work to do, and no time to worry about Dennis. Ignoring him, I forced myself to concentrate, pulling up the focus group stream in one window. Ryan was still explaining the mechanics for the game. Players rolled a giant block with numbers on the sides. Each number correlated to a stack of oversized cards that would direct the kids to do something, like make an animal sound or dance. I was lost in thought when a Facebook message popped up on my screen.

Tyler: *Hey. Is it okay if I invite my buddies over to play poker tonight?*

Me: *Sure. You don't have to ask permission. It's your apartment, too.*

Tyler: *I know. Just being polite. :-) Wouldn't want to get in the way if you had people coming over.*

Me: *Most of my friends are your friends. If I had people coming over, you'd know. But no, I'll probably be holed up in my office all night.*

Tyler: *Working on anything good?*

Me: *I have no idea...*

Tyler: *I'm sure it's great. Anyway, the guys will be showing up around 6. We'll have pizza if you want some.*

Me: *[Thumbs-up emoji]*

"Who's Tyler?" The sound of Dennis's voice in my ear made me jump about three feet. My head knocked against his jaw, sending tears into my eyes. Ouch. At least I was messaging Tyler and not applying for jobs when Dennis snuck up on me. He'd tell Jameson in a heartbeat if he spotted me job searching on company time.

Rubbing the spot where we'd collided, I spun around in my chair. By no coincidence, it rolled several inches away from him at the same time. "Do you always sneak up on people like that? You took three years off my life."

"Maybe you should pay attention to your surroundings instead of flirting at work, then." He smirked. "When I'm in charge, maybe I'll have the IT department block all social media and implement a no-phones policy."

I needed my phone at work in case something happened to Nana, but didn't see any reason to tell Dennis that. Better to pacify him. "I'm sorry. Tyler's my roommate."

"Roommate? Or roooooommmmmmmmate?" As if his tone wasn't enough to tell me what he meant, he thrust his pelvis back and forth a couple of times. I struggled not to gag at the visual, while making a note to add this moment to my list of HR complaints. If only I could manage to sneak a picture.

"Just a regular roommate, Dennis. Did you come to check the status of Project High-top?" The one and only game we currently worked on together, thankfully, and it was nearly finished. The final product went to market in six weeks, if all went well.

"I just dropped by to say hello. Can't a guy be friendly?"

Ryan caught my eye with a questioning look, as if to ask if I needed saving. I shook my head a fraction of an inch to let him know I'd be okay.

To Dennis, I put on a fake smile with forced cheerfulness. "Of course you can! Thanks for stopping by. It was great to see you!"

"Jameson also wanted me to let you know that we're doing a morale booster later."

"Oh yeah?" Morale was one thing this company lacked since the merger was announced. Too many people worried about upcoming layoffs. A booster could do wonders.

"Yup! We're all going out for drinks and apps after work. Mandatory." He named a local bar known for its female servers who wore tiny shorts and bikini tops.

"Oh, I'd love to, but I have plans with my roommate." Hopefully, he hadn't seen enough of the conversation with Tyler to know I lied.

He shrugged. "Cool. Jameson thought some of the executive game designer candidates might want to use the opportunity to let him get to know them a little better, but I'll tell him you're not interested."

Lovely. I needed the evening to work on my own game, but couldn't let Dennis capitalize on the opportunity without me. Maybe I could talk Ryan into going, too. Even though he didn't create games and didn't want to be an executive designer, we could still have a good time.

I forced a smile. "Sounds like fun. On second thought, I'll be there."

* * * *

Three hours later, I'd managed to confirm that, despite what the regulars said, no one visited this restaurant for the wings. They tasted like they'd been boiled in vinegar. The women dancing around in booty shorts and tiny shirts did nothing for me. And the conversation, which largely circled around who had the largest breasts, wasn't exactly stimulating. Clearly, the answer was the brunette in the corner. I didn't even know why the debate existed, other than that these guys wanted to hear themselves talk about boobs.

Ryan somehow got dragged to the other end of the table when we arrived, and despite my best efforts, we hadn't managed to reconfigure so we could sit together. I shot him baleful glances from my seat. The others would probably take it as evidence that we were hooking up if anyone saw me, but whatever. Shooting silent messages back and forth was by far the best thing about this excursion.

"Hey, Shannon, did you see the Red Sox game last night?" Megan asked at my elbow.

Absorbed in my thoughts, I hadn't seen her take the empty seat beside me, so the question jolted me from my semicatatonic state. "No, I'm afraid I don't have cable."

"That's too bad." She sidled closer, leaning in as if she was about to reveal a huge secret. "Tyler and I went to the game. It was a-MAZ-ing. Did he at least tell you about it?"

"No, but we haven't spoken today." A lie, but it wasn't like I could tell her about the Pact. "Besides, I'm not a huge baseball fan."

"You'd love it if you gave it a chance," she said. "I could explain the game. That way, if you could get a date, you could come along next time. We have a box."

Of course she did. Why did people always assume if you didn't like something, you didn't understand it? "I know the game, I'm just not into it. My brother played all through high school."

It wasn't even worth addressing her jab about me not being able to get a date. She was like a dog with a bone, though. She wouldn't let it go. "Maybe it was the company. What if I set you up with someone?"

Considering how obnoxious I found my brother when we were teenagers, Megan might have a point there. I used to watch with a bunch of girls giggling over how cute his butt looked in those pants. Not too different from the conversations here at the bar, actually. But the sudden interest in my personal life made me wary. "Thank you, but I'm not interested."

"Whatevs. Just trying to help," Megan said.

I sincerely doubted that, but said, "I appreciate the offer."

"So, you're not seeing anyone?"

"Why the sudden interest, Megan? You've never talked to me about anything but work, and barely that."

"As Tyler and I get more serious, it's totally normal for me to take an interest in my boyfriend's friends."

My ears perked up at the word "serious," as I'd thought they'd only been on a handful of dates. But I refused to give her the satisfaction of showing my curiosity. I picked up the menu and studied it, hoping she'd take the cue to talk to someone else.

No such luck. She put her hand on the plastic, forcing me to set it down. Good thing I was using it as a prop and not intending to actually order anything. "Let's be real here for a minute, Shannon."

"Unlike some people, Megan, I'm always real."

"I know you're after my man," she said.

The comment was so ludicrous, a hoot of laughter escaped me. She had spent a grand total of ninety seconds with the two of us together in the bookstore, where I'd talked to Megan almost the entire time. She had virtually nothing to base her conclusion on.

"Laugh if you want, but I see you messaging him at work when you think no one's looking," she said. "It's never going to happen. You're not getting my man or my job. Not when you're so basic. You'll never be extra enough to beat me."

At that point, I gave up on being polite. Shoving away from the table, I pushed myself to my feet and went to interrupt Ryan's conversation, not bothering to say good-bye. From the look on my friend's face, he wasn't having a good time, either.

Willing my legs not to shake, I continued to walk toward the other end of the table. When I got to him, I collapsed onto a stool as gracefully as possible. Which was not very.

"Everything okay?" he asked.

"She's such a piece of work." I shook my head. "Tell you later."

To avoid letting everyone at the table see my frustration, I pulled out my phone. A bunch of texts waited.

Gwen: *How's the work bonding? Need me to call in a bomb threat to the restaurant? ;-)*

Holly: *I'm desperately craving sugar. Can you have Nana make literally anything and I'll have Nathan pick it up on his way home from work?*

Tyler: *We've got pizza waiting for you when you get home. Extra cheese and mushroom.*

The messages made me smile. Sure, this outing might be a total bust, but my friends rocked. Quickly, I tapped out replies, and by the time I finished, I'd managed to push Megan out of my mind.

Chapter 7

"Being your own boss requires a lot of sacrifices. But it's worth it to do what you love." —Nathan

By the time I got home that night, I was worn out, completely exhausted. Tyler and three guys sat around the dining room table playing poker. These were work friends, not board gamers, so I didn't know anyone. My emotional tank neared empty, but I forced myself to ignore the screaming of my inner introvert in the interest of getting to know my roommate's other friends.

"Hey, I'm Shannon," I said. "Sorry to interrupt your game. I'll be in and out quick."

"Don't worry about it," one of them said. "This is the closest Craig's been to a female in weeks." The guy beside the one who spoke ducked his head, grinning.

"Hush, Tommy. Don't make my roommate uncomfortable," Tyler said. I shot him a grateful look. When witty banter turned sexual, I typically tuned it out.

"Sorry," Tommy said. "This tall bastard on my left is Skippy."

On his other side sat a guy so tall he must get people asking him constantly if he played basketball. As a fellow tall person, I refrained from commenting on his height and simply said hello, then repeated all their names. Skippy wore glasses and Tommy wore a Super Mario T-shirt. Silently, I chanted, *Skippy spectacles, Tommy T-shirt* in hopes of not having to ask again later. Craig was of average height and weight, black hair in braids, in a button-down shirt and jeans. *Cornrows Craig.*

It was the first time in my life I became aware of being the only white person in the room. Quite possibly the first time it ever happened, coming from an affluent white area and then moving to Boston. Weird.

A huge yawn brought tears to my eyes just as my stomach rumbled, reminding me that I hadn't eaten since lunch. Ducking my head, I left my musings on race for another day when I was more coherent and apologized again for interrupting their game.

"No problem," Craig said. "You want to join us?"

"Next time? It's been a long day."

"Sure. That's what they all say."

"Don't goad her," Tyler said. "She's happy to take your money, and you can't afford to lose it."

"Good thing there's no chance of you beating me, then," Craig returned.

The trash talk made me chuckle, but it was time to go. With only the tiniest bit of regret, I said my good-byes, then went into the kitchen to get my dinner.

Zombie-like, I staggered into my room, clutching a paper plate with pizza, wings, and celery sticks. I didn't even want to be in the same room as anyone else. It occurred to me that I should probably work on fixing the problems with *Speakeasy*, but I'd run out of mental energy. Anything other than pulling up YouTube videos on my tablet and noshing on my dinner took too much effort. Especially since I still had no idea where my newest game was going.

As I pondered my options for the evening, my phone beeped, reminding me that I hadn't answered Gwen's texts from earlier. Her message was short and to the point, on the thread that included Holly. *Speaking of bonding, how's the new roommate?*

The message reminded me that I'd never told my friends about Megan. Not that she existed, they knew that, but that we worked together. After running into her and Tyler in the bookstore, I'd avoided the topic, essentially hoping they broke up before he moved in.

No dice, unfortunately. This strategy proved every bit as effective as covering my ears and singing "La la la, I can't hear you" at the top of my lungs. But now, not mentioning the connection seemed weird, and it would only get more so the longer we didn't talk about it.

However, I still needed to eat my dinner, and I didn't want to text while eating chicken wings. Leaning the phone up against a stack of books on my nightstand, I started a video chat with them both to let me gossip while eating.

"Ohhh, going so well you need to talk in person?" Gwen teased.

In response, I rolled my eyes and waved a chicken wing at her, already chewing. Nana had taught me not to talk with my mouth full.

"So what's up?" Holly asked.

"I just got back from a work thing," I said, "and I was thinking... have any of you met Tyler's new girlfriend yet?"

"This is what you think about at work functions?" Gwen asked.

"We work together," I said.

"Yeouch. Awkward," Holly said. "What happened?"

"Nothing, really," I said. "I ran into them at the Harvard bookstore a couple of weeks ago. Have either of you met her?"

"Cody and I did," Gwen said. "The four of us got drinks after I got back from Baltimore. I think it was right after they started dating? A few days before my trip to Nova Scotia."

Not wanting to steer their opinions, I asked, "What did you think of her?"

"She seemed nice enough. Doesn't play games, though," Gwen said.

"I don't even understand that. She *works for a board game manufacturer.*" I didn't mention that she got the job through Daddy, because there was no sense in poisoning my friends against Megan before they got to know her. Even though I didn't like her, she deserved for Tyler's friends to give her a chance.

"Maybe she doesn't bring work home?" Holly said. "Some people are like that."

"I guess," I said. "But how can Tyler date someone who doesn't want to play board games with him?"

"She's really hot," Gwen said.

"It's not that uncommon for couples to have different interests," Holly pointed out. "He's got us to play games with, plus his poker group."

"I guess so," I said doubtfully. Tyler and I spent so much of our friendship talking about games, it was tough to picture him dating someone he couldn't do that with. Then again, we probably knew about 8 percent of each other. Maybe he and Megan enjoyed foreign films or cooking together or bird-watching.

"Or sex," Gwen said. I hadn't realized I'd spoken out loud until she responded. "You know, the one thing he can't do with his other friends."

I sighed. "Fair enough, I suppose. I just... the thing is, at work, she's awful."

From the expressions on their faces, if we'd been sitting in the same room, Gwen and Holly would've exchanged a look at my comment. "No, this isn't jealousy. We've worked together for years and—"

A knock sounded on my door. Feeling guilty for talking about Tyler while he sat less than twenty feet away, I jumped about a foot. But he couldn't hear me. I spoke quietly and this place had old wooden doors. The half-empty paper plate in my hand jerked, and I moved in time to avoid dousing myself in a pile of grease and buffalo sauce.

"Everything okay?" Holly asked.

"Yeah. I've gotta go."

In a rush, I turned the tablet off. After smoothing my skirt over my knees and moving into a sitting position, I called for Tyler to come in.

He hovered in the doorway, leaning on the frame. "Are you okay? I didn't mean for my friends to send you scurrying to your room."

"No, it's fine," I said. "Just had such a long day that I needed some alone time."

"Got it. Sorry to bother you."

"Wait. I didn't mean you. Just… a crowd of strangers was too much."

He nodded. "Yeah, I get it. Well, the guys have cleared out, so don't feel like you have to stay caged up."

"I should work on my game for a bit, now that I ate." I removed my smudged glasses and cleaned them, willing my mind to wake up a bit more. "They left already? How long have I been in here?"

"Our games don't tend to run late. Tom's got a new baby and Skippy gets up for work at something stupid like five o'clock in the morning, so we wrap up fairly early."

"Good to know. I'd love to join you next time you're here, if work doesn't completely drain me."

"You're on," he said. Then after a moment, he asked, "Want to talk about it?"

Maybe it was a bad idea, but something about Tyler made me want to say yes. Gwen and Holly listened to plenty of rants over the years, but it might be nice to get a guy's perspective. Sure, I complained to Ryan at work. He was too close to the situation for either of us to give the other any useful advice. We mostly just made up creative curses using Megan's and Dennis's names.

Throwing my legs over the side of the bed, I stood. "Yes. Let me just grab a drink first."

In the living room, Tyler listened as I reminded him about Jameson's pending retirement, how badly I wanted the promotion, and my concern that he might pick Dennis the Dick instead. Per the Pact, I didn't mention Megan. Of course, that meant my thoughts were a bit disjointed. Tyler asked a few questions, but mostly let me ramble.

When I finished, he was quiet for so long, I started to wonder if I'd bored him to sleep. Or made him rethink his offer to help. But finally, he spoke.

"I thought you wanted to start your own company, be your own boss. Isn't that why you made *The Haunted Place*?"

"It is, and I do, but I'm not ready. Before I can leave my job, I need at least a couple of other games on the shelves," I said. "Unfortunately, I have no idea what to work on next."

"Still? You mentioned that before I moved in, but you haven't said anything so I guess I assumed it got better."

"I wish," I said. "Part of the problem is that I need to come up with a killer new idea for work at the same time. Forced inspiration rarely works out for me. Trying to come up with two concepts at once is draining."

"Yeah, I can see that," he said. "Can I help?"

The biggest problem of all was his girlfriend, and I simply couldn't tell him that. Asking him to break up with her was out of the question. Even if I thought he might do it, she'd only get worse. She might even do something to wreck my chances at getting that promotion. What a mess.

To my horror, tears started trickling down my cheeks. I hadn't realized how tired and stressed out all of this had made me until I sat down and started talking about it. Poor Tyler. He didn't need me breaking down on him.

To his credit, he took the tears in stride. Setting his wineglass on the coffee table, he clasped one of my hands in both of his. "Hey, it's going to be okay. Look at me."

Our eyes met. His held only concern, no trace of the derision or judgment that I showed such "feminine" emotion. I leaned against him, letting the warmth of his body comfort me. After a moment, he put one hand on my back, holding me. My body racked with sobs as I let loose all of the stress and frustration that consumed me.

For a long time, Tyler said nothing, just stroking my hair and murmuring sympathetic sounds. His calmness, his strength, made me wish I could stay there holding him forever.

Finally, I got control of myself and sat upright. He offered me a tissue with one hand and my wineglass with the other. I opted for the tissue. "Thanks."

"Feeling better?"

"A little. I still don't know what to do."

"Sometimes you've got to let it all out before you can move forward. But it seems that your first step is to come up with a new game and form a business plan. I can help you."

"You don't have to do that." In the back of my mind, a voice whispered that this was a bad idea. For one thing, his crush wasn't that long ago. I shouldn't take advantage of any lingering feelings to help myself. Even though Megan made it seem like they were moments away from picking out china patterns, she'd been known to exaggerate to make herself look better. But also, she probably wouldn't react well if the two of us started a project together. She'd made it clear at the bar earlier that she didn't trust me around her boyfriend.

Tyler kept his word by keeping his relationship out of our apartment. We never talked about his dating life, and he left the room when making phone calls. Asking him for details would violate the Pact. I hated compartmentalizing our friendship, but didn't know what else to do. Short of telling him that his girlfriend was awful to me at work, which also violated the Pact.

"I want to. Friends help each other." He paused. "Besides, I spend most of my day looking at spreadsheets and crunching numbers. Please, give me something interesting to do."

His words made me smile. Impulsively, I leaned in and gave him a hug. His warmth enveloped me. Then he inhaled deeply, which made me wonder if I'd made a mistake. Slowly, I sat up. "Thanks for this. I'm glad you moved in."

"Me, too." He picked up the remote. "Want to watch some Twitch before bed? Good streamers playing Super Mario Maker 2 helps me relax."

I grinned at him. "Thanks. Next time. What I need now is to get some sleep."

"Sleep well. There's nothing better for making you feel human again."

"Thanks. You, too."

He leaned back on the couch and picked up the remote, so I headed for my room. For a moment, I'd been worried he might try to kiss me again. Maybe we needed to have a talk, make sure his feelings really had evaporated. I'd thought so, until he smelled my hair.

What a mess.

* * * *

Like Tyler said, a good night's sleep made me feel like a new person. Work might be stressful, but I had a good shot at the promotion. The kids who play-tested my game absolutely adored it. Not only did they have a blast playing, but several of them made astute observations we could use to improve. Little kids didn't mince words when you asked for their opinion, and my group (along with their parents) identified some opportunities to make the game even better.

Once this game was completed, I could go through my document full of ideas, shine up the best ones, and present them to Jameson. My interview was scheduled for next week, which gave me plenty of time to get ready.

Meanwhile, instead of making myself feel bad for not having a new idea, I could work on marketing *The Haunted Place*. Once I found a way to get some press for my existing game, maybe my side business could get a much-needed cash infusion. Having a real opportunity on the back burner made it easier to deal with the frustrating people at work.

Preoccupied with these thoughts, I hurried down the hall, hoping to get into the shower before Tyler woke up. Nana would be waiting to hear about yesterday's adventures, and I wanted to get down there as soon as possible.

My brain barely registered that the bathroom door stood mostly closed until I'd already grasped the handle and pushed. A shout reached my ears, but it was too late. Tyler stood in the bathroom, body glistening from the shower, completely naked.

Shock froze me in place. My mouth opened to apologize, but no sound came out. Naturally, my eyes skimmed over his body, from his broad shoulders down his largely hairless chest, all the way to the tips of his toes. Thankfully, he wasn't as slow to respond, grabbing a towel quickly from the rack and wrapping it around himself. Unfortunately, his movements drew my attention to the one part of him I should never, ever look at. But I couldn't help myself. I might be demi, but I'm not dead. I'm still curious about things.

"Eyes up here," he said, in a perfect imitation of something I'd wanted to say to my coworkers a billion times. The towel wrapped around his waist, interrupting my view so effectively I felt a small flutter of disappointment.

My face flamed. "I'm so sorry. I was distracted. I didn't know you were in here."

"It's my fault. I should've locked the door." He gestured toward the opening behind me. "If you don't mind, I need to get dressed."

Finally, my limbs unfroze. I jumped. "Oh! Yes. Let me get out of here."

"Or, you could move, and the bathroom is all yours. I'm done."

Right. Move. I could do that. I stepped back into the hallway, resisting the urge to turn and dart into my room like a scared rabbit. He stepped toward me, not meeting my eyes. I shuffled back farther, and he turned and headed for his room.

"I really am sorry," I called after him.

"It's okay," he said. "Stuff happens. I don't want this to change anything between us."

We were both adults. I knew better than to run to my friends and giggle that I'd seen his "thing" like when I was in the sixth grade. Of course, this one was much... No. Not something I could think about. "Right. Let's never talk about this."

"Sounds good."

His bedroom door slammed shut, effectively ending the conversation. My initial instinct was to fly back to my room, grab my phone, and text my mortification to Holly and Gwen. But if I didn't continue into the bathroom, Tyler would know exactly what I was doing. Somehow, him knowing that I was talking about what happened seemed more embarrassing than actually walking in on him. Not that I should be the embarrassed one. It's not like he saw me naked. But he did see me ogling him.

I closed the bathroom door, locked it, then checked and double-checked that it wouldn't open. All secure. But that didn't stop me from hurrying through my shower, one eye on the door, wondering how Tyler would have reacted if the tables had been turned.

Living with a cishet guy made everything more complicated. Especially a guy who used to have a crush on me. Work had become so uncomfortable over the past few weeks, the last thing I needed was for my home life to also become awkward.

Thinking about work reminded me of Megan. Oh, no. If she found out I forgot to knock, she'd probably demand Tyler move out. That was the last thing I wanted. He made me smile. I liked having someone around to talk board games with at all hours of the night. Watching Twitch with him before bed when he was home had turned into the highlight of my day.

Tyler and I got along well. We had similar interests, not just board games but escape rooms and Twitch and stuff like that. I'd been looking forward to joining Tyler's poker game, and disappointed when my job ruined the evening for me. Not to mention the little things, like how Tyler was looking out for job opportunities for me, always made extra for me when cooking dinner, and texted if he wasn't coming home at night so I'd know to bolt the door. I didn't want to lose him.

Once my embarrassment cooled, I'd just have to ask him not to say anything. We could be grown-ups about this. Shrugging off thoughts of doom, I turned off the shower and reached for my robe. The obvious solution to this dilemma lay less than five hundred feet away: Nana's pancakes. They cured everything.

Chapter 8

"The Beatles said love is all you need. I say you need love, health care, affordable housing, and carbs." —Nana

As expected, Nana made me feel instantly better. She and Michael were already sitting at the table when I arrived, a steaming stack of fluffy goodness on a plate between them. Coffee percolated on the stove. Seeing their domestic bliss gave me warm, fuzzy feelings.

"So, how's the new roommate?" Michael asked as I fixed myself a plate.

Luckily, I stood in the kitchen drizzling syrup when he asked, so they couldn't see my face turn red. "So far, so good."

"He's very polite," Nana said. "Saw me out in the garden last week and offered to help me pull weeds again. You never do that."

"I'd love to help, Nana, you know that. Just point me at the plants you don't really like, and I'll overwater or otherwise accidentally kill them for you."

"Shush. It's not too late to write you out of the will." She smiled, taking the bite out of her words.

"You wouldn't. You love me too much. No one else taste-tests all your bizarre creations."

"Tyler might."

"True, but would he drive you to your doctors' appointments?" Even though I knew Nana was kidding, I changed the subject. After what I'd seen earlier, I really preferred not to talk about my roommate. "How are you, Michael? My grandmother treating you well?"

"Very well." He beamed at me before glancing at her. She nodded, and the two of them clasped hands on the table. "In fact, she's agreed to do me the very great honor of becoming my wife."

What amazing news! A squeal escaped me. My plate clattered to the table in my rush to hug them both. "Nana! I can't believe you didn't tell me." Her face flushed. "It only happened last night."

"That's amazing! Congratulations! When's the big day?"

"We haven't gotten that far yet. I need to figure out what to say to your mother."

"Ah." The mood at the table shifted. My mother.

We both loved my mother very much, but she'd never exactly been supportive of Nana dating after Grandpa died. She wouldn't be nearly as excited about Nana and Michael's wedding as I was. Of course, Michael had been delivering my mail since the day I'd moved in. I'd become rather fond of him over the years.

"You haven't told her yet?" I asked. "Do you need me to run interference?" Nana rolled her eyes. "I'm a grown lady. I can talk to my own daughter."

"Theoretically, she should be ecstatic for you, considering how much she apparently wants everyone in the world to get married."

Nana snorted.

"Hey, there's an idea," I said. "Tell her it's my wedding, then after she finishes freaking out, tell her it's you and not me."

"We'll call that Plan B, dear," Nana said.

Michael said, "We're talking about doing the deed before we tell anyone, other than you. We can go to the courthouse on my day off and get it done."

"You make getting married sound like ordering groceries," I said. "Come on. At least promise I can be there?"

"Of course. You can even bring a friend." I started to open my mouth, but she held up one hand. "Hold on. I didn't say a date. We need two witnesses. Bring Gwen or Holly or anyone you like."

"Thanks." I kissed them both on the cheek before settling down to my breakfast. "Just give me a couple of hours' notice, and I'll be there. I can take a day off work to watch my favorite nana get married."

"And you promise on your inheritance not to tell your mother until I get a chance to talk to her?"

"Cross my heart."

As I ate, my gaze wandered constantly back and forth. Their love radiated across the table. A person would have to be blind not to notice their happiness. With a start, I realized that I envied them. My evenings with Tyler had shown me that, even though life was good, it would have been nice to have someone to share it with.

* * * *

Funny how quickly time moves when you're dreading something. Workdays dragged when waiting for a focus group or product launch. They hurtled by now, when I had an interview/meeting with my boss about an "amazing" new project he was guaranteed to love but that I technically hadn't the slightest idea what it was. A meeting that started in… six minutes.

Five.

Silently, I cursed myself for letting Dennis get to me. If I hadn't gotten caught talking in the meeting; hadn't made up that stupid "Dads will love this idea!"; hadn't doubled down on the lie… what a mess. This wasn't me. I wasn't a liar, a schemer. I just wanted to make awesome games that people would love. Both kids and adults.

With a nervous glance at the clock, I pulled up the document full of ideas that lived on my computer. Some of this stuff simply didn't pan out upon further exploration. Some had been pitched to Jameson and turned down back when I originally thought of them. Some got delayed or decided against when competing games entered the market. One turned out to be too expensive to manufacture. There were even a couple of really cool ideas, but none of them were likely to "especially appeal to dads."

What a stupid thing to say. What would dads even love more than moms? A game about playing sports? Drinking beer? Moms drank beer while watching sports, too. Somehow, though, I didn't think my boss would be impressed by a lecture on the importance of not reinforcing gender stereotypes in our children rather than the game idea I'd promised him.

Across the desks, Dennis watched me. In my nervousness, I imagined that he could see the inside of my computer, knew what useless ideas sat on my hard drive. But that was ridiculous. If he picked up on my feelings, it was because they emanated from me in waves. I needed to rein it in, take control of myself.

"Is everything okay?" I peered at him over the top of my glasses like a peeved schoolteacher.

"Yeah," he said with a smile that didn't reach his eyes. "Good luck in there."

Weird. But not wanting to look a gift horse in the mouth, I simply thanked him and turned back to my computer.

Two minutes to go.

This was ridiculous. I deserved this job. My ideas spoke for themselves, regardless of which parent they appealed to more. I was ten times the designer of anyone else in this building. I patted down my hair, pushed my glasses back up to the bridge of my nose where they belonged, and picked up my tea for a strong, fortifying drink before going in to blow Jameson away with my qualifications.

As the smoky liquid crossed my tongue, my eyes nearly popped out of my head. Rather than the lukewarm tea that had been in my mug when I went to the bathroom ten minutes earlier, I got a mouthful of something much stronger. Whiskey, probably, although not the good stuff. Rotgut. Nasty stuff. The floral bouquet of the tea masked some of the flavor. Absolutely alcohol, though.

The surprise jolted me into reflexively jerking back, but I managed to keep the liquid in my mouth. Good thing I liked whiskey, although not rotgut mixed with Dunkin' Donuts tea. Blech. Using extreme effort, I lowered the mug, counted to ten, and swallowed. One sip of alcohol wasn't likely to affect my meeting nearly as much as if I'd spit it out everywhere. Which was certainly what someone wanted.

My eyes roamed the room, and quickly settled on the most likely suspect. Of course. Dennis now focused a little too intently on his computer screen. He must've expected me to take one sip from the mug and spew all over my dress. A wet spot on the outfit that reeked of alcohol did not make the best impression for a job interview. Dennis apparently didn't know that I liked whiskey. Not the first time he'd underestimated me, and it wouldn't be the last.

With a newfound sense of righteousness, I popped a mouthwash tab and swished away as it dissolved. Then I swept past Dennis's desk on the way to Jameson's office for the interview. "Thanks for the liquid courage."

"What are you talking about?"

It took effort not to respond that he knew exactly what I was talking about, but now wasn't the time. When I reached Jameson's office, I turned back to sneak a peek. Dennis now scowled at his computer screen, typing furiously. Excellent.

Then my eyes settled on Megan. She looked away quickly, but not before I caught the little smirk on her face. For a moment, I wondered if Dennis's confusion had been genuine. Nah. She probably just liked seeing me flustered. Megan was snotty, but she wouldn't...would she? She knew I didn't like her. She didn't like me.

It didn't matter. I'd never be able to prove it, so I needed to let it go.

Shaking my head internally, I settled into the chair across from Jameson's desk. "Good morning!"

My boss wasn't much for small talk. Without preamble, he said, "Tell me, Shannon, what makes you the best choice for the executive game designer job?"

"Well, to start, I've got the experience," I said. "I've been with this company six years, longer than almost all the other designers."

"Except Dennis," he said with a nod.

I knew he was going to say that. "True, but there's more to experience than time in the position. Since I started here, I've worked on more games that made it to market than anyone else—including Dennis. My creations have won more awards. My games have strong rankings on BoardGameNerd. com, and I'm a hard worker."

"Good points," he said. "Why do you think your ideas have been so successful?"

"I study the markets." Well, I hang out in a game store a lot. But that's basically the same. The store's owners had kids, as did Cody's sister. Nathan had twenty-plus years of game-buying experience. People talked, I listened.

He smiled. "Very good. You clearly have been an asset to the company."

"Thank you."

"So tell me. You said you've got a new idea that should appeal to fathers in particular? Since so much of the marketing targets mothers, I like the idea of involving dads with purchasing decisions."

Oh, no. I would never live down that stupid comment. If it cost me this promotion, I might never forgive myself. Hoping for inspiration, I closed my eyes. An image of Tyler swam across my vision. Of all the days to walk in on my roommate in the shower. I needed to be thinking about kids' games and fathers, not the fascinating differences between people's bodies.

"Shannon? Are you okay?"

"Yes, absolutely. I'm sorry." I wiped my hands on my skirt. "After doing some further research, I'm afraid it doesn't seem like such a good idea."

"Oh, come on, don't be shy. You know there are multiple ways to develop an idea. Let's brainstorm."

No. No, I didn't want to brainstorm. Especially not when I had naked Tyler on the brain. "I don't want to waste your time."

"Nonsense! Megan tells me you love to bounce ideas off others, that it's where the real magic happens."

What a nightmare. Megan told her father... what? That Tyler was helping me work through a game idea in my own free time? Jameson knew most designers had their own side projects. Did she outright tell him I lied? Or just that I was a shy designer who needed a "nudge" to share my idea? Maybe I wasn't giving her enough credit for sneakiness.

It didn't matter. Whatever she'd said, I was in big trouble. My eyes cast about frantically for anything to say, but all I spotted was a billboard advertising chicken wings outside the office window. Which reminded me of the bar we went to after work that night. And what else bars served. The worst possible train of thought at the moment, but once it took off, I couldn't stop it. My mind hurtled through the tunnel, barreling toward the light of an oncoming train.

Jameson continued to stare at me. The uncomfortable silence grew. I needed to say something, anything at all.

"I was thinking about a game...based around a barbeque? Where the players collect chicken wings and beer and then whoever gets the most wins." Oh, dear. *No, Shannon. Say anything but that.* But I had the worst case of verbal diarrhea in history. My mouth wouldn't stop moving, and these useless, awful words kept tumbling out. "They could use things like special outfits to boost the value of their food. You know, more colorful or...something."

Stop talking! Stop talking now. What a total mess. With every word, I dug myself in deeper. But I couldn't back down now, so I stared at my boss, meeting his gaze fearlessly while praying for the floor to open up and swallow me.

The light went out of his eyes. "Ah, yes. Yes, you're right. That's probably not a feasible game to develop right now. Not for children, anyway."

I should've gone with the lecture on gender stereotypes. It couldn't possibly have gone worse. Or maybe spilled the tea Dennis made me in Jameson's lap. Also better than this meeting.

"No, sir," I said. "Not a kids' game. Sorry to disappoint."

As he thanked me for coming in and we said our good-byes, I knew the one I'd disappointed was myself. One stupid offhand comment, and that promotion had slipped right through my fingers.

Chapter 9

"Winning isn't everything. But it's a lot."—Cody

After my interview, all I wanted to do was go home, climb into bed, and pull the covers over my head, despite it being ninety degrees with 98 percent humidity. Unfortunately, instead, they announced another mandatory all-company meeting at the very end of the day.

I wondered if this was it, if Jameson had chosen someone to serve as his replacement. After the day I'd had, if he announced that someone else got the job, I might burst into tears. Could he possibly have made a decision so quickly? Maybe, if he already knew what he wanted to do before my meeting. Considering how badly our conversation had gone, I didn't know if it would be better or worse to find out that Jameson had known who he wanted to pick before I talked to him.

When the time came, Ryan and I entered the room together for solidarity. I needed to be able to grab his hand at the moment of truth. We scoped out two seats together at the far side of the conference table.

"Do you really think he'd decide so fast?" he asked.

"I promise he'd decided before I left the room not to give me the job."

I wanted to kick myself. Losing a job because of my merits—or the merits of the person who got hired—didn't bother me. But the idea of being passed over for a promotion because I'd let Dennis get to me left a bad taste in my mouth. The only thing worse would be losing out because I didn't happen to be the boss's daughter.

A tall, silver-haired man with an extremely dark tan entered the room. He must be the BGG vice president, since I knew everyone who worked in this office. Sure enough, Jameson strode in directly behind him and the two of them went to the front of the room. They chatted while my coworkers trickled in. The moment the clock ticked over to nine-thirty, Jameson ended the conversation and addressed the room.

"Hi, everyone. I won't take up too much of your time, because I know you've all got projects to work on. I just wanted to introduce Hans, who'll be acting as a liaison between the different branches once the merger is complete."

The stranger stepped forward. "Good morning! As Jameson said, I'm Hans and my official title is vice president of human resources. I'm here because BGG wants all company employees to work together to find the best possible team-building exercise before we combine our offices."

Ryan and I exchanged a glance. Team-building, like a retreat? With trust falls and stuff? Dennis might catch me if I fell into him, but only so he could cop a feel. No, thanks.

Maybe I could get a doctor's note to avoid the whole thing. Something vague but highly contagious. Mentally I reviewed all the conditions I could pretend to have that would get me out of team building. Lost in thought, I almost missed the rest of Hans's announcement.

"In time, we're planning to combine this office with our others. We want an environment where any BGG employee can walk into any branch, anywhere in the country, and feel right at home."

Dennis raised his hand. "What do you want us to do?"

"Well, I'm glad you asked." The clearly prepared, corny response made me smile. At least Hans was having fun with his job. "You'll work in teams of two to create a team-building exercise that will improve communication among employees. I'll be back next week for your presentations. Whichever team comes up with the best idea wins a trip to BoardGameNerd Con in Dallas at the end of next month. Paid registration, airfare, and hotel."

OMG. My mouth fell open. I'd been dying to go to BoardGameNerd Con since I first heard of board game conventions a few years ago, but Nana's health had prevented it. Now that she'd recovered, I could finally go, especially since Michael would be around. Unfortunately, I'd missed the registration for this year. The conference sold out about a week after tickets went on sale.

Gamers and game makers would gather together for three days to play, promote, market, research... a gamer's dream, but also a game *designer's* dream. It was as if the company had tailored this prize just for me. I needed to go. I could almost taste the airline cookies as Hans described the event for anyone who didn't know.

This needed to happen.

I leaned over toward Ryan and whispered in his ear. "You and me. We're doing this."

"You think we can win?"

"Oh, yeah."

At the front of the room, Dennis wore a smirk as if they'd already declared him the winner. Wiping that arrogant look from his face would be the cherry on top of my winning sundae. I couldn't wait to get started, especially after sneaking a peek at Jameson.

The boss's face said it all. When Ryan and I won this thing, I might actually manage to salvage my botched interview.

* * * *

Half an hour after work ended, my bravado evaporated. My overwhelming confidence upon hearing about the competition unfortunately had not translated into anything resembling a workable plan. I sat on my couch, staring into the space beyond my open laptop when footsteps clattered up the stairs. Keys jangled, and the door swung inward, but I barely looked up.

"Hey," Tyler said.

I flashed him a distracted hello, then went back to glaring at my email.

"Everything okay?" he asked.

"Yeah. Maybe. Sort of. I guess," I said.

"Well, glad to clear that up."

"Sorry. Work thing."

"Can I help?"

I hesitated. Megan hadn't shown the slightest bit of interest in Hans's announcement. If she wanted to go to BoardGameNerd Con, I suspected she'd have gotten her father to pay for it. Meaning we weren't in direct competition here.

Hedging, I said, "It's just that, there's this big competition at work—"

"Are you by any chance up against She-Who-Shall-Not-Be-Named?"

"I don't think so, but I can't be positive. I'm not sure if I should talk about it."

He said, "It's cool. She didn't say anything to me. If she does, I won't discuss it with her. She needs to understand that you and I were friends first."

The enormity of the relief that hit me took me a little by surprise. More than once I'd wondered what would happen if Tyler had to choose between me and Megan. Getting his help with a work project might be a small victory, but it reminded me that he cared.

"You look thrilled."

"Sorry." I wondered how to be diplomatic. "I guess it's nice to see where I rank."

"What's the saying? 'Bros before hos'?" He winced. "What a horrible expression. Let's just say, I remember that you were there for me when I needed a place to live."

"Thanks."

"No, thank you. Really. What's the problem?"

"Oh, right," I said. "They're doing a contest to welcome everyone from my company to BGG. I have to present a team-building activity or exercise that will make strangers comfortable working together."

He shuddered, which made me laugh. "Oh, no. Can't you just suggest a retreat or something and go about your regular life? You don't have to participate, do you?"

"I wish. Whoever makes the best suggestion wins a free trip to BoardGameNerd Con." I sighed. "I've been wanting to go for years."

"How much would it cost to register and go on your own?" he asked.

"Registration is closed."

"Okay, but for the sake of argument. What would it cost you to go next year?"

I gave him the number.

"Wow." He let out a low whistle. The value of the prize far exceeded the sticker price to me, but since I couldn't afford to pay, it didn't matter. "Okay, you're team building, then?"

"Yup." I turned my screen so he could scan the email we'd gotten a few minutes after the meeting.

"Any ideas?"

"Not yet. I haven't met any of the new people coming in, but I'm not about to do trust falls with Dennis the Dick."

"Fair enough," Tyler said. "What about creating an escape room?"

"That's the example they gave," I said. "Unfortunately, there's not enough time. The presentations are due Monday morning."

He rubbed his chin. "What about a board game that encourages working together? Something like *Pandemic* or even *The Haunted Place*?"

That would be amazing. Entering a work team-building competition with a board game I had created from scratch. Part of me didn't want the guys at work to know what I'd been making in my spare time (although they were certainly welcome to buy if they found it on their own). But I loved the idea of using a game as a team-building exercise. Considering we made games for a living, I suspected the big bosses would be equally impressed.

"A cooperative board game would be awesome," I said. "I could submit *The Haunted Place,* but there's always the chance one person will take over and call all the shots. Then it becomes more frustrating than team-building. We need a game where that's less likely. Also, *Haunted Place* takes like a week to play from start to finish."

"Aren't you working on a cooperative game now?"

I shook my head. "Sort of. It's social deduction, so a little different. And it's nowhere near ready." I didn't mention that it was exactly as unready as it had been when Gwen first asked me about it, more than a month ago. He knew I was struggling, but not the extent of it. Work stress plus writer's block left me frustrated and annoyed any time I sat down at the computer to work on it.

He pulled out his phone and tapped at the screen for a few minutes. "Have you ever played *Construct Me?*"

It had been a long time, but I vaguely recalled the game he mentioned. Players worked in teams of two to build objects using different-sized blocks. The catch was, only one player could see what the finished object was supposed to look like and only the other was allowed to touch the pieces. The players had to work together to get the right construction.

"Yeah, why?"

"It's one of the games being featured at the conference. They must be doing a rerelease or expansion or something. Anyway, it's also the type of game that requires teamwork."

I thought for a minute. "You think I could use that for the contest? I thought it was out of print."

"It is, but Gwen has a copy. It wouldn't be a great option if your company couldn't buy it, but according to this, it's going to be re-released soon."

"Plus, I'll get bonus points for having a hot new game before it's widely available. Even if she got it years ago."

"It's perfect," Tyler said. "By the way, never play that game against Holly and Nathan."

"Why? Gwen's the one most likely to throw pieces." Our friend was well known for her hot temper and competitive streak. She once sabotaged Cody in a game so badly, Holly still couldn't believe he'd gone out with her after.

He chuckled. "It's not that. Nathan and Holly are scarily good at it. They named all the pieces, so when they're up, it's like 'Lay Jim in the middle of Stanley. Put Dwight next to them, standing up.' They can finish the entire construction while their opponent places one piece. Plus, anyone who can hear what they're saying gets so confused, it's an added bonus."

"Who are those people?"

"Characters from *The Office*." Of course. Their favorite show, which in a weird way helped bring them together.

"That's brilliant!"

"As long as you and your partner watch the same stuff, it works."

"I'm working with Ryan," I said. "I think he only watches documentaries, but I can ask. I promised to text him to discuss ideas later, anyway."

"Excellent. Invite him over."

"Now?"

"Sure, why not? We'll order Chinese. Gwen and Cody can bring the game."

"I'll text Ryan. Get some extra crab rangoon."

"I'm hurt that you even felt the need to say that." He was already dialing, moving the phone to his ear as he spoke. "Awesome. You've got this. The guys at work won't know what hit 'em."

And when I won the team-building competition at work, that promotion was all sewn up. Take that, Dennis.

About an hour later, our friends arrived to play *Construct Me*. Despite our joking, we invited Holly and Nathan. If they really had devised an unbeatable strategy for this game, I wanted to see it in action even when that meant I'd lose. You couldn't win every game, despite what Gwen and Cody hoped. Sometimes I marveled that they'd never held a competition to determine which of them was more competitive. But every pot has a lid, and they fit well together.

Tyler set up the game while I got drinks for everyone. Wine for Gwen and Nathan, beer for Cody and Ryan, whiskey for me and Tyler, sparkling water for Holly. Chinese food containers marched down the counter, ready for the taking.

It didn't take long until we were ready to begin. The game had a straightforward mechanic. The players formed teams of two people each. Since there were seven of us, we'd take turns. One person on each team was called the "constructor," the other the "instructor." Each instructor took a card with a picture on it. They needed to walk the constructor through creating the image using the different size and shaped blocks in front of them. The cards ranged from easy to extremely difficult. After flipping through the easy stack, Tyler and I decided to skip the introductory level.

"Do you want medium or hard?" I asked Gwen.

"What kind of question is that?" She took the stack of difficult cards and handed one each to me and Nathan. "Get ready. You've got one minute once the timer is flipped."

Cody said, "On your mark...get set... go!"

At the signal, I turned to Ryan and began speaking as quickly as I could. "Okay, take the long skinny piece and place it flat. No, not that one. The oval-y one. The bigger oval-y one. Then take the smaller square piece and set it on the left end. Right, now, take the... what is that?"

"Done!" Nathan said behind me. He turned the card he was holding around to show that it perfectly matched the stack in front of Holly.

My jaw dropped. The card showed seven different pieces arranged on top of each other. Nathan and Holly managed to complete their structure before I'd directed Ryan through successfully placing two of the blocks.

"That's not possible," Ryan said. "I still haven't figured out what the second piece is."

"Told you so," Tyler said.

"How did you guys do that?" I asked.

"Watch," Holly said. "Lay Dwight flat. Put Pam on his left. Set Angela on the other end. Lay Jim across the top..."

I shook my head in admiration. Even after hearing Tyler describe it, I hadn't quite believed they were so efficient. This strategy was genius. "So that's it? Name the pieces?"

"Not exactly," Nathan said. "You have to remember which piece goes with which name. Like, the long, flat skinny piece is Jim because he's tall and thin. The shorter skinny piece is Angela. The big oval is Dwight. It all makes sense to us."

"And yet, to the rest of the world..." I couldn't possibly use this strategy without spending way too much time watching television.

"You don't have to use a TV show," Cody said. "Use anything. Call them Washington and Lincoln and Kennedy if you want. The point is, you and your partner work out a system in advance. Then you can find the pieces faster and build the structure while your opponents are left standing around scratching their heads."

"Exactly," Holly said.

A smile split my face in two. It might take a little practice, but Ryan and I could do this. "I need to watch. Gwen and Cody, take over for us."

My friends moved to my spot at the table. Ryan and I leaned against the wall where we could see both teams. Cody and Holly each picked up a card while Nathan and Gwen stacked their pieces. Tyler remained in the middle to act as judge.

"I'm glad we're past the time when I felt like I had to let you win," Nathan said.

Gwen made a face at her dad. "When was that? When I was five?"

"Three."

"Does that mean it's your fault she's so competitive?" Cody asked with a grin at his wife.

She blew him a kiss. "You love it."

"Do you guys need a handicap?" Holly asked. "Ten-second head start?"

"Man, pregnancy makes you salty," Gwen said. "We're okay. Let's just hope the pain of your loss doesn't send you into early labor."

Holly snorted in response.

Nathan shot Gwen a look. "More likely, it would be the excitement of victory. But that's not funny. She's not due for almost three months."

Without intervention, the trash talk could continue for days, especially between Gwen and her dad. To break it up, I held up the timer, although from what I'd seen so far, it wouldn't be needed. Holly and Nathan would finish building the structure long before time ran out, even if Gwen and Cody didn't. "Ready? One, two, three... Go!"

Holly started firing off instructions at Nathan. His hands flew over the pieces. They worked every bit as quickly together as it seemed when Ryan and I competed against them. That didn't surprise me. But beside them, Cody and Gwen moved just as fast.

"Stand Finn up. Put Han and Leia on either end. Balance BB-8 on top..."

Tyler snorted, but I burst out laughing. Given how competitive Gwen was, I shouldn't have been surprised that she and Cody had devised the same strategy after seeing how well Nathan and Holly did. Especially since part of the reason we'd invited everyone over was to watch and "borrow" their technique.

"Done!" Holly's voice and Cody's rang out simultaneously.

Tyler took the card and examined each structure before proclaiming a tie. So little time had passed, I flipped the hourglass-shaped minute timer back over to let the few grains of sand trickle back rather than waiting for it to run out.

"What?" Gwen said to her dad, who stared at her. "Like I've never learned anything from you?"

"Valid, I suppose. You could've warned me you've been practicing."

"What would be the fun in that?"

"Besides," Cody said, "we worked that out on the way over. We were watching *The Last Jedi* when Tyler texted."

"It might not have worked," Gwen said.

"Don't be ridiculous," Cody said.

She blew a kiss at her husband.

Watching the couples banter, a pang hit me. Sometimes I longed for the type of relationship my friends had found. It took time to meet someone and build a friendship, create a relationship that *might* turn into a romantic attachment—and even then, there were no guarantees. I loved Gwen and Holly, but I didn't want to date either of them. Tyler became a closer friend each day. Ryan and I jokingly referred to each other as "work spouse" and would do anything for each other. But that deeper attraction never developed.

Dating apps didn't work for me, because most people expected an instant connection. Setups tended to go the same way. But maybe it was time to work less, get out more. Go to more game nights, join some Meetups. Expand my friend circle in an effort to ward off the loneliness. In time, everything would work itself out.

Chapter 10

"Don't let anyone put you off your game. Whatever happens, act like it's exactly what you wanted to happen. Unless the Red Sox lose." —Nana

Monday morning finally arrived. It had to be the first time in the history of office buildings that someone couldn't wait for their workweek to begin. During breakfast with Nana, I was so antsy, she finally suggested I walk to work to burn off my nerves.

Not the worst idea, but considering it was August, I decided to drive. The competition didn't start until eleven, but I couldn't wait. As a result, I wound up twenty minutes earlier than my usual start time, with nothing to do but sip my tea and munch the donut holes I picked up to share with Ryan. Neither the caffeine nor the sugar made me feel any better.

On my way in from the parking lot, I spotted Dennis off to the side in what used to be the Smoker's Corner. The past few years, people used it primarily to hold private conversations. From my vantage point, there was no way to tell who he spoke with, but if he felt the need to hide, I wanted to hear him. I inched closer, hating that I cared enough to eavesdrop but not quite willing to stop myself. A lot rode on this competition. If Dennis beat us, he'd probably also get the executive game designer job, especially considering how badly my interview had gone.

Dennis would become even more of an arrogant jerk. Every day, he'd find a way to remind me that he didn't just get the job, he *beat me*. Since his skills made it easier for him to find a new job, Ryan would probably quit, and I didn't know what I'd do if I lost my only friend and ally in the company. I didn't want to leave until my board game business took off, but

I also didn't want to work for the guy who made jokes about our company's single-stall unisex restrooms being a great place for "you and I sex."

Dennis's voice carried through the hedges to my ears. "No way. We've got this in the bag."

A female voice responded. Megan. "You better. Daddy refuses to promote me because I haven't been here long enough to 'prove myself.' I'm okay with you getting the job, but I can't stand the idea of working for *her*."

Megan absolutely wasn't getting named executive game designer? What amazing news! Her words made me wonder exactly what I did to make her hate me, but it didn't matter. We rarely worked together, and when Tyler was around she pretended we were BFFs. I could avoid being alone with her until they broke up, I found a new job, or both.

Speaking of Tyler, I inched closer. Maybe Megan would say something that would finally give me a reason to tell him about my reservations. I couldn't say "I don't like your girlfriend" without coming across as petty and jealous. But if I had something concrete, maybe I could convince him that he'd be better off without her.

"What did she do to you, anyway?" Dennis asked.

"She's trying to steal my boyfriend."

"No, she isn't," Dennis said, echoing my thoughts. "You had it in for her long before you started dating that guy."

It surprised me to hear my number-one nemesis standing up for me, but then I realized he wasn't really. He was letting Megan know he could tell she was lying, which was a power move. Most likely, he didn't care why she didn't like me.

"It doesn't matter."

"It matters to me," he said. "You want me to beat her, and at the moment, our goals happen to align. That's great. But when I'm in charge, I need to know if there's some reason I shouldn't keep her around."

"We're not some great sisterhood, you know. I don't have to like her just because she's the only other woman."

"No, I suppose that's true." A silence settled, as if he waited for her to say something else.

A heavy sigh drifted to my ears, so loud I expected Megan to fall over from the effort of exhaling so much. "Fine, okay. I asked Daddy to give me the designer job at the same time Shannon applied. For some reason, he gave it to her instead of me."

Her explanation surprised me. She acted like she'd had no interest whatsoever in making games. And how was it my fault that her father hired me because I was qualified? I certainly hadn't known that she also wanted the job or that she felt entitled to it.

Megan continued, "He gave me the market research job instead, which is totally boring and pays crap. Worse, everyone likes her better."

Because I'm not fake and completely two-faced.

"Thank you," Dennis said.

"Whatevs. Just make sure you win."

"Relax. Justin and I are going first. She's not going to beat us."

Ugh. Bragging about his victory before we'd even presented. What a tool. I resisted the urge to chuck a Munchkin at him through a hole in the bushes. Instead I bent down, peeking between the branches so I could see.

Megan tossed her head, sending blond curls cascading down her back. "She better not. I gotta go."

"You're not staying to watch?"

"I wish I could, but I'm not that interested," she said.

Dennis asked, "Why do you even work here if you don't like games?"

She shrugged, examining her fingernails. "It's a job. Daddy refused to continue my allowance unless I started working. And it's easy. He lets me mostly do what I want."

No surprises there. Except that, apparently, I wasn't the only one who noticed Megan didn't have an actual role with the company. I reached for my phone to text Ryan, but it vibrated in my hand before I unlocked it.

Ryan: *I hate to do this to you, but I can't come in today.*

The bottom dropped out of my stomach. He couldn't possibly be bowing out of the contest at the last minute. I needed him. On my own, I could explain how to use *Construct Me* as a team-building exercise, but the game required at least two people to demonstrate it. Hans needed to see our full presentation to understand how we anticipated using the game to help with team-building and camaraderie.

Maybe Ryan was joking? With great trepidation, I texted back.

Me: *Noooooooo! What? I need you!*

My initial instinct was to pick up the phone and call him, but I stood close enough for Dennis and Megan to overhear. Nowhere in the office felt safe from curious ears. My second instinct was to scream at him via text. But this was Ryan. We'd been friends for years. If he was going to bail on me for something so important, he must have a good reason.

Ryan: *I'm sorry. I want to beat Dennis more than anything, but Zoe got hit by a car. We're at the vet now.*

My heart sank. Poor guy. He loved that little beagle with all his heart.

OMG. What happened?

Ryan: *The leash broke. She darted after a squirrel, ran right into traffic. :-(I couldn't stop her.*

Me: *I'm so sorry. Do you need me to come sit with you?*

Ryan: *What about the competition?*

Me: *You and Zoe are more important than winning a team-building contest. I can pay for the conference next year.* I didn't add that it would take a huge chunk out of my savings. He had enough to worry about.

Ryan sent back a series of heart-eyed emojis. Then: *Dennis will be insufferable if we don't show up and he wins.*

Me: *He's been insufferable for years. Together, we can deal with him.*

Ryan: *No. Do the presentation without me. Maybe one of your friends can stand in under the circumstances?*

I had no idea if using a third party to help me would be allowed, but I had to at least ask. Talking about the game wouldn't be good enough to win the prize. I kicked myself for not making a video of our practice sessions, but it was too late now. Gwen was traveling for work as usual, Holly's pregnancy heartburn kept her in bed until noon most days now, and I didn't feel comfortable asking Nathan or Cody to drop everything and come help me. But someone else might. Unless his girlfriend told him not to.

"Where are you going?" Dennis's voice permeated my thoughts.

"To get a pedicure," Megan said. "If I'm here, Hans might try to rope me into presenting something, and I'd rather not."

Too bad Megan was so awful, because I could use a pedicure, too. We could go together, if we were friends—and if my work ethic let me skip out in the middle of the day whenever I wanted.

"What are you going to do once your dad retires?" Dennis asked.

"I'm going to work for *you*. Duh."

Her heels clacked against the ground, headed toward the parking lot. I faded back into the shadows, as close to the wall as I could get. My mind raced as she walked away. I needed someone to go through the presentation with me, and while she'd probably be pissed once she found out, that wasn't my problem. The question was, did I want to put Tyler in a position to fight with his girlfriend?

My initial instinct was, no, that wasn't fair. Why ask my friend to help me, knowing it would cause problems in his relationship? On the flip side, my internal voice argued, I wasn't supposed to know how badly Megan wanted me to lose this thing. How Tyler managed his relationship wasn't my problem. Besides, if he worried about how she'd react, he could say no. It wasn't my job to protect him.

Sometimes my internal voice sounded a lot like Gwen.

With a nervous glance at the time, I texted Tyler to tell him what happened. Before I could even finish my request, he'd replied.

Tyler: *Competition starts at 11, right? I'll be there at 10:45.*

I should've known he wouldn't let me down. The fact that he didn't even need to take any time to think about coming to help lifted a huge weight off my shoulders.

Me: *My hero. :-)*

At exactly quarter to eleven, Tyler's Civic pulled into the parking lot. I met him at the driver's door.

"How's Zoe?" he asked.

I loved that he asked about the dog of a guy he'd met once before even getting out of the car. "Still in surgery, but Ryan says the vet is hopeful she'll make a full recovery."

Taking the game from him, I led the way into the building and up the central staircase to my office. Outside the main doors, I took a deep breath. "You ready?"

"I am. Are you?"

"As ready as I'll ever be."

He squeezed my hand. "You've got this."

"No, we've got this."

Inside the conference room, we found Hans and explained why Tyler would be standing in to assist with my presentation. Lucky for me, our new vice president had three dogs of his own. Dennis objected to the last-minute substitution, but he quickly realized he didn't want to be the guy getting pissed about the injured dog. Without Megan there to back him up, when everyone called him out as an unfeeling monster, he changed his tune.

Once Dennis stopped complaining, Hans stood and clapped his hands together. "Okay, everyone, let's get started."

The people who had been milling around the room took their seats at the conference table. The presentation order had been predetermined by a random draw, leaving me and Ryan—well, Tyler now—last. I settled in to watch my coworkers' ideas, thinking about what Dennis said about going before me and wondering if he'd somehow rigged the drawing. Was winning that important to him, or was it just bad luck?

I forced myself to shrug the thought away. If Dennis had somehow cheated, there was nothing I could do about it now. His deception would only make beating him even sweeter.

First up, this guy who worked in Accounting stood and discussed trust falls. Not a big surprise—someone always made that suggestion. But also not groundbreaking, and he wouldn't win. I suspected, based on his monotone presentation, that Ragnar didn't care much about going to the conference, anyway. He probably only showed up because management provided free lunch at the end.

Next up, Stuart from Marketing wanted to do an entire weekend at this local questing warehouse. The place advertised something like a hundred different rooms to explore, requiring teams of three to five players to beat them. My friends and I had visited a few times over the years, and we loved it. Nothing beat spending the day solving puzzles with your favorite people. For a major corporation with unlimited funds, this was an awesome idea. However, it far exceeded the budget we'd been given by Hans for the project. That's why I hadn't suggested the same thing.

Finally, it was Dennis's turn. He swaggered to the front of the room. "Thanks, everyone, for coming today. I can't wait to close things out so we can all enjoy the delicious sandwich spread kindly provided by our fearless leaders."

Suck-up. He glanced over as if to gauge my reaction, knowing damn well I hadn't presented yet. I didn't give him the satisfaction of reacting. Stared back at him as calmly and coolly as if he'd asked about the weather.

With a smirk, he made a big show of pulling a board game out of his backpack. A square yellow box with blue letters. He waved it above his head, looking directly at me the entire time. *Construct Me.*

A gasp rose in my throat, and I managed to swallow it through sheer willpower, turning the sound into a cough instead. Somehow Dennis had gotten wind of my idea. Now he presented it to the partners as his own, leaving me with nothing to show them. Tyler patted me on the back as I sputtered, a reassuring reminder that he was on my side.

Dennis provided a brief overview of the game. His teammate, Justin, explained how the mechanic forced people to work together. Then they thanked everyone and sat. To my surprise, they didn't demonstrate the game. Did that mean they didn't know how to play? Or maybe they thought it wasn't important.

Hans thanked them, then turned to me. "Last but not least, we have Shannon. What did you bring to show us?"

My mouth went dry. I couldn't present the same idea as Dennis, not thirty seconds later. At the same time, after asking them to let Tyler fill in for Ryan, we couldn't say we'd come empty-handed. The tea I'd recently finished rose in my throat. The room spun around me. It was only one convention, sure. Only one team-building exercise, one meaningless day at the office. That's how most people saw it. The game came out years ago, after all. It won some major awards. I shouldn't have assumed no one else would be familiar with it. Of course one of my coworkers would have had the same idea. We were a bunch of board game makers; we knew the market. But for me, this competition was more than a team-building exercise. It was my chance to show everyone that I belonged here, despite being female. It was a chance to let the people transferring in know that I was serious about this job and not to discount me because of my gender. To show Jameson why he should pick me to run things once he retired. And being left empty-handed on my turn to present gave Dennis one more thing to lord over me. To my horror, tears pricked the edges of my vision. I couldn't cry. I wouldn't. That's what Dennis wanted.

Beside me, Tyler squeezed my hand and whispered in my ear, "It'll be fine."

"How?" I whispered back.

"Watch this." He stood, and the partners who looked expectantly at me turned to him. He raised his voice to address the room. "Playing *Construct Me* as a team-building exercise really is a great idea. So great that Shannon and Ryan thought of it as soon as they heard about this exercise."

"No way," Dennis said, a little too loudly. "If she's got the same game, she must have gotten the idea from us."

Until that moment, I'd naïvely believed this whole thing was one unfortunate coincidence. But the practiced disbelief in his tone told me he'd known all along what activity I planned to present this morning. I couldn't explain how I knew, but I'd have bet Nana's house that Dennis set me up on purpose. The only question was how he figured out my plan, and I didn't like the obvious answer.

Dennis was friends with Megan. Megan didn't want me to win this competition. Tyler and Megan were dating. I hated myself for even thinking my friend might have told her about my presentation. It couldn't be. But it was the most obvious conclusion.

A stupid conclusion, though. Why would Tyler come to bail me out if he'd helped to sabotage me? He could've not responded to my text, pretended he didn't see it. Or made up a meeting, some reason he couldn't come help. No. I refused to believe he had anything to do with this.

As I stood trying to figure out what was happening, Tyler asked Dennis, "You're a hard worker, right? Show up early, work late?"

Dennis puffed up his chest. "You know it. And who are you, anyway?"

"I'm the guy who came to help demonstrate the game, to show everyone how it's done," he said. "I'm also the guy who understands office dynamics. Shannon, do you always lock your computer when you walk away?"

"It's policy," I said automatically. But in my heart, I knew immediately where Tyler was going with his question.

"Sure. And most people shut down or lock their computers at night when they go home. But what about when you walk away for a minute? To go to the bathroom or greet a focus group or even to go to a meeting? Is your computer locked right now?"

I felt the color drain from my face. How very stupid of me. Even knowing Dennis would seize any advantage over me, I never thought to lock my computer when I walked away for a few minutes. No one did, because small offices like this tended to be trusting. It's not like we dealt in state secrets. Suddenly, I remembered the day my chair seemed out of place, and I cursed myself for not paying more attention. I'd even figured Dennis moved it, but so I would look silly, not to steal my ideas.

Now I wondered what other information Dennis had "found" on my computer when I wasn't around. Unbelievable. The second I got back to my desk, I was changing my password.

"How dare you? What are you suggesting?" As Dennis sputtered, his face turned purple. To Hans, he said, "Can you believe this guy? Are you really going to believe Shannon's roommate's lies?"

I stepped forward. "I never mentioned how I know Tyler."

"M-Megan told me," he said.

"How did you know I know Megan?" Tyler asked.

"I guessed. I know Megan is dating a guy named Tyler, and you know Shannon. I put the pieces together." His tone grew more confident with each word. We couldn't prove he lied, and he knew it. And maybe it wasn't him, but someone had been in my computer. It could have been Megan. It's not like BGG was going to dust for prints.

During this entire conversation, Hans's head swiveled back and forth. Now, he spoke up. "Let's simmer down, everyone. Dennis, Shannon, this game has been around awhile. I played it myself years ago. Using *Construct Me* for team building is a great idea, but not exactly like inventing the wheel. Especially since we all make games here, we should be familiar with what's already available. It's completely plausible that you both thought of it independently."

Begrudgingly, I agreed that it was possible, although unlikely. Dennis snorted and nodded a bit while staring at the ground.

"Great. Glad that's resolved," Hans said. "Now, you've got an excellent idea, but we can only have one winner. You can't share the prize, because there are four of you and only two conference passes available."

I repressed a shudder. As if I'd go to a convention with Dennis. Especially when the prize package included only one hotel room. "What do you suggest?"

"Let's play," he said. "You're both familiar with the game. You've each got a partner. Three rounds. First team to win two gets the grand prize."

Tyler had to be thrilled at this turn of events, but he maintained a perfect poker face. "I'm in if you are."

"Let's do this," I said.

It only took a moment to set up. Dennis and I moved to opposite sides of the conference table with a pile of pieces in front of each of us. Tyler and Justin stood at the head of the table, each holding a card so we couldn't see the picture on the other side.

When I looked at Dennis, he swiped at his forehead with the arm of his hoodie. I bared my teeth at him in a grin, cool as a cucumber. Nathan and Holly's method for playing this game wouldn't have worked for me and Tyler, since we weren't big fans of *The Office*. But over the weekend, my roommate had helped Ryan and me come up with a similar strategy.

Hans held up one hand for attention. "Everyone ready?"

Tyler and I exchanged a smile before we both looked at him and nodded. Dennis grunted, which Hans apparently took for agreement, and Justin said, "Yup."

"Excellent. On the count of three, then," Hans said. "One... two... three... go!"

"Okay," Tyler said. "Lay Mr. Darcy flat. Place Jane on one end in the middle. Balance Mr. Knightly on top. Stand Lydia up against the whole thing, touching Darcy and Knightly."

As he spoke, my hands flew. Knowing which name went to each piece let me grab them with ease, turning and stacking without hesitation.

"Time out!" Dennis yelled. "What they're saying doesn't even make sense."

I ignored him. To my left, Tyler kept calling out instructions, which I followed until he said, "That's it!"

"No fair," Dennis said, "they cheated."

My hands went to my hips as I turned to face him. "How?"

"Your partner is saying weird stuff to distract me."

"No, he's telling me which pieces to use. We're *working together*, which is the point of the exercise."

Behind him, Hans grinned. "Nothing Shannon did is inconsistent with the rules of the game or the spirit of the contest. They just came up with a more effective method of communication."

I resisted the urge to stick my tongue out at him. Something about Dennis made me want to act like a five-year-old. Sticking my fingers in my ears and saying "Nyah nyah nyah" would have been a slight step up, but with a superhero effort, I refrained from that, too.

Tyler, who didn't have to work at the company, apparently saw no reason to respond with maturity. He put his thumb to his nose and wiggled his fingers at Dennis. I could've hugged him for displaying exactly the sentiment I couldn't.

Hans cleared his throat. "The agreement was that the winners are whoever wins two out of three rounds, yes? Let's set up for round two."

With a grin, I pushed Tyler the pieces so he could build the next structure and took one of the identical cards Hans held out to me and Dennis. He counted down, and when he gave the signal, I started firing instructions.

"Start with Mrs. Bennet, lying along the ground. Line up Bingley and Lady Catherine on either end, with space in the middle. Stretch Elizabeth between them like a bridge."

Tyler followed my words with no hesitation, quickly replicating the image on my card. Meanwhile, Dennis glared at me, so angry that we completed the exercise before he'd uttered a single word to his partner. "Done!"

Hans quickly confirmed our victory, and this time I didn't hold back my joy. I whooped loudly and launched myself at Tyler, knocking him off balance with my exuberant hug. He recovered quickly, scooping me up and twirling me around before setting me back on the ground. The air around us sizzled with my excitement.

I didn't care that we were at my workplace. Or that the guys would tease me for acting "girly" for the next week, as if I should be ashamed of being female. Beating Dennis in this game, by so much that he found himself at a loss for words, meant more to me in that moment than all of it.

If I could turn that emotion into a board game, I'd be a billionaire.

Chapter 11

"When life gives you lemons, chuck 'em out and make chocolate cupcakes." —Nana

A week later, Tyler popped into my home office with a mug of steaming tea in each hand. "How's the new game going?"

"It's not." I glanced guiltily at the computer screen, where I'd been adjusting the fonts on half a page of text in an effort to feel productive. The euphoria at beating Dennis should have given my mojo a boost. Unfortunately, I couldn't get past wanting to use the one idea I had. Everything kept circling back around to trying to convince myself to produce it, despite there being a very similar game already available. Which I couldn't do. With a sigh, I took a long gulp of the tea. "Thanks for this."

"You're welcome. Is there anything I can do to help?"

"Maybe. It's early, though, so this is totally secret, okay? You can't tell anyone the details, not even Cody." *Or your girlfriend.*

"My lips are sealed," he said.

"Okay, great. I'm determined to come up with a new social deduction theme, but it's not easy. A lot of my ideas wouldn't work as a game."

"I liked the speakeasy idea you had," he said. "The Roaring Twenties are cool."

"Thanks. So did I. I wish there was a way to make it work, but it's been done." I sipped my tea, brow wrinkled. "And I'm unfortunately so stuck on that idea, it's hard to come up with anything else. There has to be something I can do so my work isn't wasted."

"Okay, so you don't want to put out the same themed game as someone else. I get that," Tyler said. "But their game is meant for at least a dozen people to walk around and chat with each other in one-on-one conversations. It's basically a role-playing game, much more like a murder mystery dinner party than a board game. Yours is a group discussion around a table, with as few as four people. Right?"

"That largely sums it up."

"What are the other differences?"

"In my game, one of the speakeasy patrons gets hauled off to jail in the middle of each night. In theirs, people have time to talk and all make their guesses at the end."

"See? You've got the same theme, but the actual games aren't *that* similar."

"True," I said. "I don't know, though. For some reason, it still bothers me."

"Fair enough. What if you expanded? Do a dual release, one the pure social deduction game you've been working on. But then also, what if you used that social deduction element in some other type of game? Instead of talking to the other players to find the undercover cops, give people something else to do."

"Like *Shadows over Camelot*?" The game I mentioned was one of the most complicated, longest games my friends owned (other than campaign-based games like *Dungeons & Dragons* or legacy games, which could last ages), but we enjoyed it. Although the game came out several years ago, it was still the most difficult cooperative game I'd ever played. Even when you didn't have someone secretly working to undermine everyone else, we routinely lost. "That game is painful."

"Well, your game doesn't have to be *exactly* like that," Tyler pointed out. "I was thinking of something like *Werewords*."

Ohhhh. The only social deduction word game I'd come across, *Werewords* had mass appeal because people who enjoyed both word games and social deduction games could play together. The entire game lasted only five minutes, but you could play over and over. It also required people to use an app, which appealed to a lot of millennials.

"Hmmm… What if we had players trying to guess the 'passcode' to get into the speakeasy?" I said. "Where one person is an undercover cop, and if they figure it out, everyone gets busted? The passcode could be a word or a phrase, which adds a bit of complexity."

"Exactly."

"I'd need Holly's help with an app at some point. But we could make the game function without it. Like, put the words on cards. That way, there's a low-tech version for people who want to be true to the 1920s theme." The more I spoke, the more excited I became.

"Excellent point," he said. "I like it."

"And we'd need other roles. The waitress, the band leader..." I made notes on my computer as we talked, until I realized I'd been typing for several minutes while Tyler stood in the doorway. "Sorry. I got a little carried away."

"No problem. You've been so stressed, it's nice to see you enthusiastic about something."

The compliment flustered me, so I went back to typing. Then I realized Tyler was still waiting for me to say something. I could thank him and send him away, but I remembered his initial offer of help. "Do you think you could sketch me some basic cartoons of what the characters might look like? Not right now, but whenever you have time."

"I've got time now," he said. "Let me grab my sketch pad."

He disappeared and returned a moment later, settling into an overstuffed armchair I'd shoved into the corner when Tyler moved in to make room for his leather recliner in the living room. I usually had trouble working at home when someone else was in the room, but ideas flowed freely back and forth between us. Having a collaborator was very different from having a distraction.

"Speak Easy!" he shouted, out of nowhere. "That's it."

"I thought I told you the game's name before? Anyway, we can't use it. It's taken."

"No. I mean, yes," he said. "Speak Easy, not speakeasy. Two words, because it's about speaking the passcode, not about the venue itself. It's a play on words."

"I love it. Tyler, you're a genius!"

Our eyes met over the top of his computer screen, and my heart pounded with excitement. To me, nothing compared to the joy of being creative, and I'd been blocked for so long that getting unstuck felt like Christmas morning.

Soon, the welcome sound of fingers clacking across a keyboard filled my tiny office for the first time in weeks. Behind me, Tyler's pencil scratched across the paper, quickly and surely. This sure beat the arrhythmic clicking of my mouse button while I dejectedly played online hidden object games, praying for an idea.

Next thing I knew, my stomach growled, pulling me out of the Zen-like state I'd fallen into as we worked.

"Sorry," I said with a glance at the time. "Wow, we've been working for almost two hours."

"Uh-oh," Tyler said. "I've got to get out of here."

"Is something wrong?

"No. I'm supposed to meet someone for dinner. I can still make it, but it'll be tight." He stood and stretched, wincing. "Speaking of tight. Oh, man."

"You okay?"

He tried to shrug it off, but failed to conceal the flash of pain crossing his face. "It's an old injury. Flares up sometimes when I sit the wrong way for too long."

"I'm sorry," I said. "That chair isn't terribly ergonomic."

"My fault," he said. "I should've sat at the kitchen table. Even the recliner would have been better."

"Is there anything I can do?"

He bent down, touching his toes, then rolled up one vertebrae at a time, like in yoga. "I'm way past due for a massage. Maybe I should cancel my dinner."

"Come here." I wiggled my fingers at him. "I can help you work out the kinks."

"Really?"

"Really. Come on, I've been caring for Nana for years. I can do a mean massage. Or, you know, a nice one."

"We've got to talk about these jokes."

"At least I didn't mention a boy band." I stood and walked behind him, grateful that my height left me eye level with the back of his neck. Flexing my fingers, I said, "Show me where it hurts."

Gingerly, he brought his hand to the right side of his lower back. I touched him softly, hearing a sharp intake of breath. "There?"

"Yeah."

Lifting the edge of his shirt, I kneaded the muscles, adding more pressure as I went. He let out a groan. "Sorry, am I hurting you?"

"No. That's good. Keep going."

I continued the pressure, using my thumbs to dig in, noting the stark contrast between my pale hands and his ebony skin. His back was taut, smooth. I'd always thought Tyler was a bit on the skinny side, but as I massaged him, I realized that he had more muscle than it seemed. He was thin, but strong. Without even realizing it, my fingers slid around his side, cupping his hip. More of a hold than a massage.

He coughed, and I jerked back as if he'd burnt me.

"Sorry," I said.

"No, it's good. I'm good," he said, pulling his shirt back into place. "Thanks."

"No problem. Let me know if you need anything else."

"Yeah, well, I'm late for dinner. I'll see you later?"

"Absolutely. I'm going to keep working, but I'll show you what I've got when you get back, if it's not too late," I said.

"Awesome. Sorry for running out on you like this."

"Don't be silly. You spent all afternoon helping me with work. I didn't expect you to spend more than five minutes talking about this game with me."

"I really enjoyed it."

"Me, too. I'm so excited about this project now."

"Right." Was it my imagination or did his smile falter, just a bit? He cleared his throat. "Have fun tonight."

"You, too." Fun with Megan. Ugh. He didn't say it, but that had to be who he was meeting.

"You okay?" he asked. "You look like you're smelling a raunchy fart."

I chuckled. "Yeah. Just... thought of a particularly unpleasant character. For the game."

"Cool." He glanced at his phone. "Can't wait to hear about it."

After he left, I turned back to the computer, but somehow my excitement had fizzled. I could, of course, write in an unpleasant character like Megan, as long as I didn't name her.

The Sneak: Completely two-faced. Pretends to be your best friend, but she's not. Lies constantly.

But I'd lost my taste for the game. When Tyler and I were working together, the room buzzed with energy. Now the lights seemed muted... I must be hungry. Or more likely, I needed water. Before Tyler came in, I'd worked for several hours without a break.

Time to recharge, get some dinner, review what I'd worked on, and maybe catch a streamer on Twitch. Not think about what an amazing afternoon I'd had collaborating with Tyler.

Chapter 12

"I'm not a poor loser. Come on, no one *likes* losing." —Gwen

Between my excitement at attending the conference and planning for Nana's upcoming wedding, the next few weeks flew by. I managed to bury my humiliation at the botched interview. Spending all my spare time working on *Speak Easy* with Tyler even made waiting for Jameson to announce his replacement bearable. With luck, the game would be ready to go to play testers by the end of the summer.

As long as we competed for the same promotion, Dennis remained on his best behavior. Mostly that meant he ignored me, but I'd take a total lack of discussion over ogling my boobs, making thinly veiled sexual references, or snidely questioning my competence. He and Megan spent more and more time together, working on some secret project, and I enjoyed the temporary reprieve.

Before I knew it, the weekend of the conference arrived. Although technically Ryan had been my partner for the team-building exercise, he agreed that Tyler deserved to go with me. He'd not only come up with the winning idea, but he'd helped me present it. Besides, Ryan didn't want to leave Zoe before she'd fully recovered.

When the first day of BoardGameNerd Con arrived, we woke up early to fly to Dallas. I couldn't contain myself. Two days of playing games, conversations with manufacturers (some of whom might be hiring remotely, if I was very lucky), and a chance to get out of the office for a few days. Throw in the fact that I'd be traveling with a good friend and that the trip was free for both of us, and it was my perfect weekend.

If I needed anything else to be happy about, Nana and Michael were getting married the day after we returned. A four-day weekend of relaxation, games, and celebrating love. What more could a person need?

My happiness shone back at me from Tyler's face every time I looked at him. Even though he didn't make games, he loved playing as much as I did. When our flight landed, we rushed to the taxi line, then headed straight for the hotel, eager to get checked in and start exploring the conference as soon as possible.

After we got our keys, we took the elevator up to the seventh floor. Tyler opened the door and went ahead of me into the room. In my eagerness, I plowed straight into his back. "Oof! Ow. What are you doing?"

"Sorry," he said. "Take a look."

He moved out of the way, and I rolled my suitcase up beside him. The room looked nice. Thick, heavy navy-blue drapes held open with silver cords. A plush dark-blue patterned carpet that would eat my high heels if I weren't careful. Inside the bathroom door, I glimpsed a tub roughly the size of my entire bathroom at home. So what was the problem? I didn't spend nearly as much time in hotels as, say, Gwen, but this place met all my needs and then some. Did he have some way of detecting bedbugs?

When I turned back to Tyler, I realized he'd been watching my face while I surveyed the room. He saw my confusion and pointed. My eyes followed his finger, and finally realization dawned. A massive king-sized bed sat between two wooden nightstands.

One bed, not two.

"I asked for a double room," I said. "They didn't have a two-bedroom suite, but they said I could get double beds."

"I know," he said.

"It's not a big deal. I'll call the front desk, and they'll move us."

"If they can. This is a big conference. The hotel block probably sold out months ago. Rooms with double beds tend to go fast because everyone wants to share to save money."

"Thanks, Mr. Negativity. This is clearly a mistake. They'll fix it, I'm sure." Confidently, I strode to the phone by the far nightstand and dialed the front desk.

Three minutes later, I replaced the receiver and turned back to Tyler, who stood tapping away on his phone, apparently disinterested in my conversation. Negative Tyler might have been, but he was also correct. The very polite concierge apologized and informed me that they could give us a free breakfast at the hotel buffet as an apology for the mix-up.

Conference-goers had bought out the entire hotel, and they didn't have anywhere else for us to sleep.

Not only were all the double rooms booked, but they didn't even have an extra king or queen room if the two of us wanted to split up and pay for one room so we wouldn't have to share a bed. Also no suites. We could sleep in this room paid for by BGG or go somewhere else.

To his credit, Tyler put his phone away without saying "*I told you so.*"

"It's no big deal. I'll sleep on the couch."

I glanced at the couch in the living area next to the bed. My inner feminist bristled at the idea of getting the bed because I was the woman. But the couch was narrow, not really suited to someone with my frame. Tyler would sleep more comfortably on it than I would. Besides, my company had paid for the trip. We wouldn't be here at all if not for me, and it wasn't like I'd messed up the reservation. I absolutely, 100 percent, had asked for a room with two double beds. My confirmation email said so.

"Thanks," I said. "Let's go downstairs."

Excitement perfumed the air of the convention hall. I'd attended the local American Board Game Championships with Gwen and Holly in the past, but this was different. People came to play (and buy) new games or talk to their favorite game designers. Some manufacturers hosted daylong tournaments for various games, but not all attendees entered. Vendors also ringed the room with dozens of different games, most of them brand new to me. Some not even available in the United States yet.

Beside me, a smile just about split Tyler's face in two. He looked like a kid in a candy store. I bounced up and down on my toes as I peered around the room, even though I already towered over most of the other attendees.

"Glad we came?" Tyler asked.

"This is unbelievable!"

He glanced down at my feet. "Are you going to be okay in those shoes? The conference lasts all day."

"I don't know about you, but I play most board games sitting down." I offered him a teasing smile. "But yeah, I'll be fine. I wear these at work all the time."

"You also sit at work."

"Sure, but the bathroom is wicked far from my desk," I said. "Really, don't worry about me. We'll be sitting and playing games at least some of the day."

"Speaking of work, any news on the executive game designer job yet?"

"No," I said. "When we won this trip, I figured I had it all sewn up. But no one has talked to me. Everyone has been on their best behavior, working hard to come up with new ideas for the big bosses. Rumor has it there will be an announcement next week, but that scares me. If Jameson makes an announcement without talking to me first, it's probably going to be Dennis. He's such a weasel. He doesn't deserve it."

"I'm sorry. That must be hard for you."

It *was* hard. Mostly, I got through the workday by ignoring my less supportive coworkers. As long as we worked on different projects, we were fine. A thousand times over, I'd earned that promotion. My newest ideas weren't a hundred percent ready to show off yet, but I'd been working hard all summer. Jameson would love the concept I'd come up with recently—not just one game but an entire new product line. With my help, BGG could explore a largely untapped market. After we got back, I'd scheduled a second meeting to discuss my new suggestions, but recent whispers made me worry it might be too late. I cringed every time I thought of how badly I'd botched the interview. Then I thought about how Megan convinced her father to poke at me until I blurted out a terrible idea, and I saw red.

I reminded myself that Tyler didn't know what she did, and I couldn't tell him when it was my word against hers. Instead, I decided to focus on the positive. "Overall, work is pretty good. I've got Ryan. Plus, I mean, I get to make games for a living. Six-year-old Shannon is ecstatic to do what I do every day. If I don't think about Dennis, I love my job."

"I'm sorry he's so terrible." His sharp eyes saw through my pretense, looking at me with concern that melted my heart. Tyler always gave me the impression that if he could, he would make everything better. But we weren't here to talk about my problems.

"Thank you." I paused long enough for him to see that I truly appreciated the fact that he cared. "Want to play a game?"

Not waiting for him to reply, I headed for the first booth on my left. Inside, vendors sold an expansion pack to a board game about building train lines. Gwen hated expansions, said they ruined the "purity" of the game. Personally, I liked getting new adventures or goals in a game I'd already learned. As a designer, I understood the need to create continuing income streams from the same game whenever possible. It was typically much easier to get people to buy an expansion for a game they knew and loved than to hook them on a completely new, untried concept.

That was the one drawback of *The Haunted Place*. As a legacy-style game, the campaign could be played exactly once. Each campaign took place over multiple gaming sessions, but once completed, that was it. The base set couldn't be expanded because the board changed with every level played. I could write a sequel, and hoped to, if the first game did well. Already, ideas swirled in my head. But no expansions.

Still, legacy games typically sold for more than your average game because they took significantly longer to play. They were hot at the moment, as a relatively new concept. With a bit of luck and some good press, everything would work out. Maybe I could try writing a new set of rules that would apply to the changed game players found themselves with when the campaign ended. Let those who already owned the game download it for free. Hmm.

According to the sign-up sheet, the creators of the game we looked at would be presenting it for play in the room across the hall in five minutes. Several seats remained. Just enough time to refill my water bottle and grab a seat. After dashing our names across the sheet, I took Tyler's hand and headed for the other room. Once the designers finished their spiel, we sat across from each other and started setting up seamlessly, as one.

From the moment we sat down, the day flew by in a flurry of games and laughing and piece placement and dice rolling and networking. We played games alone and games with strangers. We found competitive games, cooperative games, social deduction games, and some with elements of all three. I talked to every game designer who had a few minutes to spare while Tyler made a list of Christmas gifts. I loved every second of it.

By the time we took a break for dinner, I'd come up with about fifteen games I wanted to buy and seven ideas for new games to make, both for adults and kids. Nothing to appeal to dads, unfortunately, but I'd get over that someday. Probably.

I'd gotten the contact information for the convention organizers to see about setting up a booth for myself next year and obtained the names of three distributors who might be able to make my games cheaply enough to increase my profit margins. We'd even found a tournament with the new version of *Construct Me* taking place the next day and put our names on the list before it filled up.

All in all, it was the best day I possibly could have hoped for.

By the time we stumbled back to our room, I exhibited the kind of delirium that only came from having an amazing, exhausting day. I moved as if drunk, despite not having anything other than water and tea all day.

"You can use the bathroom first," Tyler said, kicking off his shoes into the closet. "I'll change out here and go in when you're done."

"Thanks." Since it took me longer to go through my nightly makeup removal and skin-care ritual than it took Tyler to change into his pajamas, that made sense. I gathered up my things and staggered toward the door. Then I turned back. "Hey, we can share the bed if you want."

"Really? You sure?"

"Yeah. It's enormous, and it's got to be way more comfortable than the couch. We had a long day, and we both need to get a good night's sleep. Tomorrow will be even longer. Just throw a couple of pillows or the extra blanket down the middle. We're adults, we'll be fine."

"Thanks." He smiled at me, a lopsided grin that made my stomach do unexpected flip-flops.

It hit me like a lightning bolt between the eyes. That smile was so sexy. Especially the way his eyes lit... What was I doing?

Oh, no. This was *Tyler*. My roommate. I couldn't suddenly find myself attracted to him. Not now. Not after all the times I'd pretended not to notice his feelings or outright rejected him. And not when he had a girlfriend, for the first time in the two years I'd known him. Why couldn't my traitorous body have decided to want him six months ago?

Something must've shown on my face, because Tyler's face fell. "You okay? I'm good on the couch. It's no big deal."

I couldn't let him know about the thoughts swirling in my head, about the possibility that I might be attracted to him. Most likely, I just needed to get some rest. We'd gotten up at five o'clock in the morning Boston time to catch our flight. We spent an awesome, fun day together. Having warm, fuzzy feelings toward him at the end was perfectly natural. That little jolt meant nothing. It should evaporate by morning. "Sorry, it's not you. The day sort of caught up with me all at once. Definitely, we can share."

Before he could say anything else, I swept up my pajamas and raced into the bathroom, shutting the door firmly, as if that would also shut out the new maelstrom of emotions raging inside me.

By the time I came out, he'd crawled into the bed on the side closest to the door. A line of pillows marched down the center. I climbed in on the other side, willing myself not to think of how flimsy that barrier was or what lay on the other side.

I needed a good night's sleep. Tomorrow, everything would go back to normal. Tyler would just be Tyler, my friend and nothing more. Or so I told myself.

Chapter 13

"With the right person, love is always worth the risk. Never give up."
—Cody

"Unless they get a restraining order." —Gwen

The *Construct Me* tournament started bright and early Saturday morning at eight. Not wanting to be late, I set alarms on my phone for six-thirty and six-forty-five. Tyler set up a fail-safe wakeup call at seven. We dominated this game, and we weren't about to let someone claim the title of champion because we overslept. I didn't know what it was, but something about this particular game brought out my inner Gwen.

After a hard time getting to sleep, I woke up twice before finally overcoming my discomfort with Tyler sleeping so close to me. The row of pillows between us seemed as easily destroyed as wet tissue paper. It wouldn't take much to toss the barrier aside if either of us wanted to. A few months ago, absolutely Tyler wanted to. This morning, I wished we could. But now, he'd moved on, and I needed to respect his new relationship. Throwing myself into his arms would ruin everything.

When I finally drifted off, I lay on the edge of the bed, rolled onto my left side, facing the air conditioner and the far wall. Herculean effort kept my spine ramrod straight. Tyler lay on his back when I got up in the night to go to the bathroom, but he maintained the same uncomfortable-looking stiffness as me. He didn't appear to be asleep, but I couldn't bring myself to ask.

He was probably wondering if he'd made a mistake sharing a bed with me, or if Megan would get mad when she found out. I had no idea whether he'd told her about the hotel's mistake. She wouldn't be pleased at the thought of me and Tyler even sleeping in the same room, much less a bed. In fact, it surprised me that she'd let Tyler come to the conference in the first place now that I thought about it. I certainly wouldn't be the one to enlighten her. Not my relationship, not my problem.

These thoughts clung to me until the sun's rays peeked into the room, slowly waking me before the alarm went off. I moved in and out of dreams, seeing Tyler and his girlfriend in one (in my dream, oddly enough, he was dating Lana from my roommate search, of all people), eating dinner with Tyler and Nana in another. When I finally opened my eyes, I was dreaming that we'd lost today's tournament and Tyler was comforting me with a hug. His strong arms embraced me, making me feel completely safe. I leaned back against him, savoring the feel and smell of him.

The smell? My dreams never involved scents. Images, yes. Smells, no.

My eyes flew open at the realization. The masculine scent in my nose wasn't part of a dream, and neither were the strong arms holding me in place. At some point during the night, our pillow barrier had vanished. Tyler and I lay in the center of the bed, his arms wrapped firmly around my torso, one hand making my breasts tingle under his fingers. Meanwhile, my hips wiggled backward. His pelvis cradled my bottom in a way that made me feel safe, secure. From the sound of his breath, he remained asleep.

Being held left me warm and comfortable. I wanted to stay there, savoring the imprint of his body against mine. The body I couldn't have, since I'd rejected him and sent him to another woman. The body I'd sworn to myself last night to stop thinking about.

This was wrong. I shouldn't be lying here, thinking about the firmness against my lower back. Wondering about what would happen if I turned in his arms and pressed my lips against his. I tried not to remember the morning I walked in on his shower, but the sudden mental image made my thighs ache.

Why couldn't I have experienced all these feelings when Tyler kissed me? It was too late to make my move now.

With a stifled groan of disappointment, I slowly lifted his lower hand from where it lay against my stomach and inched away from him, toward the edge of the bed. I barely breathed, too focused on not jiggling the bed and waking him. It seemed like hours passed before I made it to my destination. A glance at my phone told me that the alarms would go off soon, so I might as well get up. There would be no going back to sleep now, too afraid of wiggling back toward the temptation in the middle of the bed. On the other hand, if I replaced the pillows, I'd either wake Tyler or leave myself so little room to lie down I'd have to balance on one edge and wind up toppling onto the floor. Probably both.

Sighing softly to myself, I sat up and swung my legs toward the ground. My feet landed on one of the pillows that should have been in the middle of the bed. Tyler's breath remained the same, slow and steady. As quietly as possible, I pulled a bra and panties out of my suitcase, then grabbed a sundress and matching cardigan from the closet.

On my way to the bathroom to shower, I sneaked a peek at him. He looked so peaceful with those long, inky lashes against his cheeks. As I watched, he stirred, licking his lips. The movement jerked me back to reality. The only thing more awkward than waking up in Tyler's arms would be if he opened his eyes now and caught me standing there, mooning over him like some schoolgirl.

Inside the bathroom, I turned the water on as cold as I could stand, swallowing a shriek when I stepped under the icy blast. It brought me back to reality. We couldn't be together. It didn't matter. Tyler was a friend, my roommate, my tenant.

To calm my raging libido, while I shampooed my hair, I listed all the things about Tyler I didn't like: He was usually right. I couldn't figure out when he bluffed at poker. He tiptoed around me like a guest in my home rather than a roommate. He put olives on his pizza. Four not-at-all good reasons to forget about him.

By the time I finished getting ready, I'd managed to refocus on my energy on our plans for the day.

"You done in there?" Tyler asked when I finally emerged from the bathroom.

"Yeah, sorry it took so long." I avoided his eyes, but he didn't seem to notice. In fact, from the way he hummed as he showered, he seemed perfectly happy. He must have slept better than I did.

Of course, it helped that he had no idea about the way our bodies snuggled together in the night. How well we fit. What would have happened if we'd woken up at the same time?

The bathroom door opened, saving me from that particular brand of mental torture. It didn't matter. We were here to game.

I forced myself to act natural, determined not to betray the path my thoughts kept taking. "Ready?"

"Yeah, you?"

"Just need my shoes." Before I even finished my sentence, I'd stepped into them, grabbed my conference badge, and headed for the door.

He grinned and held it open for me, one hand sweeping out. "After you."

The conference didn't serve breakfast, but the hotel included a buffet. Thanks to the hotel's mistake in our rooms, we now had two free tickets. With the regular price at nineteen dollars, I couldn't wait to see what kind of delicacies awaited. Due to my unfortunate lingering, though, we had barely enough time before the tournament to drop in and pick up something to munch on the way. To his credit, Tyler didn't mention our late start or bemoan the virtually wasted meal vouchers.

We arrived at the conference room with a few minutes to spare. From what I could tell, the new version of *Construct Me* didn't differ in any important way from the original. Same number of pieces, same shapes, and still all the same color. These pieces might not be exactly the same sizes as in the original game, but I couldn't imagine that mattered to our strategy. The only other difference I noted was that the manufacturer used plastic instead of wood. Maybe they'd updated the pictures on the cards with additional structures.

No big deal. We still had a plan, and in a few short hours, with luck, Tyler and I would celebrate our victory.

The tournament used double elimination, so we'd be guaranteed to play at least two games. But with the system we'd worked out, I expected to go all the way. So did Tyler.

We took our places and waited for our opponents to join us. Mentally, I reviewed our names for each piece while we waited. From the way Tyler examined the table, he did the same thing. We didn't speak, not wanting to give away our strategy to any competitors who happened to overhear.

To make things fair, in each round of the tournament, every team sought to create the same structure. Twenty teams scattered around the room, with two teams per table directly competing against each other. The tables were spaced widely enough that players at one wouldn't be able to easily see or overhear what happened at the others. The winning pair would move on to the next round. The losing teams dropped into a second bracket where they'd play each other until only one team remained. Then that final team would then return to the top bracket and play an undefeated team.

In the first round, we wound up facing off against two women, Hilary from Austin and Liz from Sacramento. I didn't get a chance to ask how they knew each other. About thirty seconds after we took our places, an Asian woman with long, dark brown hair and an official-looking clipboard held her hand up for silence.

"Good morning, everyone, and welcome to the *Construct Me* tournament!" Scattered applause popped up around the room. After a moment, she continued, "I'm Shana, the head judge. Bear with me a minute while I explain the rules for those of you who haven't played before, and we'll be starting soon."

"Why would anyone play a tournament if they don't know the rules?" I whispered to Tyler.

"For fun." He smiled at me. "You sound like Cody. It's not always about winning."

He was right, of course. For me, games were about the journey, not the destination. I usually didn't care who won, even in cooperative games, as long as the process kept me entertained. Yet, for some reason, I wanted the excitement of winning together, the exhilaration of seeing what a great team the two of us made. Playing brought us closer together, but winning an entire tournament would cement our bond in a way I very much wanted.

If I were a petty person, I'd say it was to give me the ability to lord our win over Megan. As much as I tried to get along with everyone, our encounters always left a bad taste in my mouth. Tyler was smart, funny, and caring. Loyal. He could find a woman so much better for him. Someone who loved games as much as he did. Someone who was standing about six inches away from him...

"Also," he said, breaking into my unhelpful thoughts, "the bystanders need to know what we're doing."

Shana spoke into the microphone. "Is everyone ready? Instructors, draw your cards."

From the table, I picked up a card with a picture of an object in it. It contained more pieces than the games Tyler and I played when we practiced, but didn't seem too challenging. Across the table from me, my partner looked up from the pieces he organized and smiled at me.

"A reminder," Shana said, "that your construction must remain stable long enough for a judge to come around and check it for accuracy. If the structure falls before we get there, you must rebuild it. The other team can continue working during this time. Anyone who intentionally topples another team's construction will be disqualified."

Yikes. Intentional toppling? This was serious business.

"Ready? On your mark, get set... construct me!"

I started firing instructions at Tyler. This object contained multiple pieces, some of which balanced a bit precariously, but our routine let us work together as quickly and seamlessly as when we practiced.

Beside me, one of the women spoke in a Texas accent. "A5. G7. 2."

What? Part of me wanted to turn to see what they were doing, but I couldn't take my eyes off my task. Our gazes met over the top of the card when I paused, and he glanced at our opponents. Only a slight widening of his eyes told me that what he saw worried him. But it didn't matter. We needed to keep going. I opened my mouth.

"Check!" The word rang out from Hilary, who stood beside me.

My mouth dropped. We'd been doing well, but he'd placed less than two-thirds of the total pieces needed, even using our previously thought foolproof strategy. How could the other team have finished so fast?

Even before the tournament judge made it to our table to check, it became clear we'd been solidly trounced. Our strategy of naming the pieces worked well, but these women had also come up with a shorthand for the orientation and placement.

The second round went every bit as quickly. We made a valiant effort to keep up, but our strategy simply couldn't beat theirs.

"Nice job!" I said when their victory was confirmed. Despite my disappointment, I couldn't ignore how impressive they were. They deserved to win.

"Seriously," Tyler said. "You totally spanked us."

The shorter of the two, who I thought was Liz, winked at him, blue eyes dancing. "It's been a long time since I spanked anyone. Hope you enjoyed it."

He laughed, flashing those perfect white teeth, and it hit me that she was flirting with him. How dare she? She didn't know we weren't a couple! She didn't know Tyler was seeing someone else. She didn't know...

"Are you guys free for lunch later?" Liz asked. "We'd love to meet up."

I opened my mouth to tell them we had plans, but Tyler beat me to it. "Sounds great. We'll meet you at the double doors at noon."

I fumed silently, but arguing would only make me look petty and insecure. Neither of which was true. I was fine, just frustrated to lose so badly, so fast. Instead, I forced a smile. "Sounds like fun."

The organizers returned to set up for the next round, so we left our former competitors to play again and went to the seats along the edge of the room to watch until someone called us for our next game.

Snippets of conversation from the games still taking place drifted to my ears. "Take the long, hard piece…that's it, baby, and thrust it into the hole."

In my head, I heard Holly's voice. *That's what she said.* I suppressed a giggle that turned into a frustrated moan when I realized that, if we'd been paired against that team, Tyler and I would have won our first game by now.

"Are you okay?" Tyler asked me. "I know you wanted to win, but we have another shot. They just have to set up the second bracket."

I forced myself to take a deep breath. He didn't know what upset me, couldn't know. Liz hadn't done anything wrong. Maybe everyone in Sacramento talked to people like that. Neither had Tyler. Normally, I'd enjoy a friendly lunch getting to know fellow board gamers. If nothing else, talking to people about games they enjoyed gave me important market research. Tyler knew that; it was probably why he agreed in the first place. Instead of being inexplicably annoyed, I resolved to enjoy this opportunity.

* * * *

Five minutes into lunch, my resolve to focus on the positive dwindled. Liz was practically drooling in Tyler's lap while we ate, and he wasn't doing anything to dissuade her. Like, I don't know, mentioning his girlfriend. It didn't matter, I kept telling myself. I wasn't the relationship police. Tyler wasn't available to me, and if he wanted to flirt with someone else while he dated Megan, it was none of my business. I certainly wasn't going to inject her name into the conversation, especially not when we had a Pact never to mention her.

Plastering a smile on my face, I turned to Hilary. "Is this your first board game conference?"

"Oh, no! We come every year. It's the only time we get to see each other, since we live so far apart."

"That's got to be rough. Where did you meet, college?"

"No, we met through mutual friends." She paused. "We're both members of an organization for people who do well on standardized tests."

"What, like Mensa?"

"Yeah." A wariness entered her eyes, and I wondered what type of reaction she expected from me. "Exactly like that."

"Cool," I said. "Tyler's best friend and my best friend met at the American Board Game Conference a couple of years ago. They're married now."

"And how long have the two of you been together?" Hilary asked.

Tyler's face turned red. "Oh, no. We're not a couple. No, sorry. We're just friends."

Something about his protestations hurt a bit. Was the idea of the two of us so horrible? After all, he was the one who'd kissed me, all those months ago. Maybe he forgot. Maybe he kissed so many girls while drinking, it didn't make any impression on him. Maybe he hated the kiss, so he repressed it.

Maybe I need to stop feeling sorry for myself and remember that I have some self-respect. The voice in my head sounded an awful lot like Nana, and she was right.

"So you're not together?" Liz asked. The small, satisfied smile on her face made me want to snarl at her, but I forced myself to be the bigger person. She didn't know the history.

Forcing myself to keep a neutral face and voice, I said, "We've been friends for about a year and a half. Maybe a little longer. Roommates for a few months now."

"I had a male roommate once." Liz shuddered. "He's still programmed into my phone as Jerk Wad."

"Uh-oh." Tyler turned to me. "Please tell me you haven't named me Jerk Wad in your phone."

"Of course not! You're still My Hero." The smile that lit up his face brightened my mood considerably. To Liz, I said, "What was so bad about him?"

Until our food arrived, she regaled us with stories of used condoms left lying around, food blown up in the microwave, people parading in and out of the apartment at all hours. By the time I started eating, she had me laughing so hard, I'd forgotten why I didn't want to come to this lunch. Maybe Tyler was right, and I needed a break. Getting out, away from work, spending time with people outside our tiny circle for a change.

After we finished eating, we returned to the conference room for the remainder of the tournament. The games would run constantly until they declared one team the winner. I wished Liz and Hilary luck, despite secretly thinking they didn't need it, before pulling Tyler over to the table where we'd meet our next match.

"Okay, do we have time to revise our strategy?" I asked.

He shrugged. "It doesn't matter, does it? We're here to have a good time, and that's what we're doing."

"You're certainly having a good time," I muttered before I could stop myself.

"What's that supposed to mean?"

"Nothing," I said. "I'm sorry. Let's focus on the game."

"You really want to devise a new strategy when our next round starts in four minutes?"

I glanced at the whiteboard in the front of the room where someone had drawn two brackets. My name and Tyler's now appeared on the lower bracket, the one for teams that had lost one game. We would play until we lost another game or until we won the next four rounds. If we defeated all the other teams in our bracket, we would move back to the top and face whoever won their five games. Quite honestly, after playing against Liz and Hilary, I didn't want to meet any team that defeated them. My mind still reeled when I replayed our initial game, trying to think how we could have done better.

"Can we do what they did?" I asked. Tyler knew instantly who I meant. "I mean, sure, we can shorten the names of the pieces from Mr. Bingley to Bingley or even B. That's easy. Assuming we remember, that would save some time. But to create shorthand for every possible orientation of the pieces in the next few minutes seems impossible."

"Then let's not try," he said. "One thing at a time. For the next game, I'll leave out unnecessary words. So, instead of: 'Lay Mr. Bingley flat,' I'll say 'Bingley flat.' Things like that. Okay?"

I nodded. "And if we win, we can refine for the next game?"

"Exactly. Seriously, how many other people have come up with any sort of strategy, much less an unbeatable one? Chances are, half the people in the lower bracket never played the game at all before this morning."

His words gave me a huge boost. With a smile, I leaned over and squeezed his hand. Our eyes met, and butterflies fluttered in my stomach. "Thanks. We've got this."

If he felt the same rush of sensation I did at the contact, he didn't show it. Which was fine, as I reminded myself for the fifteenth time that we were just friends. I didn't need or want to be more, and neither did he.

A bell rang at the front of the room, and the chatter around us stopped. "Two-minute warning! Everyone take your places and get set up."

A couple joined us, both older than Nathan, so probably in their fifties. The man looked at me with an intensity that made me pull my cardigan tighter around my breasts to cover them. Tyler cocked his head at me, and I gave an exaggerated shiver. "It's cold in here."

He raised one eyebrow, but didn't comment. Creepy Guy let out a bit of a huff, which his partner pretended not to notice. Something told me we wouldn't be meeting this team for drinks after our game ended. In fact, I couldn't beat them and move on to the next table fast enough.

I pushed a stack of pieces in front of Tyler and grabbed our cards. "You're up first."

"You sure?"

I didn't want to stand next to Creepy Guy, and he stood arranging his own pieces on the table in front of him, so I nodded. "I've got this."

By the time the bell rang, I'd regained my confidence. "Jane flat. Lydia upright left. Bingley bridge."

As I spoke, Tyler's hands flew across the table. Beside him, Creepy Guy stood with his mouth open, looking back and forth between us. A furious look on her face, his partner kicked the table to get his attention. Unfortunately, when she did, Tyler's carefully constructed stack toppled.

I groaned. We'd almost finished re-creating the picture, and now we had to start from scratch. But I refused to let them faze me. Taking a deep breath, I met Tyler's eyes. "We've still got this."

"Pause!" A voice near my ear interrupted, causing me to jump. Turning, I saw a guy holding a clipboard and wearing a badge that identified him as Adam, one of the tournament judges.

Dazed, I turned to look at Creepy Guy, but he couldn't have finished. Not in the few seconds it took Tyler to rebuild. I asked Adam, "Is everything okay?"

"Touching the table is a rule violation," he said. "Your opponent caused your structure to topple. They're disqualified. You don't have to rebuild— you'll automatically move to the next round."

A wave of relief hit me. Here we'd been on the verge of elimination, but instead we took out the guy who made my flesh crawl when he looked at me. A double win!

With a squeal, I jumped around the table and gave Tyler a full-body hug. He returned it enthusiastically. Our eyes met, and my pulse quickened. He swallowed hard as his arms tightened around me. My breath caught.

He wanted to kiss me. I didn't just know it, I felt it with every fiber of my being. No matter what he felt for Megan, some feelings for me lingered beneath the surface. All I had to do was lean toward him, press my lips against his, and I'd find out how deep those feelings ran.

The air crackled, and everything else faded away. Nothing else mattered. Not the game, our current opponents, or Liz and Hilary. In that moment, Tyler and I were the only two people in the world, and we felt exactly the same shot of desire.

Shana cleared her throat behind us. The two of us jerked apart, the moment ruined.

Tyler released me, and something flashed across his face. It looked an awful lot like the same flicker of disappointment I felt. But that was impossible. He had a girlfriend, and we had a tournament to play. We couldn't let the excitement of an unexpected and quick victory to sweep away our common sense. I didn't kiss guys who had girlfriends, anyway, because I didn't have any interest in dating a cheater. It might be good to remind myself of that fact more often.

When Tyler turned to clean up the pieces, his hands moved steadily. He didn't seem to feel any of the emotional chaos coursing through my veins. Taking a deep breath to steady myself, I turned toward the woman beside me and held out one hand. "Sorry about that."

"No problem," she said as we shook. "Sorry for knocking the table."

"We would've reset," Tyler said.

"Rules are rules," she replied. "Good game."

Chapter 14

"Always keep your opponents off guard." —Cody

Our third game paired us against the duo I'd overheard earlier, lacing every instruction with sexual innuendo. We beat them handily. Even without our new and improved system, they didn't pose much of a threat. Still, the easy victory gave us a boost of confidence for the next round.

The next two games flew by in a blur of piece placement and instruction giving. Before we knew it, Tyler and I found ourselves filling in the last position on the lower bracket. Our performance after lunch confirmed my suspicion that we'd have remained in the top bracket if not for the bad luck of facing off against Liz and Hilary in the first game. Not that it mattered at this point. In about half an hour, we'd face the champions in one final nail-biting game.

Seeing the way Tyler's face lit up upon realizing that we'd be playing the final game made me extra happy for our victory. With a start, I realized the impetus for my newfound competitiveness: I wanted to win because doing well at this game made Tyler happy.

The tournament coordinators still worked to fill in the names on the top bracket, but a sweep of the room told me what I suspected: We'd be facing off against Liz and Hilary for the second time in the final round. We'd had only a few minutes here and there to bootleg their strategy, and I didn't know if it would work. They'd clearly spent a lot of time practicing. I didn't begrudge them that. Win or lose, I'd had a fun day and an awesome tournament with a good friend. Winning would only be the icing on the cake.

During the break, we celebrated our afternoon successes with mochas from the coffee bar in the hotel lobby. Tyler insisted on paying. "You're paying for everything else."

"Well, technically, my company paid for everything else," I said. "And I wouldn't be here without you. I'd be home, texting Ryan about this week's episode of *RuPaul's Drag Race*."

"I wouldn't be here without you, either, so don't argue," he said. "By the way, how's Nana? I barely saw her last week."

"Oh, she's great!" Quickly, I filled him in on the wedding plans. The small ceremony would take place on Monday morning at the courthouse, followed by lunch at a local restaurant. Me, Tyler, and Michael's children would be the only guests. With the addition of Michael's family, I no longer needed to bring a friend to serve as witness, but Nana adored Tyler.

"I'm so happy for her," he said when I finished. "Your nana is a neat lady."

"Michael's a great guy, too. It's so tough to find that right person, especially later in life."

"It's not exactly easy to find the right person at our age, either."

I shot him a sideways glance. Maybe things with Megan weren't going as well as I thought. "Yeah? I thought things were going well for you."

He shrugged. "I guess time will tell. Sometimes a person seems right, but things don't work out for reasons beyond your control. There's no way to know how someone feels unless they tell you. All I can do is keep doing what I'm doing and hope it works out."

His words surprised me, because until now, his relationship with Megan appeared to be smooth sailing. Sure, I never saw her, but he stayed out a couple of nights a week. I never heard them arguing over the phone, and our other friends never hinted at relationship troubles. For her part, she swanned around the office gloating about her perfect boyfriend whenever the opportunity presented itself.

Their unspecified problems explained why he flirted with Liz at lunch, although it still rubbed me the wrong way. Then again, I didn't have any right to judge, especially without knowing what obstacles they faced. It wasn't like he hit on Liz in front of Megan or took it beyond conversation. Maybe he just needed to blow off some steam.

The last thing I wanted after realizing my attraction the night before was to listen to Tyler talk about another woman, especially after waking up in his arms. The memory still brought a wistful smile to my face. But friends helped each other, even when it made one of them uncomfortable. "Well, if you want to talk about it, I'm a good listener."

An odd look crossed his face, but he quickly hid it. "Thanks, but I'm okay. We should get back to the tournament."

As suspected, when we returned to the conference room, Hilary and Liz stood at the table set up in the center of the room to host the final round. I forced myself to meet their eyes steadily and smile broadly. They couldn't see how nervous they made me. Tyler walked around the table to stand by the stack of cards while I went to sort the playing pieces. My hands shook the tiniest bit, but one glance at Liz's face told me she noticed. I took a deep breath, counted to ten, and forced my hands to still.

Like before, we'd play three rounds. Best of two took the crown. This time, I knew what to expect from my co-competitors, so they wouldn't have the advantage of surprise. They didn't know we'd been refining our strategy.

The moment the timer flipped, Tyler began to speak rapidly. My hands flew in an effort to keep up with him. Hilary spoke at the same time, but Liz turned to look at Tyler and faltered. Whether it was surprise at our new and improved game play or something else, I didn't know. But she paused, for just a second, and dropped one of the pieces. It ricocheted off the table, landing with a soft thud on the carpet. By the time she recovered, I was placing the last piece.

"Done!" Tyler called to the judges.

I held my breath, unable to believe we'd managed to beat them. Head judge Shana came and examined my structure carefully, comparing it to the card she'd taken from Tyler. Finally, she nodded. "Round one goes to Tyler and Shannon!"

A shriek of joy escaped me, but we didn't have time to celebrate. Round two started in twenty seconds. Tyler and I switched places at the table, and he rearranged the pieces the way he preferred them.

I drew the card, then squinted at it for a moment. With each round, the structures depicted grew more complicated. In this version of the game, some of the pieces were similarly shaped enough that it took a moment to figure out which instructions to give. A moment we didn't have. It didn't help that the pieces were all the same color.

Ten seconds after Liz and I received the pictures, the timer flipped and the round began. I fired off words at Tyler so fast I barely registered them in my brain, but it wasn't enough. Liz simply spoke faster. We still had two pieces to go before completion when her voice rang out.

"Done!"

Shana confirmed the structure while I drank water and tried to calm my stampeding heart. Just like that, the competition was tied.

Tyler clasped my hands across the table and met my eyes. "We've got this. Breathe."

In and out, I inhaled while he counted to ten, then exhaled for another ten seconds. We didn't have much time, but the slight break calmed my nerves. When he released me, I wiped my now-clammy hands on my dress.

Beside us, Liz and Hilary waited as calmly as if they stood in line at the movie theater. I refused to let their confidence faze me. Instead, I focused on stacking the objects in front of me.

"Ready?" Shana asked. We all nodded, but she wasn't waiting for confirmation. "On your mark... get set... go!"

Tyler squinted at the card in front of him while my heart pounded in my ears. We couldn't afford any mistakes, but if we waited too long to start, this thing would be over before it began. Beside him, Hilary did the same. Neither of them said a word. An eternity stretched by.

"Come on!" Liz snapped. "Give me anything."

"Right." Hilary jumped upright. "A14."

As if the sound of her voice shook him out of a trance, Tyler started speaking. "Elizabeth flat. Darcy right. Lydia left. Jane on Lydia, long way."

I followed his instructions as fast as I could. The structure started to take shape. Most of the cards didn't use more than eight or nine pieces, so I sensed when we must be nearing the end, although Tyler said nothing. My hands shook as I lifted the ninth piece.

To my dismay, Hilary's voice rang out. "Done!"

A wave of disappointment hit me, but I tried not to show it. "Good game, guys."

"Thanks!" Liz's excitement bubbled over as she bounced around and hugged all three of us. Her hair smelled like strawberries, a scent I used to love. I resisted the urge to shove her away.

"Not so fast," Tyler said, looking from the card in his hand to their structure. "The judge has to confirm."

I shot him a confused look. All day, he'd never once waited for confirmation before assuming that the first team finished had won the round. Was it because we'd reached the final of the tournament, no matter what? Or did I dare hope...?

"I'm sorry, but this is incorrect," Shana said as she inspected Liz's creation. "The timer starts again in three...two...one!"

Tyler spoke instantly, as if he'd been waiting for the cue. "Put Knightly on top of Darcy, standing upright. And... done!"

My heart still danced in my chest as I looked between our structures. Immediately, I saw the difference. Liz and Hilary had placed the longest of the three cylindrical pieces on top of their structure, whereas Tyler had directed me to use the medium-sized one. It was a minor difference, but that was all it took.

Shana hadn't had time to move away from the table, so she quickly reviewed my structure. "That's a match! Victory to Tyler and Shannon. Congratulations!"

A squeal escaped me. From the moment we'd met Hilary and Liz, I hadn't dared to hope we'd win the tournament. I didn't even know why it had become so important to me, but seeing how well Tyler and I worked together made me stupidly happy.

"Hell, yeah!" Tyler cheered. "We did it."

I put my arms up in the air, expecting a massive hug, but he slapped my hands instead. I bounced up and down and spun around, pretending to only have wanted a high five. Our big moment had no room for disappointment.

"First and second place, that's amazing!" Hilary said to us.

I offered her a sincere smile. "Congratulations. That system you two worked out was pure genius. We tried to copy it, but there wasn't enough time."

"Thanks," Liz said, "it was all Hilary's idea. She's the brains of the operation."

"Hush. We're a great team."

"And so are we," Tyler said to me. "I can't believe we won a tournament for a game we discovered a few weeks ago."

"Yeah. Good job, everyone."

"Let's go celebrate!" Liz spoke as if her invitation extended to the entire group, but her gaze was fixated on Tyler. "Drinks at the hotel bar?"

"No, thanks," I said quickly. "I'm wiped, and we've got an early flight tomorrow." What I didn't say was that watching her flirt with Tyler all day had made me into a person I didn't like very much. Time to recharge would do wonders to restore my personality.

"I'd love to," Tyler said, with a glance at me. "If you don't mind?"

"Of course not. Why would I mind? I could use some introvert time, anyway."

"Great," he said. "Hilary?"

"Oh, you know I wouldn't let Liz go without me."

I couldn't tell if Tyler seemed disappointed to have a chaperone or not, and I didn't want to find out. "Good game, everyone. I'm going to head over to the pool for a bit to unwind."

After we said our good-byes, I walked away. In another universe, we could all be friends, but I was too annoyed by Liz and Tyler's flirtation to allow that to happen in this one. Part of me wanted to call Megan and tell her what was happening, but since we weren't exactly friends, I didn't have her phone number. I couldn't even stalk her on Facebook, since Tyler didn't have a relationship status posted and hadn't updated a thing on his account since 2015. He might not have even accepted my friend request when we first met. If I could reach her, she'd probably call me jealous and then hang up on me, but at least I'd have felt like I tried.

About fifteen feet down the hall, Tyler caught up with me. "Hey. Are you okay? Did you want to celebrate with just the two of us?"

"I'm fine." I didn't even know how to put into words what bothered me without sounding jealous. "Have fun. We've done a lot of peopling the last two days, and I'm happy to curl up in bed and watch Twitch for a few hours."

"Okay. You're not mad at me?"

"Why would I be mad?"

"I don't know. Something seems off. You're less…Shannon than usual. Less vibrant."

"I said I'm fine," I snapped. "Are you planning to come back to the room tonight?"

"Why do you care?" he asked. Finally, I'd pushed him too far. "You've been barely polite to Liz and Hilary all day. That's not like you. Now you're mad at me because I want to go have a drink with them?"

"I'm not mad," I said. "It's none of my business what you do."

"That's right." He sighed. "Look, you can't get all weird and jealous whenever I talk to another woman."

"I'm not jealous!" I snapped. Good one. Getting angry was a great way to convince Tyler I wasn't lying. Silently, I counted to ten before continuing. "I just wanted to know if I should leave the dead bolt open when I go to sleep. The room is more secure with it engaged."

He deflated a bit, running one hand over his hair. "I'm sorry. Of course. I didn't think of that. Yes, please leave the lock open. I'm only going for one drink. But if it makes you feel safer, engage it, and I'll text you when I get back."

"Thank you."

Because of course, I cared what he did. As much as I didn't want to, I cared. Part of me hated finding out that the guy I'd been developing feelings for wasn't trustworthy after all. A small, darker part was upset that he might cheat on his girlfriend, but not with me. A stupid emotion, really, because he didn't have any reason to think I liked him. Also, I didn't want him that way. But you can't control your feelings, even when you dislike them, so there we were. Me, pissed at Tyler, annoyed with myself because of it, and him not having any inkling what was going on inside me. When I got back to the room, housekeeping had moved the dozen or so tiny pillows back to the head of the bed. Thinking about how I woke in Tyler's arms, I rolled up a spare blanket from the closet and put it in the middle before re-creating the pillow wall. An extra barrier might help. Then I changed into my pajamas, turned on the TV, and crawled into bed, trying to ignore my loneliness.

Maybe I should've headed to the bar for a drink, too. Found some other conference-goers to join, or even pretended to have a good time with Tyler, Liz, and Hilary. A good, stiff drink might have helped me sleep, but it was too late now. My eyes darted to the fridge located under the TV, but I didn't need to pay fifteen dollars for a shot of mediocre whiskey, or worse, twenty dollars for a mediocre whiskey mixed with soda.

Briefly, I considered calling room service for some dessert. Cake might also help me sleep. But I wasn't hungry. This was stupid. None of it mattered. We had to get up for the airport at the crack of dawn. With a frown, I clicked the TV off and slapped the remote down on my nightstand. I double-checked that my phone was plugged into the charger, then chucked my glasses beside it on the table.

Sleep would ease my frustrations. Sleep, and a little distance. Tyler and I had been spending a lot of time together recently. Between his help at work and seeing him at home every day, it was too much. We needed some time apart. I'd hang out more with Ryan, ask Holly and Gwen for some girl time... everything would be fine. Tyler and I were friends. My feelings would go away. I didn't care if he was out having sex with Liz at that very moment.

But as I tossed and turned, listening futilely with one ear for his key card in the door, the same words kept running through my head. *I shouldn't care... but I do.*

Chapter 15

"Some people get more than one great love in a lifetime. Some don't. You never know, so when you find someone who makes you happy, grab them and hold on with both hands." —Michael

The morning after we got back from the conference, Tyler and I had both scheduled vacation days. Despite not needing to go to work, I got up at my normal time, showered, put on my favorite vintage sundress, and bounded down the stairs to Nana's apartment as usual.

"Good morning!" I yelled through the open doorway. "Someone's getting married today!"

Nana appeared in the door to her bedroom, face flushed. "Hush. You'll wake the whole neighborhood."

"And why shouldn't I? This is exciting!"

"We appreciate your support. At my age, if I let myself get as worked up as you are, I'd have to worry about a heart attack."

"Not funny," I told her. "Especially given your history."

"You worry too much," she said.

"I worry exactly the right amount for someone who adores you. Where's Michael?"

"Oh, he's a bit of a traditionalist. Thought it would be bad luck to see the bride before the wedding. He spent the night at his place, and we'll meet him at the courthouse."

Just when I thought I couldn't love my future stepgrandfather any more, the gesture warmed my heart. "That's sweet of him."

"I found a good one," Nana said. "Speaking of, where's Tyler?"

"He'll be at the wedding, but I thought you'd want one last girls' morning before the wedding. From now on, it'll never be just the two of us. You won't have time for me." I pretended to pout, pushing out my lower lip.

"Don't be ridiculous," she said. "Now come make your favorite grandmother breakfast."

The familiarity of cooking in Nana's kitchen, just the two of us, enveloped me like a warm hug. As much as I liked Michael, and even enjoyed the mornings Tyler had eaten with the three of us, I missed our girls' time. Nana talked about her honeymoon plans while I mixed batter and heated the waffle iron.

By the time the scent of sizzling bacon filled the air, she stopped abruptly. "Listen to me rattling on about my beau like a schoolgirl. How was the conference?"

"Amazing!" I regaled her with lists of the games we played, an explanation of the tournament, and the story of how we'd finally won, despite nearly being defeated.

"That's wonderful, dear. And how was spending the weekend with Tyler?"

A knot formed in the pit of my stomach. Thankfully, cooking gave me an excuse to avoid her eyes. I gave Nana an abbreviated version of the weekend's events, making it sound like we'd made some great new friends rather than me getting pissed at Tyler's probably-completely-innocent flirting. With luck, she wouldn't pick up on my changed feelings for him.

"Well, I'm glad you two had a good time, dear," she said when I finished. "I'm still rooting for the two of you."

A hollow laugh escaped me. "He's got a girlfriend, Nana. There's no point in hoping for us to get together."

"Hmmm."

"What, hmmm? It's pretty simple."

"I'm not so sure about that," she said. "The past few months, I've seen the two of you together several times. You and I have talked about Tyler more than once. And before this morning, you constantly reminded me that you're not attracted to him. Every single time he came up in conversation. Until now."

That was the problem with spending time with your relatives. They got to know you better than everyone else and figured out stuff you'd rather not tell them. My mouth opened and shut, but I couldn't think of anything to say.

Keeping my face carefully turned to avoid her keen eyes, I focused on serving. Nana watched silently while I slid a steaming waffle onto her plate and dropped three slices of bacon next to it before handing her the syrup. Finally, I said, "Eat up. You have a big day ahead."

"This conversation isn't over." She poured the sweet maple liquid over her breakfast, then took a bite. "But I'm willing to put it on hold temporarily."

"Thanks." To distract her from me and Tyler, I asked Nana about Michael's family, who I still hadn't met. I knew he had three adult children a few years younger than Mom, but not much else.

The hot coffee, bacon, and waffles fortified me. By the time we finished breakfast, I'd pushed my unrequited crush on Tyler aside, ready to focus on enjoying the day. I couldn't change how I felt about him or the fact that he was unavailable. Tomorrow, I would figure out a way to bury my feelings permanently. Today was about family.

As I was leaving Nana's, I heard the upstairs door click shut softly. A moment later, I turned the corner of the landing and came face-to-face with Megan. It took me a minute to register her standing there. Why would Tyler choose now, of all times, to violate the Pact? We'd been pretty clear: the apartment, and our friendship, was a Megan-free zone.

"Hi," I said, trying not to show my surprise. I'd stayed up until after midnight working on *Speak Easy*, and I hadn't realized Tyler invited her over. She must have shown up pretty late. "How are you?"

Her face turned bright red. "Hello. Aren't you gone for your grandmother's wedding today?"

"I'm off work," I said. "Nana lives downstairs. The wedding is in Boston."

"Okay." She shifted from one foot to the other, then looked past me out the front door. "I gotta go to work. Busy day today."

I moved toward the wall to give her room to pass in the narrow staircase. She walked down the center, sending me squeezing up against the wall, despite having plenty of room to walk by me on the other side. My opinion of this woman fell every moment we spent together, and it hadn't started out that high.

Shaking my head, I resisted the urge to go straight to Tyler and ask what on earth he saw in her. He'd broken the Pact by allowing her to come over, so he couldn't get mad if I confronted him about it. Then I heard the shower running and the answer became clear: Like Gwen said a few weeks ago, Megan slept with him. It killed me that some people didn't need any more than that in a partner, but whatever. We needed to talk about her, and we would, but not today. Today was about love. Tomorrow we could talk about friendship and keeping your word.

By the time I double-checked my hair and reapplied my lipstick, the bathroom door clicked open. From the sounds in Tyler's room, he was looking for something to wear. I went down the hall to grab my purse, then headed down the hall toward his room. The door was cracked, but I was very careful not to peek.

"Hey, Tyler?" I rapped lightly on the door frame so the door wouldn't swing farther into the room. The last thing I needed was the torture of having to see his partially clothed body and think about what he and Megan had been doing.

"Yeah?"

"You ready? I told Nana we'd leave in five minutes."

"Almost. Have you seen my lilac tie? The one I wore on the day you showed me the apartment."

You mean the one your girlfriend bought you? I didn't say that. Instead, I considered the question. "I honestly don't remember seeing it since right after you moved in. Maybe call the dry cleaners to see if one of us left it there by mistake?"

"Yeah, I'll try them. Thanks."

I shouldn't open this can of worms, but I couldn't resist asking. "Can't you wear a different one?"

"Yeah, but it's my lucky tie. Seemed like Nana's wedding was a good time to wear it. You know, bring good fortune to the marriage?"

His lucky tie was the one Megan bought him? How sweet, and not at all annoying. "What a nice thought. I hope you find it."

Less than an hour after we finished breakfast, Nana and I arrived at the courthouse with Tyler. Michael's children and the justice of the peace waited for us along with the groom. His face broke into a radiant smile at the sight of Nana in her wedding dress, a simple knee-length ivory sheath with lace along the sleeves and collar. Her expression mirrored his.

Wondering if anyone would ever look at me that way again, I pretended to clean my glasses while sneaking a glance at Tyler. Once, we might've had a chance, but it was too late. The window for making my move had closed. My heart panged at the thought.

To focus on something else, I introduced myself to Michael's family and the officiant. Nana's sharp eyes darted between me and Tyler. With determination, I ignored her. Poor Nana wanted this relationship so badly, but some things weren't meant to be.

On the flight home from the conference, I'd daydreamed about holding Tyler's hand during the ceremony, about our eyes meeting over the vows and him understanding how I felt about him, without me having to say a word. I'd even imagined him coming to me after Nana and Michael walked out, telling me that he'd broken up with Megan and kissing me gently before walking back down the aisle with me.

Naturally, none of that happened. In my fantasies, Megan hadn't been in my house this morning.

The memory of those dreams filled me with embarrassment. Going away for the weekend with my roommate had been a huge mistake. At least Tyler had no idea that I now found him extremely attractive. If he realized that I pined for him, his pity would only make everything worse.

"Everything ready?" the justice of the peace asked.

Pasting a smile on my face, I nodded. Today wasn't about me and Tyler, it was about Nana and Michael. They were so lucky to have found each other, and I was grateful to be able to share in their joy.

At the front of the room, a clerk pressed a button on an old iPod, and music filled the room. Nana and Michael walked down the aisle together, hand in hand. My eyes met Michael's son's across the aisle, and we exchanged polite smiles. He reached over and squeezed the hand of the man standing beside him, drawing my attention to their matching wedding bands.

A familiar pang hit me. People thought demisexuals didn't want love, but that wasn't true at all. I believed in love, in relationships, in finding the right person to spend the rest of my life with. Plenty of demisexuals or asexuals also believed in marriages of convenience and companionship, but I wanted the whole package. Maybe someday I'd find myself attracted to someone at the same time they wanted me, but today wasn't that day.

Once again, my eyes darted involuntarily to the man sitting beside me. He smiled, a friendly gesture I knew better than to read anything into. Pushing my sadness aside, I returned a smile of equal wattage, then turned to focus on the happy couple.

Their vows turned my smile from forced to genuine. This wasn't the time or the place to think about my own relationship problems. Nana had been on her own for almost twenty years since my grandfather died, and she deserved to find happiness again.

The ceremony was short and sweet, followed by a luncheon at Nana's favorite brunch place. I'd offered to host something in our backyard, but between me being gone for the conference and the two of them getting ready to leave for their honeymoon, Nana decided to leave the preparations and cleanup to someone else. No reason to argue with that logic.

Tyler accompanied us to the restaurant, but wound up sitting with Michael's daughter, who worked as a tax attorney. They had plenty to talk about. I settled into my chair between Nana and Michael's son-in-law quite happily. If the past weekend had taught me anything, it was that Tyler and I should probably spend a little less time together, at least temporarily.

After the waitress brought champagne, I stood to give my maid-of-honor toast. "To Nana and Michael. I am ecstatic that the two of you found each other. Nana, I love you so much. You're my best friend, truly, and you've taught me everything I know. Michael, I liked you when you were only my mailman. Today I'm proud to be able to call you my grandfather. Be good to one another."

Everyone clinked glasses and cheered, but I avoided meeting Tyler's gaze. His eyes bored into me, and I wondered if he somehow sensed that I wanted him now. It didn't matter, because we couldn't be together. Loving someone meant wishing them happiness, with or without you.

* * * *

After lunch, Tyler and I drove home while Michael and Nana headed to Maine for their "mini-moon." They planned to spend the night in Bar Harbor before returning home. Later this year, they'd take a longer trip to Florida when Nana could arrange for Mom to come take care of her bakery. My mom might have weird ideas about food and be kind of a health nut, but she also liked money and knew how to run a store. She'd helped manage Nana's Bakery for years before moving to Florida.

Nana had also hinted that she might be thinking about retiring, which made me wonder if she'd try to entice Mom into moving back. I'd believe it when it happened. What must it be like to love your job so much that you never, ever wanted it to end? I didn't even want to go back to the office tomorrow after four days off, and I loved what I did.

"You're awfully quiet," Tyler said.

"Just thinking about how hard it'll be to go back to work after such an excellent long weekend away."

"At least you can gloat to Dennis about how awesome the conference was. Remind him that you went and he didn't."

"Yeah." I sighed. "If only I didn't hate stooping to his level."

"He's hot garbage. You could never bend low enough to wind up at his level."

"Thanks." I squeezed his hand where it rested on the gear shift, wishing I had a reason to keep touching him.

He turned his wrist, running his thumb over my fingers, sending a lightning bolt down my spine. I turned to look at him, and something passed between us. All this time, I'd assumed that his feelings for me changed before he started seeing Megan. Suddenly, I wondered if some possibility for romance still lurked between the surface.

The car stopped at a light. Our hands still touched. At this point, it would be weird to pull back, but it was weirder to stay the way we were, frozen together. The longer we touched, the more my skin burned, calling my attention to the spot. I wanted to lean over and kiss him; I wanted him to lean over and kiss me. From the look on Tyler's face, he wanted it, too.

But I wasn't a boyfriend stealer. Tyler wasn't a cheater. If anything were to ever happen between us, he'd have to break up with Megan first.

Summoning an admirable amount of self-restraint, I faked a sneeze, pulling my hand back. Then I dug in my purse under the pretext of needing a tissue. Tyler exhaled, releasing a breath I hadn't realized he'd been holding.

Behind us, a car honked. Ahead, empty road stretched between us and the green light. Tyler shifted into gear, and the car started moving. For the rest of the trip home, I clutched my purse in my lap, keeping my gaze focused firmly out the side window. As the buildings whizzed by, I racked my brain for something to say, some way to tell Tyler how I felt about him. The words never came.

At the end of the day, I had no business meddling in his relationship. Confessing my feelings would only create a mess. I couldn't do that to my friend.

Chapter 16

"Some people are such dicks, it's not worth wasting your time on them."
—Gwen

The next morning, I lay in bed staring up at the ceiling until after Tyler left for work. Memories of the prior day swirled through my head until I simply couldn't face him. For a shining moment, I'd allowed myself to think he wanted me as badly as I wanted him. But when we got home, he gave me no hint of any interest. In fact, he dropped me off and left, probably to go see his girlfriend. I'd missed my chance.

The reminder of how desperately I'd wanted to kiss him made me roll over and bury my head under the covers. The only thing more embarrassing than my uncharacteristic behavior after the wedding was knowing how he would have reacted if I'd gone a step further and pressed my lips to his.

He'd have pulled away. Informed me that he was happy with Megan and that he didn't want to be anything but roommates. Then, if Megan found out, she'd probably make him move out and I'd be stuck back on Craigslist. Or worse, she'd talk Jameson into firing me.

A reminder popped up on my phone, informing me that while I'd love to hide in bed all day, my boss expected me to show up at work in time for the staff meeting at eight o'clock. Being heartsick wasn't an excuse for missing work, so I forced myself out of bed.

Since Nana and Michael were in Maine, no one expected me to show up at their apartment for breakfast. A pang of loneliness hit me. Nana never took a vacation. Other than when I went to Mexico for Gwen's wedding and to the conference, we'd eaten breakfast together every morning for years. Even when Nana got sick, I brought food to the hospital. Never had I missed a day and stayed in my own apartment. I didn't like it.

Not even stopping at Dunkin' Donuts on the way made me feel any better. Their coffee cake muffins didn't hold a candle to Nana's recipe.

I hoped her getting married wouldn't change everything. What if Nana moved into Michael's condo? Would I walk a mile to his place for breakfast every morning? The thought of eating breakfast alone after all these years made me sad.

Work was exactly what the doctor ordered after the last few days, a distraction from this maelstrom of emotion.

With a start, I realized that an all-staff meeting meant seeing Megan first thing as soon as I got back. Even though she hadn't said anything yet, she couldn't have been happy that Tyler and I went away together, or that we attended a wedding together when we got back. From Day One, she'd been worried that I had feelings for him, that I might try to steal him away. Having realized that her concerns were right on target, I didn't know how to face her.

Not that I'd ever tell her about my feelings—or Tyler, for that matter. No one ever needed to know. The concern was simply that I'd never been a talented liar. With my luck, Megan would take one look at me and see my change of heart branded on me like a big scarlet *A*.

I stopped dead in my tracks and pulled out my phone. Ten minutes until the meeting started. Our office building towered above me at the end of the block. In less than two minutes, I'd enter the lobby. The elevator took about another forty-five seconds. When I arrived at my desk, Megan would be there. I knew it.

Like a coward, I turned and headed for the nearest Dunkin' Donuts to make my second stop of the morning. It might make me a few minutes late for the meeting, but if I brought Munchkins for the group, Jameson would forgive me.

Twelve minutes later, I slunk into the office. As expected, a sea of empty desks awaited me. The conference room door stood shut. Through the glass panes beside the door, I saw Jameson standing in the front of the room, up by the whiteboard.

With an apologetic smile, I cracked the door open and popped my head through. "Good morning, everyone. Sorry I'm late."

"How nice of you to join us," Megan said snidely.

I held up the small cardboard box in my hand like a shield. "I brought donut holes."

"What a lovely gesture!" Jameson said. "Thank you! These are perfect, because this meeting involves a celebration of sorts."

A celebration? Suddenly, my mouth went dry. Although I hadn't checked my work messages since leaving for the conference, if Jameson wanted to promote me, he'd have called my cell. The likelihood of me entering this meeting with a promotion waiting that I didn't know about approached zero. He must have made the decision over the weekend, without waiting for our second meeting. My heart dropped like a stone.

Everyone was watching me, so I smiled and murmured wordlessly at Jameson, holding out the box. Hopefully he wouldn't realize I hadn't said anything. He took it, and I headed toward the sole empty seat at the conference table. Ryan met my eyes quizzically. I shook my head slightly. No idea who we were celebrating, which meant it wasn't me.

The cardboard box of treats went in the middle, and I grabbed two before settling back with my hot tea. Taking a long sip, I braced myself.

"As I was about to say," Jameson said, "congratulations are in order."

I froze, looking around the room. Sitting next to her father as usual, Megan wore her regular plastic smile, the one that didn't meet her eyes. She always looked like she thought people should give her awards just for breathing, so that told me nothing. But across the table, I spotted the corners of Dennis's mouth turning ever so slightly upward. My stomach rolled over, and I pushed the food in front of me away.

"Last week, an idea for a new game came to my attention," Jameson said. "Something new, something fun: social deduction games for kids."

Hold on a second. No one knew what I'd been fleshing out since finishing my last project. I'd guarded the idea closely, because I wanted everything to be perfect before I took it to Jameson. I spent hours poring over the file, polishing it, making sure there weren't any mistakes. It wasn't just one game, but an entire new line, with simplified rules and themes more appropriate for kids than speakeasies or Nazis or mafia members. I loved the idea; had trouble keeping it to myself. Not wanting to spoil the surprise, I didn't even mention it to Ryan or Tyler. But then how had Jameson found out?

The days before I left had been a bit of a whirlwind, but could I have been so busy that I forgot telling Jameson my plan? Maybe in one of the emails about the days I'd need off? No. Impossible.

"Kids aren't that different from adults," Jameson said. "They like the same types of games. And one thing kids love is outsmarting other people—especially their parents."

Now he was quoting directly from my notes. I thought back to the mess on my desk, trying to remember if I'd printed anything. Since we shared a printer, it was entirely possible Jameson would have found my notes if I'd forgotten to pick them up. The only thing was, those notes shouldn't have been on the printer in the first place. I was very sure I'd never printed anything, and I couldn't have been distracted enough to do it by mistake.

"In fact, I know these new games are going to be a hit," he continued. "I love this concept so much that I've decided to promote the person who came up with it."

At his words, a massive smile crossed my face. This was really happening. He was going to give me the promotion! I'd worked so long, so hard. Between winning the team-building exercise and creating this new game, I'd absolutely earned the title of executive game designer. In my excitement, I almost forgot that my boss shouldn't know these games existed. We were scheduled to talk about them tomorrow.

Everyone in the room held their breath, waiting to hear who Jameson would name. I sat up a bit straighter in my seat, savoring this moment.

As I shifted, my eyes met Dennis's. All of a sudden, I knew exactly how Jameson learned about this game. My mind went back to the day I tripped over my chair, to Dennis's watching eyes. I thought about how he'd read my emails to Tyler and found out about my plans to present *Construct Me.*

With horror, I realized exactly what was about to happen, and I didn't know any way to stop it. Desperately, I jumped to my feet. "Jameson, can I talk to you for a moment privately?"

"After the meeting. Come on, Shannon, you know better than to try to steal someone else's thunder."

Yes, unlike the other people in this office, stealing wasn't my style. With a huff, I slumped back into my chair, mind racing.

"As I was saying," Jameson continued, "let's all give a hand to our new executive game designer. Congratulations, Dennis! What a great new product line you've come up with!"

* * * *

After the meeting, I remained in my chair, red-hot rage blinding me. My mind raced. Dennis stole my idea. No question. But how did he get the details? Back when he first searched my computer, I'd only sketched out some of the basics. Since the day of the competition, when I realized what happened, I'd not only been extremely careful about locking my computer, I'd changed my password to something random, obtained from a random password generator online. They'd never guess it—I'd had to walk around with it written down on a slip of paper in my bra for a week before memorizing it.

A thought occurred to me. Shoving my chair backward, I grabbed my phone and stuck it in a pocket of my dress. Then I snuck outside to call Holly, walking deep into an empty section of the parking lot where I could see if anyone approached.

"Calling on the phone? Wow, I must be a high-level friend!" she said when I answered. "Are we hiding bodies?"

I chuckled. "Not yet. Maybe. But also, this is too complicated for text. I need your IT expertise."

"Sure. What's up?"

Quickly, I explained how Dennis stole my project idea, and how I suspected he'd managed to access my computer. "Typically, in an office, could the big boss—or, I don't know, the big boss's daughter—access passwords?"

Holly hesitated. "I'm not sure how to put this delicately."

"This isn't about Megan and Tyler." Well, probably not. If she broke into my computer to steal my ideas, he absolutely was going to finally hear about what a snake his girlfriend was. The only reason I'd been waiting to speak up was lack of proof.

"You're sure?"

"Positive. This is about my career, which is way more important."

"Okay." She didn't sound like she believed me, but we had more important things to talk about. "Does your company have an IT department?"

"Sort of," I said. "It's two guys who install updates and tell us to restart when things freeze. They're not even full-time; they also work for the app development company upstairs and a couple other places."

"In that case, I'm going to say no. The big boss wouldn't have any ability to see passwords. That sort of thing is handled by the IT guys, even part-timers, and they don't maintain lists."

"Could the IT guys see my password? Or could they go to the password generator site where I found it and use my history to retrieve it?"

"Unlikely. I mean, yes, they could see you went to that site by checking your browser history. They shouldn't be able to see your results, though, not if it's a reputable site. If they went back, it would reload and produce a new, totally random password. Unless you took a screenshot and saved it on your desktop."

"Well, that's a relief," I said. "Except I still don't know what happened."

"Did you share your ideas with anyone else? I hate to ask, but did Tyler know?"

Pain lanced my heart at the thought, but no, it wasn't possible for him to have sold me out like that. "No. I kept all the data on my work computer, and we never discussed it. He's been helping me with a solo project."

Across the lot, Dennis and Megan left the building and snuck around the corner. Probably to celebrate their victory. If only I could somehow get them to admit what they'd done. As if of their own volition, my feet carried me back toward the building, slowly and quietly.

Holly sighed. "I don't really know what to tell you. Unless you wrote down your password and left it lying around, they shouldn't have been able to get in. But if you give me the name of the site you used, I'll do some research."

Something she said rang a bell. "Hold on a sec. What did you say again?"

"Oh, no." Disbelief filled her voice. "Tell me you didn't write down your password."

"It was like fifteen characters, half random symbols!" The excuse sounded weak, even to my own ears. "But it should've been fine. At work, since most of my dresses don't have pockets, I carried it in my bra. At home, there's no way…"

My voice trailed off, not wanting to finish that sentence. There was a way for Dennis to have gotten my password at home. More specifically, there was a way for Megan to have given it to him. That explained why she showed up at our apartment yesterday morning. It would've only taken her a second to take a picture of the slip of paper with her phone; no need to even touch it and risk me noticing anything out of place, like with the chair.

"Holly, I have to go," I said.

"Tell me you don't think Tyler had anything to do with this," she said.

"Not directly. I'll call you later." Not giving her a chance to respond, I hung up.

The wind carried voices around the corner. I sidled between the hedges and the building, hoping to sneak through the shadows. My ears strained, but by the time I got into a good position, they'd gone silent. I fumed. What now?

Then I realized that while Megan and Dennis weren't speaking, they weren't exactly being silent. Noises absolutely came from their direction; noises I recognized. Ducking slightly, I peeked through a gap in the hedges. A soft gasp escaped me, and my hand went to my mouth as if to pull the sound back.

It didn't matter. They weren't paying any attention to anything but each other. Megan stood with her arms wrapped around Dennis's neck. He held her off the ground, and they were kissing like the act was about to be outlawed.

The sight of Megan and Dennis locked in an embrace shouldn't have filled me with glee. My reaction made me a horrible friend; Tyler was going to be crushed when he found out Megan was cheating on him. At the same time, he needed to know the truth about her, and this was something concrete I could share with him. It was one thing to tell Tyler that Megan and I didn't get along. But her cheating on him was on an entirely different level.

A picture was worth a thousand words, right? As much as I didn't want to hurt Tyler, he needed to know about this. Finally, I had proof that his girlfriend wasn't who he thought. Lifting my phone toward the opening, I double-checked that it was on silent and snapped a couple of pictures. Sliding the device back into my pocket, I turned to sneak back into the office.

Halfway there, my heel caught on a root, and I stumbled. My hands shot out, steadying me against the wall. I only prayed that Dennis and Megan remained too wrapped up in each other to hear the quiet thud of the impact and my soft grunt of surprise. It took me a minute to steady myself and disentangle my shoes. At the corner, there was no sign of either of them, so I shot through the lobby and into the single-stall restroom by the elevators to clean up.

First things first. They'd invaded my technology before, and they apparently knew at least one of my passwords. I texted the picture to Ryan, as a backup in case they somehow got to my phone. Tyler needed to see it, and he would, but I wanted to think up a nicer way to break the news to him than a texted picture while he was at work.

In the mirror, a wild woman looked back at me. The hedges had caught my long hair, giving me a bird's nest on my head. I knew I shouldn't have grown it out. Redness tinged my cheeks. If I walked back into the office now, everyone would know something was wrong.

With a deep breath, I washed my hands and splashed cool water on my face, savoring the sensation on such a humid day. With wet hands, I smoothed my hair into something resembling where it belonged. Then I forced myself to count to one hundred before leaving the room, hoping Dennis and Megan would have already gone back to work.

No such luck. When I opened the door, Megan stood directly outside, hands clasped primly in front of her. With not a hair out of place, she looked as fresh as if she'd just stepped off of Instagram. No idea how she did it.

"Hi," I said awkwardly.

"Nice dress," she replied.

"Thanks!" It was on the tip of my tongue to add, "It has pockets!" but Megan wasn't a friend who would get excited for me, and I didn't see any reason to prolong this conversation. I needed to get back upstairs and tell Jameson what I'd figured out. And I needed to decide what to say to Tyler when I got home.

"What were you doing back behind the hedges?"

"I, uh, lost an earring last week, and thought it might have fallen when I was out walking."

"Riiiiiiiight."

Silently, I cursed myself for being such a terrible liar. Moving to walk around her, I said, "I'll see you later."

"Actually, I think we should chat now," Megan said. "Come with me."

It was on the tip of my tongue to refuse, but what if I could get her to admit something? My phone was in my pocket, maybe I could record her. I didn't know if it was legal, but that was the least of my concerns. I made a sweeping gesture with one hand. "After you."

As she turned and walked back around the corner, I reached into my pocket and pulled out enough of my phone to see the screen. A few quick taps and it started to record a voice memo. Now I just needed to keep my right hip pointed at Megan and hope she said something incriminating.

When we got to where I'd seen her with Dennis, Megan spun around to face me. "Look, I know you're not stupid and you know I'm not stupid, so let's not mince words."

"Great!" I said. "I don't like you."

"That's cool, I don't like you, either," she said. "But I do like my life right now, and I can't have you messing with it."

I blinked at her. "What are you talking about?"

"I thought we agreed not to play dumb."

"Look, if you're happy with Dennis, I'm happy for you. I certainly have no intention of standing in the way." After all, if she broke up with Tyler to see someone else, I didn't have to be the one to break his heart.

"Of course I'm not happy with Dennis!" Her voice sounded harsh, ragged. "He's a means to an end. Daddy wanted to give one of you the executive designer job. Dennis told me that if I helped him get it, he'd have my back."

"What do you even do here?"

"Listen, I'm going to cut to the chase," she said, ignoring my question. "I know you saw me kissing Dennis. He means nothing to me, yet I doubt Tyler would understand."

I shrugged. "Plenty of people have open relationships. I don't judge." She gave me a look of derision so strong, I almost laughed. "You're not going to tell Tyler what you saw. And you're not going to tell Daddy how Dennis and I came up with the idea for our kids' social deduction product line."

"Oh, really?" I arched an eyebrow and looked down at her, enjoying our height difference. I rarely used my size to intimidate people, but that's because it usually wasn't necessary to keep the upper hand. "'Came up with' is quite a euphemism for 'stole.'"

But Megan's next words took the wind right out of my sails. "That's right. Because if you do, I'll tell everyone about your trans friend. Things could get very uncomfortable for *her* if people find out the truth."

Chapter 17

"It's all well and good to be nice, but don't let anyone take advantage of you." —Holly

I simply stared at Megan, letting her threat sink in. This couldn't be happening. After everything I'd worked for, putting in so many hours for this company, I had to sit back and watch someone else steal the credit for my idea. Not just the credit—the promotion. Dennis didn't earn the executive game designer title; he stole it.

"I don't understand," I said. "What do you get from any of this? You were never up for the promotion. What do you care who gets it?"

"Dennis and I made certain agreements. The details are none of your business."

"You're cheating on one of my closest friends. It's a little my business."

"This has nothing to do with Tyler. I really do care about him."

"But you're sleeping with Dennis."

"Whatever. Like you're such an expert on relationships." She rolled her eyes at me. "Look, before you came along, I was the only female working here. The guys latched on to my every word. They worshiped me. Then, suddenly there are two girls, and I have to split the attention."

"So, you're sabotaging my career for... your ego?" A horrible thought occurred to me. "Is that why you're dating my roommate? To prove that you're somehow better than me?"

"Oh, I don't have to prove it, sweetheart. I *am* better than you. Look at this!" She swept her arms out to show off the greatness of her appearance. The gesture was largely lost on me. "That's why Tyler is with me instead of you."

"Get out of my way," I said, ignoring the jab of pain in my heart. "Some of us actually work around here. We can't all depend on Daddy to cover up our incompetence."

By the time I made it up to my desk, I was shaking with rage. My phone held the proof of Megan's deception. It should be enough to convince Jameson that she and Dennis stole my ideas. But I couldn't use it if the result was outing Ryan to our entire company. I hated Megan for making me decide whether to be a terrible friend to him or Tyler, who both deserved better.

I also couldn't just sit here. I needed to get out, go for a walk, clear my head. Watching people parade over to Dennis's desk to congratulate him all day, while Megan smirked at me from her desk in the corner, made me want to throw up. What sadist invented open office plans, anyway?

Without meeting anyone's eyes, I pulled up a blank email and sent a quick message to Jameson. Without elaborating, I told him I felt sick and needed to take the rest of the day off. He should assume women's troubles, which I supposed it was in a way. The troublesome woman just happened to be his daughter.

Then I held my head high and walked out. Waiting for the elevator took too long, and the thought of making forced small talk with anyone on the way down gave me a headache. Down the stairs I went, through the lobby, and straight out the front door. I made it about ten steps beyond the building toward the parking lot before my legs collapsed. There was no way I could make it to the T in my current state. Not knowing what else to do, I picked up the phone and called Tyler's work number. His office was only a few miles away, so while I could have called Gwen or Holly, no one else could make it here as quickly.

I needed to get out of here before Megan or Dennis came outside to gloat.

Tyler picked up instantly. "What's wrong?"

"How did you know?"

"Well, you've never called me at work before, for a start. And the only time you've ever called instead of texting was when Ryan canceled the presentation at the last minute."

"Oh." The fact that he paid attention to that stuff touched me. "I can't go into detail right now, but would you come pick me up?"

"Right now?"

"Yeah."

He didn't hesitate. "No problem. You okay?"

I thought about lying, but he was a pretty smart guy. "No. I'll tell you on the way home."

"I'm on my way."

"Okay. Thanks."

"No problem. See you soon." He hung up before I could say anything else. While we spoke, it seemed like everything might be okay. Until I heard his voice, I'd felt like someone had dunked me in ice water. But Tyler's deep voice comforted me, like sipping a mug of chamomile while soaking in a hot bath.

Before I could evaluate that feeling, Ryan appeared in front of me. "Okay, what just happened? I know you don't want to work for Dennis, but storming out dramatically is not your style. And what was with that picture?"

The story came spilling out. Ryan knew Dennis had been in my work computer—he was the one who'd suggested the random password generator—and that I'd been working on a new social deduction game with Tyler, but not everything else. By the time I got to Megan and Dennis kissing in the bushes, steam practically poured from his ears.

"Okay, you're pissed," he said. "I get it. But if you walk away, they've won. Why not tell Jameson?"

I couldn't tell him the truth. Ryan was already so upset on my behalf. Instead, I grasped for the easy answer. "I can't prove Dennis did anything wrong without implicating Megan. Who's Jameson going to believe? Me or his sweet, innocent daughter?"

Ryan sat heavily on the bench beside me. "You've got a point there. This sucks. It sucks so hard. Why do the bad guys always win?"

"Because life isn't an action movie?"

"You've got that right," he said.

Tyler's car turned into the parking lot, effectively ending our conversation. Even if I'd been inclined to tell Ryan about my chat with Megan, I couldn't get the story out in the next fifteen seconds. I stood and slung my bag over my shoulder. "That's my ride."

"You called Megan's boyfriend to pick you up?"

"He's my roommate."

"I know, but giiirrrrrrl." He shook his head. "What a tangled web, I guess. I can't believe you're leaving."

"I'll be back," I said.

"You better. We're not going to let Dennis get away with this. We'll figure something out."

Tyler's car pulled to a stop at the curb, so I said good-bye to Ryan, keeping my face bland in case anyone else watched through the windows. Neither of us spoke until his car turned out of the parking lot and down the street.

The shoulders I'd been holding so stiffly collapsed. I let out a sigh that filled the car, swirling around us both.

"That bad, huh?" Tyler asked, shooting me a look.

"I can't even," I said.

He got a carefully edited version of the story, ending before I called Holly.

"I get why you're so upset," he said, "especially after what happened with *Construct Me*. Can you prove Dennis was in your computer?"

"I can prove the contents of the file were on my desktop on the day Dennis accessed my computer, thanks to my dated backups."

"But you can't prove he accessed it."

"Nope. Not without a witness," I said. There was a witness, of course, but she wasn't about to tell anyone what she knew. What a mess. How had all this office romance drama come to affect me, of all people? I wasn't dating anyone! With a frustrated groan, I dropped my head into my hands.

A moment later, Tyler's warm hand touched my back, tentatively at first. When I didn't shrug him away, he rubbed a small circle on my back. I let out a small sound of appreciation, and the circle grew larger. Mmm. His touch relaxed me, eased some of the tension of the morning.

It also made me crave more. Which I couldn't have. Instead, I needed to tell him about Megan, but I didn't know how to do it without risking Ryan. Reluctantly, I sat up.

"Is there anything I can do?" he asked. "Want to stop by Game On! instead of going straight home?"

Ordinarily, walking the rows of my favorite store and chatting with John and Carla made me feel much better. But the morning had sapped all my energy. "Thanks, but no. Just take me home?"

"You got it."

As we drove, my mind swirled over the morning's events and how quickly Tyler came to my aid when I needed him. As much as being the damsel in distress sucked, knowing that he had my back meant the world to me. I shot a glance at his profile as he drove, looking at the strong line of his jaw and those strong, high cheekbones.

When I realized what I was doing, a wave of embarrassment hit me. After everything I'd been through, here I sat ogling my friend. I still couldn't believe I'd found myself attracted to him over the course of the weekend. And now, of course, I couldn't turn it off. What terrible timing. I couldn't have had this epiphany before Tyler started seeing someone else? It had been months; things probably were getting serious, especially if he'd let Megan into our apartment after promising not to invite her over unless I was okay with it.

His phone chimed with a text. His lips quirked as he glanced at it at the next stoplight. Megan, probably. I honestly didn't want to know, but some small sadistic part of my mind had to ask. "Something funny?"

"It's nothing," he said. "Liz sent me a joke."

My spine stiffened involuntarily. "Liz. Sacramento Liz from the conference Liz?"

"Yeah, that's her full name."

His chuckle only infuriated me more. Sacramento was a long way from Boston, but I hated thinking that the two of them kept in touch after the conference. She lived so far away, it had to be innocent, but I couldn't shake my memory of the way she looked at Tyler. "Seriously? You exchanged numbers?"

He shrugged. "She sent me a friend request on Facebook. After I accepted, she messaged me. Why?"

"Huh. She didn't send me one," I said pointedly.

"She probably thought you didn't want to be her friend," he said, pointing out the obvious. "Is something wrong?"

Yes, of course. I'd developed a crush on my roommate and close friend while he was in a serious relationship with one woman and flirting with another, meaning that he probably wouldn't want to be with me even if I hadn't blown my chance with him six months ago when he kissed me and I rejected him. None of which I could confess.

The car sped up after we passed an accident by the side of the road. Tyler let the silence stretch between us as he drove the rest of the way home. The minutes ticked by. Finally he turned to face me. "Seriously, Shannon, have I upset you somehow?"

"No. Everything's fine," I lied.

"See, I know you're lying. You've been weird since the conference," he said. "I figured you were tired, and I know you got a bad break at work this morning, but I can't shake the feeling that you're upset with me. You're mad Liz and I are Facebook friends? Or that she sent me a message?"

"I'm sorry. I shouldn't be upset with you, and I very much appreciate you coming to get me this morning." I ignored his other questions.

"So what's wrong?"

"I don't know." I sighed. Maybe it would be easier to let everything out in the open, clear the air between us. "I don't know why it bothered me so much to watch you flirt with Liz all weekend."

"I wasn't flirt—" He hit the brakes and the car came to a hard stop. "Hold on. It bothered you when we were talking?"

My breath caught at the look on his face. I didn't want to admit my jealousy, not when he could have any woman he wanted. He didn't want me anymore, and who could blame him? I saw no reason to tell Tyler about my feelings. So instead I reached for a partial truth. "It's nothing. It's just that you seem like such a nice guy. Loyal, trustworthy…"

"I'm not sure if I should say thank you or ask if you're describing a dog. But those are good things. What's wrong with being loyal and trustworthy?"

"You're not! You spent all weekend flirting with Liz when you have a girlfriend. She was sitting at home waiting for you to call her while you were out flitting around the conference breaking hearts."

He snorted. "I wasn't flirting with Liz, at least not intentionally. Just being friendly. I wish you'd said something earlier, because I'd have stopped. I hate thinking I led her on without meaning to."

"Sorry. I guess I shouldn't have jumped to conclusions," I said. "But then why keep in touch?"

"I've always had female friends. It doesn't mean anything."

"Megan doesn't mind?"

"She doesn't mind me living with you, does she?" Actually, she did, but I couldn't tell him that. "Anyway, I don't need her permission to make friends. And Liz is a fellow accountant. She's looking for work out west, so I told her I'd hook her up with the hiring manager in our San Francisco office."

"Oh. That was nice of you."

"Yeah." He paused. "Seriously, next time you want to know something, just ask. Don't jump to conclusions. Especially conclusions that make me seem like a dog."

"Sorry," I said. "I should've known better."

The car turned onto our street, and suddenly all thoughts of Liz and Megan and conferences and even Tyler flew out of my head. A choking sound escaped me, and both hands flew to my face. I couldn't breathe.

"Are you…" Tyler's voice trailed off, telling me exactly when he saw the same thing that had sent my heart slamming into my throat.

An ambulance sitting in our driveway, rear doors open and lights flashing.

Chapter 18

"It's never too late to tell someone you love them." —Nathan

Tyler stomped the accelerator, sending us leaping forward. He screeched to a halt on the street before slamming into Park. Something in me snapped, and I flung the door open practically before the car halted, barely remembering to remove my seat belt before it choked me. I raced for the front of the house, screaming Nana's name repeatedly.

Tyler caught up with me at the door. He caught my arms, bringing me out of the middle of the hall.

"NANA!" The word came out half as a yell, half as a sob.

He was talking to me, but I couldn't hear anything. All I saw was the ambulance with the flashing lights, my mental image of Nana on the floor. If I could get to her side, she'd be okay. But Tyler was in the way and he refused to move, no matter how I shoved or kicked at him.

Finally, he pulled me close, wrapping me in arms of steel. "Shhh. Shannon, it's okay. She's okay."

"Let go of me!"

"Sorry, I can't," he said. "Hear that? The paramedics are down there, talking to her. They'll help, but you have to let them do their job."

"I need to see her." In that moment, I hated him. I wanted to kick and punch and pull his hair until he fell to one side, giving me access to Nana.

"I know, and you will. But listen. They're coming up the stairs now. We're in the way. Come outside with me."

The notion of preventing the paramedics from getting Nana to the ambulance permeated the fog in my mind. I allowed Tyler to lead me down the front steps to the side of the driveway.

Voices came through the open door. A moment later, a man and a woman carried a stretcher over the threshold and onto the front porch. Nana looked so tiny, with an oxygen mask on her face. Her painted fingernails lay on top of the sheet, so vibrant against the stark white fabric. Her face more closely resembled the fabric of that sheet than the red of her fingernails. At least she was breathing.

A choked sob escaped me, and the woman looked over. "Are you Shannon O'Rourke?"

I couldn't speak, but Tyler answered. "She is."

The male paramedic said, "Next of kin? You can ride with us if you'd like."

I nodded dumbly, my eyes never leaving the slow rise and fall of Nana's chest. "What happened? And where's Michael?"

Tyler held up his phone. "Michael is at the grocery store. He'll start walking back immediately, but I'm going to go pick him up and meet you at the hospital."

"Meet me?"

"Yeah. You're going in the ambulance, remember?"

Right.

"Unless you don't want to," he said.

"No, I do. Thanks."

While we spoke, the paramedics had finished putting Nana in the back. The female now sat in the driver's seat, while the male stood with one hand on the back door.

"You ready?" he asked me.

With a nod, I climbed in beside her and grabbed her hand. She squeezed back, which lifted my spirits about 10,000 percent. For the next several minutes, I held her hand and whispered silent prayers.

The paramedics adjusted a few things before slamming the rear doors shut. The last thing I saw was Tyler, getting into his car and driving back the direction we came.

Finally, we started moving, and I felt comfortable enough to speak. "Hold on, Nana. I'm not ready to lose you yet."

"She can't talk to you," one of the paramedics said. "She's sedated."

It didn't matter. Being near her was enough. Sitting here and watching her breathe, as if the weight of my stare would be enough to keep her chest rising and falling rhythmically.

Michael showed up at the hospital not long after we arrived, while Nana was still getting settled. I'd been directed to the waiting room, clicking through the channels on the TV purely to have something to do. Focusing on the changing screens kept me from losing it while I waited to find out what was going on.

"Here," he said, holding out an object. "Tyler said you left this in his car."

My phone. He not only noticed that I'd left my phone behind, but he'd taken the time to make sure I got it back. Even though we were having a stupid argument when we spotted the ambulance.

I glanced at the door. "Where is he, looking for a parking space?"

"No, he went home. Said this is a time for family."

It was on the tip of my tongue to state that Tyler *was* family, but I stopped myself. He wasn't. He was Megan's family, for as long as she wanted him to be. If Michael saw the sadness that crossed my face, he didn't comment. Good, because I didn't know what to say.

"Do you know what happened?" I asked instead.

He shook his head. "The doctors haven't said anything yet. The paramedics said she called nine-one-one herself, which is a good sign. Now we wait."

"Right. We wait." And wish, and hope.

"Rose is very lucky to have you, you know."

"Thanks," I said. "You, too."

"No," he said with a sad smile. "I'm the lucky one."

The look on his face made me realize exactly how untrue that statement was. Nana's life changed for the better when she met Michael. Just like my life changed when I started spending more time with Tyler. He wasn't the person I should want to comfort me in moments like this, but I couldn't help wishing he sat in the empty chair beside me, holding my hand.

A doctor approached, pulling Michael to the side for a conversation. I eavesdropped long enough to determine that Nana should make a full recovery. My entire body sagged with relief. She would live. With a few basic lifestyle changes, she would be fine. Nana wasn't that old; she could have many years left if she took care of herself.

Only one person could go in to visit her at a time, so Michael went through the double doors first. While waiting for my turn, I picked up my phone. I needed to say something to Tyler, but didn't even know where to start. *Sorry for flying into a weird jealous rage for no reason?*

My first instinct should have been to text one of my best friends, but Tyler had been the one to find Nana with me. He was the one to compliment her roses the day they met, to put her trash bins down at the curb every week, to treat her with the same care and consideration he'd show his own grandmother.

But I didn't need Tyler by my side. I shouldn't call him for comfort. Michael and I would be fine. Instead, I needed to talk to the rest of my family.

Now that we had an update on Nana's condition, I stepped outside to call Mom and let her know what was happening. She and Dad had been prepared to board the next flight to Boston after Michael called them from the grocery store.

"Thanks. Sometimes it's hard being so far away from family," she said after I gave the update.

"I get it, but everything is fine. I promise, when you need to be here, I'll let you know."

"Let's hope that's not for a very long time."

After we said our good-byes, I called the manager of Nana's bakery to let her know what happened. Nana still did most of the baking but only worked the counter a couple of days a week; Deana handled the shop the rest of the time. She assured me that she'd take care of everything and let me know she'd swing by after the shop closed for the night.

Once we finished, I weighed my phone in one hand, studying it as if doing so would cause another text to appear. I wanted to talk to Tyler—no, I *needed* the contact—but after our argument in the car and my conversation with Megan, I didn't know what to say to him. I needed to put some distance between us, without letting him know why, even though it would break my heart.

But I didn't need to ghost him. At the very least, he deserved to know that Nana was going to be okay. He probably wasn't texting because he knew I'd be busy and distracted. Of course he'd assume I'd text an update without waiting for him to ask for it.

Me: *She's out of the woods. Will be home later. Thank you for everything.*
The reply came seconds later. *You're welcome.*

Somehow those two words on the screen made my heart lighter than any moment since I'd turned onto my street that afternoon. Tyler was only a text away, and he'd show up for me if I asked.

Ask I would, as soon as I came up with a way to avoid the wrath of Megan. Once I did, I'd force myself to summon the courage to tell my friend and roommate that I'd fallen in love with him.

Chapter 19

"You can't turn attraction off any more than you can turn it on. When you find someone who gets you excited, go for it." —Gwen

A couple of hours later, the doctors told me Nana was in stable enough condition that it made no sense for me to stay with her overnight. She insisted I leave rather than "moping over" her bed all night long while she slept. Begrudgingly, I dropped Michael off before heading home in Tyler's car, which he'd left in the parking garage for us.

By the time I got home, my body felt like I'd run multiple marathons. The shock of Nana's incident followed by all the waiting wiped me out, especially after the emotional drain of work that morning. Huh. My conversation with Megan seemed weeks ago. The second Michael dropped me off, I dragged myself to my room and fell on top of the bedspread, fully clothed.

A moment later, a knock sounded.

Tyler. I stifled a groan, too worn out to pretend to be okay. It wasn't that I didn't want to see him. It's that I wanted to see him too much. But this wasn't the time to confess my feelings—I was much too exhausted out for an emotionally heavy conversation.

"Come in." I called, because it was such an ingrained response and not because of any desire to see or talk to anyone.

The door opened slowly. Tyler poked his head in.

At his concerned look, the well of tears I'd managed to suppress ever since seeing the ambulance in the driveway threatened to overflow. I nodded through blurred vision. A moment later, Tyler's weight sank onto the bed beside me. "I'm so sorry, Shannon. How is she?"

"She's going to be okay," I said. "The doctors are predicting a full recovery."

"Oh, thank goodness." Relief filled his voice. He spoke quietly, almost reverently, as if afraid to consider what might have happened. "Is there anything I can do for you?"

"Stay with me for a bit?" My voice sounded so plaintive, I barely recognized it. "I don't want to be alone."

Leaning over, I put my head on his shoulder. He put his arms around me, and finally, I let myself sob. He sniffled. Tears fell into our laps, mingling until I didn't know who shed what. For a long time, we sat in silence together, joined by our shock at almost losing the most important person in my life, our relief that I'd been given the gift of more time with her. The rest of the world fell away.

His arms felt so warm around me, so right. It reminded me of the morning when we woke up together at the conference. But this time, we were both fully awake and aware of the way our bodies fit together.

Even after our argument earlier, he wanted to take care of me. He could have left me to suffer alone. Instead, he sat on the bed, stroking my hair with one hand. As time passed, we'd nestled and adjusted until the two of us were half-lying, half-sitting on top of the covers.

This was my moment. The turning point in our relationship. All I had to do was lift my head, look up, and lean toward him. My lips would find his. My actions would show Tyler how I felt about him. He'd know that I'd realized I wanted to be with him.

Indecision kept me frozen in place. He hadn't given me any indication that he wanted to be with me now. Still, I couldn't afford to repress my feelings. It was so difficult to find someone, especially in this day of dating apps and people spending all their time online. He was good and sweet and handsome and smart and charming. Those things were what mattered. Not to mention the way I felt when we were together. No one else made everything I did a genuine joy. The apartment felt cold when he wasn't home. He was the person I looked to for advice or comfort, and the only person I ever wanted in my bed.

That's why, finally, with a deep breath, I wiped my eyes, and turned toward Tyler, lips parted in anticipation. His breath warmed my face. My mouth suddenly felt paper dry, but I couldn't back out now. We'd been moving toward this moment for too long.

A loud snore emerged from his lips, moving me backward. While I'd been lying on the bed, searching my soul, he'd fallen asleep.

Poor guy. He'd had a long and emotionally exhausting few days, too. Of course he'd be wiped out. It had been selfish of me to ask him to come in and stay with me when he also needed to rest. I couldn't bring myself to wake him up. Morning would come soon enough. I planted a gentle kiss on his check and smoothed an errant lock of my hair behind my ear so it wouldn't tickle his nose, then nestled back against him.

He jerked awake, eyes fluttering open. "What's going on?"

"I don't know. I, um, think you fell asleep," I said.

"Sorry, yeah. Was I snoring?" He shifted on the bed, putting some distance between us.

"No." I took a deep breath, then said the only thing I could think of to ease into the conversation we needed to have. "I was thinking about that night in Mexico."

He winced. "I thought we put that behind us."

"We did. Or at least I did. But there's something I wanted to ask you."

"About the thing we don't talk about?"

"No. When I got to the beach, you were sitting in a hammock, looking at the ground. You looked so sad."

"Did I?" He stiffened slightly, betraying the casualness of his words.

"Yeah," I said. "What happened before I got there?"

"I don't remember." The words came out too quickly. If he really didn't remember, he'd have spent a couple of seconds thinking about it.

"That's not true," I said. "Come on, I thought we were having a moment."

"Okay, fine. It's really not a big deal. A few minutes before you came out onto the beach, I saw on Facebook that my ex got engaged to the guy she cheated on me with."

"Ouch. That's gotta be rough."

"Yeah." He paused. "I mean, it's fine. We broke up a long time ago, and I got over any feelings probably a year before that. But something about seeing that he was the one...I don't know."

"I guess when someone cheats on you, you don't want to think about them living happily ever after. Especially not with the cheatee."

"No, you don't," he said quietly. "My dad cheated on my mom. A lot. Loads of different women. She refused to leave him. But every day of my life, I saw how miserable he made her."

Reaching over, I squeezed his hand. "Oh, Tyler. I'm so sorry."

He didn't answer right away, and then a lightning bolt hit me. He would never, ever kiss me while in a relationship, and he'd probably think less of me if I'd made a move on him. Thank goodness we'd had this conversation.

At the same time, he needed to know about Megan. Even though my first reaction had been to tell him, I hadn't known then how important it was. A lot of couples moved past cheating. Some decided to have open relationships. But watching Tyler as he spoke about his past, I became very aware that he wasn't one of those people. If he knew about Megan and Dennis, he'd dump her. My fingers stretched involuntarily toward my phone before I yanked them back.

This was torture. I couldn't tell Tyler the truth without ruining things for Ryan. His gender identity wasn't mine to share, and I would never dream of outing someone against their will. Telling Tyler, knowing what Megan would do, would be the same as telling everyone myself.

I didn't know what to do. I couldn't let my friend stay with that snake. There had to be a way to help him see who she was without spelling it out. If he broke up with her on his own, in a way that didn't implicate me, maybe Megan wouldn't take her revenge. What was the alternative? Sit back and let Megan manipulate him down the aisle, through buying a big house with a picket fence and having 2.5 kids? No way.

With a deep breath, I sat up and faced him. "Tyler, we need to talk."

"Sure. Did the hospital call while I was out?"

"No, this isn't about Nana," I said. My heart broke at what I knew had to be done. "It's about Megan. She's not who you think."

Tyler let out a breath, then nodded, standing slowly. "Yeah, I thought you might say that."

"You mean you knew?"

"We went out to dinner after I dropped you at the hospital. She told me you might come to me with some story, try to make her look bad because she and Dennis got so much praise at work this morning." He shook his head sadly. "I didn't want to believe it. Honestly, Shannon, I thought you were better than this. But let's hear it."

I couldn't believe my ears. She'd gotten to him first. Now, no matter what I said, it would look like petty work jealousy. Unless I showed him the picture, which I absolutely could not do. Two paths diverged in front of me, and no matter which one I picked, someone got hurt. Tyler might not be hurt for months, or even years. Ryan would be hurt immediately. Either way, it broke my heart to be forced to sit back and watch.

"She told you that I'm jealous of her work performance and that I was going to come to you and make up a nasty story about her?"

"Yeah. I assumed she was being paranoid until just now."

I swallowed and counted to ten, trying to regain control of myself. "You didn't think she knew I had something to tell you about her?"

"What's there to tell?"

Earlier, I'd thought about what to say to Tyler, tried to guess how he would react and what to say. Not once had I considered that he might give me flat-out disbelief. He didn't even want to listen to me.

A few weeks ago, before the team builder challenge, we'd joked that his decision to help me instead of Megan showed how he valued me over her. Whether that was true then, I clearly saw where I ranked now. Our friendship meant so little compared to what they had, he assumed the worst of me.

All the wind went out of my sails. If he believed Megan over me without even listening to me talk, maybe they deserved each other.

Instead of answering his question, I said, "She wouldn't like you sitting here, on my bed."

"No, she wouldn't." he said. "I should go."

I made no move to stop him. If he didn't want to know the truth about his girlfriend, I couldn't force him to listen. I couldn't show him the photographs, knowing how he felt about cheaters. Not when Ryan would pay the price. All I could do was sit and watch as he got up and left the room.

Then I threw myself facedown into the pillows and cried myself to sleep.

* * * *

When I woke up, the spot on the bed where Tyler once sat with me felt cold. I lay there, staring at it. Even after we fought, he comforted me. He held me, although he was also worried about Nana. He never asked me for anything, only offered to let me take what I needed from him. But then I ruined everything by trying to warn him about Megan.

A red light blinked up at me from my phone. A slew of texts from my friends.

Gwen: *Tyler called us. Glad to hear Nana is going to be OK. Is there anything I can do for either of you? Do you want me to come over?*

Similar messages came from Holly, Cody, and Nathan. Tyler had even reached out to Ryan. Not having the energy to have the same conversation over and over, I texted one update to everyone, then turned my phone to "Do Not Disturb."

I got out of bed, determined to find Tyler. We needed to talk, as soon as possible. But the apartment was still, silent. The clock on my phone told me that I'd slept long past the time he normally left for work. If I wanted an in-person conversation, I'd have to drive to his office and talk to him there.

My mouth tasted like sand since I fell asleep without brushing my teeth. Maybe not getting to kiss Tyler was a mixed blessing. My entire body felt stiff and achy, both from falling asleep in a bra and from lying in a weird position all night. Even the bridge of my nose hurt from where my glasses dug in while I slept.

A shower might make me feel better. I staggered down the hall, stopping to grab clean towels from the linen closet. After I closed the doors, something tickled the back of my mind. Halfway to the bathroom, I realized what it was. There seemed to be an awful lot of room in the closet. Great. Because I wanted to do laundry right now.

For a long time, the water beat down on me. For once, I didn't have to worry about using all the hot water. Instead, I curled into a ball on the floor of the tub and let myself wail, releasing a deluge of emotions.

Nana took care of me. She loved me. When I moved to Boston, she was the only person I knew. She gave me a place to live, encouraged me to go out and make friends. She taught me a love for games, the rules of poker, how to bake. She showed me what unconditional love felt like. And I'd almost lost her. Worse, one day I would lose her, and there was nothing I could do about it.

When I finally felt as worn and wrung out as a dishrag, I turned off the water. Then I stood for a long time toweling off. Something still felt wrong. The same brain tickle I got at the linen closet returned. Nana was going to be fine. Wasn't that enough for me?

With a shrug, I wrapped myself in a towel and headed back to my room. No one else would be here, so I didn't much care that I didn't have any clothes on. The thought reminded me of the time I walked in on Tyler naked, and for a second, I allowed myself to contemplate how I might respond if the tables turned on me. One thing could lead to another very easily. That would certainly make it easier to confess my feelings.

Except for all the reasons it couldn't happen. Sigh.

About ten feet down the hall, my sense of wrongness got stronger. I stopped and turned to my left. The door to Tyler's room stood open, which wasn't terribly unusual. For once, clothes didn't lay strewn across the carpet, threatening to spill out the door, but I didn't care about the mess. As long as he kept it within those walls, whatever.

My gaze moved slowly upward across the freshly vacuumed carpet. Light flooded the room, odd since the curtains usually remained shut. The closet door also stood open, which was normal. Except for one thing.

No clothes hung inside. No clothes on the floor. Now that I stopped to look, no other signs of life. No clutter on top of the dresser. All dresser drawers firmly shut. No sheets on the bed. No signs of Tyler at all. The room looked exactly the same as the day before he moved in.

A strangled sound escaped me. Turning, I ran to the kitchen and starting flinging doors open. No beer in the fridge. No poker chips in the china cabinet I used to store games. No games, period, other than mine. No Mario Brothers on the shelves under the TV. No signs of Tyler, anywhere.

Then I spotted a paper on the kitchen table. Twelve thumbnail sketches: The Flapper, The Cop, The Mob Boss, the Bartender, and several plain old mob members with names like "Dirty Harry" and "Murderous Morty." In full color, with all kinds of detail. Stuff we'd never discussed, like Morty holding a semiautomatic gun. Those extra bits told me how much time Tyler must've spent on this beyond when we worked together. He'd finished the images at some point, and they were perfect.

That, more than anything, told me that he wasn't coming back. With a low moan, I fell to my knees. The single sheet of paper was his way of saying "good-bye."

Chapter 20

"When opportunity knocks, open the door. It might not come back later."
—Holly

There wasn't time to grieve over Tyler's leaving. As badly as I wanted to talk to him, see if we could work things out, Nana still waited in the hospital to be released, and she needed me. Being sad was a luxury I couldn't afford.

"What are you doing here?" she demanded when I walked in.

"Visiting you? I want to make sure you're okay."

"Of course I'm okay," she said. "It takes more than one fall to take out this old lady. You should be at work, sticking it to the man."

Her comment reminded me that Nana had no idea what transpired yesterday. I brought her up to speed quickly, leaving out the bits that might send her blood pressure skyrocketing, but including my argument with Tyler. By the time I finished, her eyes flashed with indignation. "So that's it? You're not friends anymore? He just moved out?"

"Honestly, I don't know," I said. "Looks like it."

"What a jerk." Her statement caught me off guard, so I shot her a questioning look. "He didn't mention a word of this when visiting me earlier."

"Tyler was here?"

She nodded. "Snuck me in a cupcake left over from the wedding. He's a good one, you know. I was kidding about the jerk thing."

"Yeah." A good one who'd ditched me. But I didn't want to argue with my grandmother in her hospital bed, so I went to look out the window instead.

"What are you going to do?" Nana said.

"What do you mean?"

"Well, you're obviously in love with him."

I sighed. Hearing someone else say the words didn't make it any easier than me thinking them myself. Not when I couldn't act on them without destroying Ryan's career. "We're friends. I love him as a friend."

"And you admitted that you're attracted to him, so you might as well tell me you want more."

"Loving someone and being attracted to them doesn't mean..." Except maybe it did. What was romantic love if not a combination of those things? "Huh."

"Told you so," Nana said proudly.

"It doesn't matter. He moved out. He chose Megan."

"Bullshit."

Her words made my mouth fall open in a nervous laugh. "Nana!"

"Well, it is, and you know it. He thought you were attacking his girlfriend and he defended her, like any good partner. He didn't 'choose' her over you, because he doesn't have any idea how you feel about him. To make a choice, a person needs to know their options."

"He knows we're friends. He spent last night comforting me, but when I tried to warn him about Megan, he wouldn't even listen. He acted like I'd make up lies just because I don't like her. Then he took off without a word. No good-bye, no note, no text."

"Maybe he didn't know what to say," she said. "Why didn't you stop him from leaving?"

"I didn't hear him gathering his stuff. I must have been completely exhausted."

"He was probably tired, too. Too tired for an emotional good-bye. Or maybe he didn't know what to say."

"Why are you defending him?" I asked. The question came out a little harsh, but it stung that my own grandmother wasn't taking my side.

"Because you're in love with him. Because nothing you've said changes that fact."

Maybe not, but it hurt that he didn't care enough about our friendship to finish our conversation about Megan, much less tell me that he'd decided to bail.

Suddenly, the hospital room felt claustrophobic. Promising Nana that I'd think about what she said, I gave her a kiss good-bye and told her to get some rest.

"Rest? Ha! I'm lookin' to blow this joint," she said. "The doctors promised to release me before lunch. I'll see you at home later."

Time to go back to work. Avoiding Megan and Dennis wouldn't work forever, and the longer I stayed away, the harder it would be to walk in there. Everyone would know I was sitting at home sulking. Not to mention, I'd never come up with a way to prove Dennis stole my promotion from my living room. All the files sat on my desktop. Maybe if I pored over everything, I could find something making it clear that these were my ideas. The voice, the artwork suggestions, anything.

If I turned around and went home, sulking was precisely what I would wind up doing. Sitting so close to Tyler's empty room, wondering what I could have said or done differently, sounded like a horrible way to spend the day. Maybe I should have told him my suspicions about Megan at the very beginning. Things never should have gotten to this point. At the very least, then he could have decided not to move in if his relationship was more important than our friendship.

It was easy to beat myself up, but I still didn't know what I should have said. He'd have assumed I was jealous and dismissed my concerns out of hand. Much like he did yesterday. I didn't have a time turner, so there was no point in dwelling on it. At least I had a plan to maybe fix my work problems. One thing at a time.

With no better options, I hopped on the T and rode to the office. The whole way there, I replayed the recording I'd made of Megan yesterday morning. This conversation gave me exactly what I needed to show Tyler how his girlfriend acted when no one else was around. The picture of her with Dennis showed how little she cared about him and their relationship. Too bad I couldn't give him either file.

With a groan of dismay, I shoved the phone into my bag and buried my head in my hands until the train reached my stop. There had to be a solution I wasn't seeing.

Ryan spotted me on the way in and waved me over to his desk. "What's wrong? You should look like the cat that swallowed the canary right about now."

In all the confusion surrounding Nana, I'd completely forgotten to update my friend. With a glance around, I pulled over a spare chair, lowered my voice, and told him about her episode and my subsequent conversation with Tyler, ending with the fact that he left when I tried to tell him about Megan.

"I don't understand," Ryan said. "You know Megan and Dennis worked together to sabotage you. You got Megan on tape, admitting it. Why didn't you play the tape for him? Show him the picture you texted me?"

I bit my lip. That was the twenty-five-thousand-dollar question, and the answer he couldn't hear. Instead, I deflected. "He didn't want to see it. He got so mad when I even hinted that his girlfriend might not be perfect."

"That's why you need to make him listen," he insisted. "And why aren't you in there now playing that tape for Jameson? He needs to know what happened before Dennis starts what should be your job."

"I'm not positive what I have is enough. She never says that Dennis knew she stole my password or who broke into my computer."

"It's enough to try, right? Are you worried he won't believe you? Go to Hans. Or better yet, go to the full board of directors."

All excellent ideas. All things I would do in a heartbeat, but for Megan's threats. I tried to change the subject. "I'm starting to think the board doesn't exist. We haven't seen or heard anything from any of them except Hans."

Ryan watched me carefully for a minute. "What aren't you telling me?"

"I don't know what you're talking about."

"Yes, you do," he said. "There's a reason you're not turning them in. You're a nice person, but you're not a doormat. You don't let people treat you like this, not without a good reason. And don't feed me more garbage about people not believing you. They *can't* believe you if you don't tell them. The fact that someone's not likely to listen isn't a good reason not to tell them what they need to hear."

"I know."

"Hold on. Did Tyler tell Megan you're demi? Is that the problem? You're worried that she'll tell all the guys, and they'll give you a hard time?"

He'd come so close to hitting the nail on the head. But if this were only about me, I'd deal with the fallout. "No."

"Hmmm." Ryan held out one hand. "Give me your phone."

"What? Why?"

"I want to hear that tape for myself. There's something on it you don't want me to know."

I lowered my gaze to the desk. "You don't want to hear it."

"Yes, I do. Give it to me. Now."

Our eyes met, but Ryan's gaze didn't waver. I saw the determination on his face, knew I couldn't win this battle. Finally, with a sigh, I unlocked my phone and pulled up the file. Then I slid the device into his hand and averted my eyes. "It's near the end, if you want to skip ahead."

"Think I'll listen to the whole thing, thanks." He air-dropped the file into his own phone, then popped earbuds into his ears. Then he leaned back and closed his eyes to listen.

We sat in silence. The rest of the office was fairly busy, with Dennis leading a focus group in the middle of the room. He had several kids who appeared to be about eight to twelve years old running around and making animal noises, so no one paid any attention to us.

A quiet gasp told me when Ryan reached the relevant part of the tape. A moment later, he slammed his phone onto the table. "No. Shannon, you're not doing this."

"Doing what?"

"You're not going to let them get away with stealing your ideas to protect me."

I lowered my voice. "I can't out you to save myself. Even if you weren't a good friend, I would never do that to anyone."

"You wouldn't be outing me. You don't control Megan. You're not telling her what to do."

"But if I know she's going to do it, and I allow it to happen, then I'm partially responsible."

We stared at each other, locked in a stalemate. Finally, Ryan nodded. "I get why you would think that. And I absolutely appreciate what you're doing."

"Thanks. So you understand—"

Abruptly, Ryan stood, so fast his chair careened backward into the desk. Then he climbed on top of it, teetering for a second before stepping onto the desk instead. He waved his arms over his head and cupped his hands around his mouth. "Everyone, may I have your attention please? I have an announcement."

Too late, I realized what he intended. Oh, no. I grabbed his hand and hissed at him. "Stop. Get down."

From the middle of the room, Dennis's voice boomed out. "What going on? You two getting married?"

A few nervous laughs skittered around the room. Ryan smiled thinly. "No, but thank you for asking. I wanted to let everyone in the office know that I'm trans."

I sought out Megan in the crowd. She stood with her arms crossed, lips pressed so firmly together, they disappeared.

Someone asked, "What?"

Ryan repeated himself. "I am a trans man. Assigned female at birth, raised as a girl. A few years ago, I realized my truth, that I am a man. I just thought everyone should know."

Stuart looked over from the next desk. "Um, thanks?"

A high-pitched voice sounded from the direction of the kids playing Dennis's game. "Cooooooooooool!"

"Any questions?" When no one said anything, Ryan stepped down, and sat. A moment later, he popped back to his feet. "Oh, and also, Megan and Dennis stole Shannon's idea for the kids' social deduction games, and Megan told everyone she'd out me if Shannon turned her in. So, here we are. Have a good day."

My mouth fell open. "I can't believe you did that."

Megan let out a series of outraged shrieks, but everyone else fell silent. The kids all stared, apparently having decided our interoffice drama was more interesting than Dennis's game. It took me a minute to find Dennis in the crowd. His stood trembling, hands clenched at his sides.

Jameson appeared behind us. "Excuse me, but those are some serious allegations, young man."

"Yes, I know," Ryan said. "But she has proof. Shannon?"

"Get it," Jameson said. "I want all of you in my office in two minutes."

Since the evidence I needed resided on the phone in my pocket, I followed him into his office. Megan and Dennis appeared a moment later. Ryan stood against the back wall, arms folded.

"Who wants to go first?" Jameson asked.

"Shannon will," Ryan said. "She's the one who figured it all out."

It didn't take long to lay out my evidence: the moved chair, the *Construct Me* coincidence, the changed password, Megan leaving my apartment early in the morning before work, and Dennis magically knowing all of my ideas by the end of that day.

Jameson listened to all of it, silencing Megan each time she tried to interrupt. "I always thought the two of you coming up with the same idea was a bit fishy. But it is an old game, and I didn't want to believe one of my employees was sneaking around, looking in other people's computers. The fact that it's my own daughter...I'm appalled. You said you have proof?"

"I do, sir." Pulling out my phone, I opened the audio file.

Before I could tap the Play button, Megan stopped me. "Daddy, you can't listen to that. It's illegal in Massachusetts to record a private conversation. Or to ask someone else to play one for you."

"After everything I've done for you, are you going to have your father arrested for listening to a recording?" Megan visibly shrank under the scrutiny of her father's gaze. "How do you know what Shannon is about to play for me if she's lying?"

Dennis cleared his throat. "I have no idea what Shannon thinks she has, but if she's secretly recorded me on video, I will be pressing criminal charges."

His words seemed to give Megan strength. "Me, too. Not against you, Daddy, but against Shannon."

For a long moment, everyone stared at me. Finally, I stood, walking to the water cooler in the corner and taking a long drink. Then I turned and faced the others. "Ryan did something very brave and difficult out there. He stood up and announced something very private, to ensure that Megan and Dennis didn't get away with what they did."

"And I'd do it again," Ryan said. "I'm not cool with blackmail."

I nodded. "It's time for me to be brave, too. I'm willing to accept the consequences of my actions."

"You're sure about this?" Jameson said.

"Yeah." With a deep breath, I pressed Play.

Megan shrieked and dove for my phone, knocking it out of my hand. She continued to make noise until Dennis stood, wrapping his arms around her and putting a hand over her mouth. On the floor, my phone played.

"This game is so much fun!" Preston's voice emanated from the speakers. A recording from my focus group. Legally obtained, and not remotely incriminating. The real tape wasn't needed, in light of Megan's actions. Her desperate attempt to stop me from playing the recording made her deception obvious.

"My daughter's reaction shows me everything I need to know. Sweetheart, you're fired. Get your stuff, and I'll see you at home."

She went pale, stilling instantly in Dennis's arms. He coughed. "What about me?"

"Take the rest of the week off," Jameson said. "I want to compare Shannon's files with what you gave me, and I'll be in touch in a few days."

It was bad form to smirk at other people's misfortune, so I struggled to maintain a straight face as I turned to Jameson. "Thank you for listening to me."

He put out one hand, which I shook. "Thank you for bringing this to my attention. That took a lot of nerve."

My heart sang as I watched the two of them leave together. Megan continued to shoot me scathing looks through the window of Jameson's office as Dennis practically dragged her to her desk to get her stuff, then out the front door.

He might be back, since my illegal recording didn't prove he knew what Megan had done. Producing the actual tape wasn't worth going to jail when it didn't give me the needed confession. I needed to prove not only when I came up with the idea, but why Jameson should make me executive game designer over Dennis.

The Haunted Place was doing well. Thanks to John's help, copies at Game On! sold quickly. With the resources of BGG, it could become as popular as *Betrayal at House at the Hill*. It would take me years to get my social deduction game on the shelves without BGG's distribution and marketing connections.

My heart wrenched at the thought, but I knew what I needed to do. There was only one way to convince my boss that my game ideas were better than Dennis's.

I took a deep breath and counted to ten, not entirely believing what I was about to say. "If you have another moment, sir, I have a couple of things I'd like to show you."

Chapter 21

"Don't be a ninny. When someone gives you a gift, accept it." —Nana

At the end of the day, I left the office, my steps heavy. My conversation with Jameson should have left me feeling optimistic about the future, but for some reason, I felt hollow. A month ago, or even a week ago, I'd been desperate for the executive game designer job. Finally, my boss recognized that I was the best candidate, once I started talking about branching out into making adult games. He loved the ideas I'd shown him and thought *The Haunted Place* could be ready for a relaunch before Christmas.

After printing out all my original notes with the screenshots and a few emails, he believed that Dennis had used my ideas to get the promotion. As of two o'clock this afternoon, the title officially did not belong to him, and he'd received a written warning. I wanted him fired, but Jameson strongly suspected that Megan masterminded the deception. I still couldn't prove Dennis stole my password or that he asked her to do it. For now, I needed to accept that a slap on the wrist was all he was going to get. Completely unfair, but sadly not unexpected. I supposed I should be grateful he didn't get to keep the promotion.

If I took the executive game designer job, I'd get everything I ever wanted. I could even devise a mentorship program aimed at finding people from underrepresented groups and teaching them to make games. There was so much good to be done.

But as I rode the T home that afternoon, it didn't feel like enough. Handing over the drawings Tyler and I made in order to get a promotion left me hollow. We worked on that game together, intending for it to be marketed and sold as one of my products. Not as part of BGG's line. Sure,

Tyler gave me all the pictures. He wasn't likely to raise a fuss, especially since he wasn't speaking to me. But using *Speak Easy* to get the promotion I'd earned a dozen other ways felt wrong. Did I want the job that badly?

One thing always helped me think: Nana's kitchen. More accurately, a conversation with Nana, coffee, and one of her homemade cupcakes. It was almost five o'clock, so she should be home from the hospital. I shuddered to think of the earful the doctors would have received if they tried to stop her from leaving.

"Nana, it's your favorite granddaughter!" I announced from the entryway. "Are you decent?"

She appeared in the doorway to the bedroom, fully dressed and wearing gloves. "Am I decent? What kind of a question is that? Michael and I were expecting you."

"Well, you're wearing rubber gloves, so maybe a valid one."

Playfully, she swatted at my arm, but her cheeks were turning pink. "Shush. Now give me a hug."

Dutifully, I crossed the room to wrap my arms around her, relieved to see her dressed and upright and not attached to any tubes. "How are you feeling?"

"Like a million bucks," she said. "Don't you worry about me. How are you?"

"You won't believe what just happened." Pacing the living room, I recounted my afternoon at the office. Halfway through, Nana brought me coffee, which I gratefully accepted.

"That's quite the offer," Nana said when I finally stopped to take a breath. "What are you going to do?"

"I have no idea," I said. "Honestly, I should probably take it. Take the raise, take the promotion, and get my games into the market. They don't need my name on them, do they?"

"Only you can answer that," she said. "That sounds like a solid plan."

"Yeah, it does." This coffee tasted good, but I needed something more. "I know you've had a lot going on, but do you have any cupcakes in the freezer?"

Before she could answer, I headed for the kitchen. According to Mom, there had been a revolving tray of baked goods in Nana's freezer since the Ford administration. The fact that she hadn't been home for a couple of days meant nothing. But when I entered the room, I stopped dead at the sight awaiting me. "What's going on?"

A massive stack of cardboard boxes leaned against the far wall. The cabinet doors stood open, and a medium-sized box sat on the ground, half full of brown-paper wrapped bundles that could only contain dishes. Michael knelt in front of the box, wrapping china.

"Oh, dear," Nana said. "I didn't want you to find out like this."

"Find out?" I repeated in a daze. For about three seconds, I'd let myself believe she just bought new dishes. "Are you moving?"

"Why don't you tell me your news first?"

"I already told you my news! Nana, tell me you're not selling the house."

"Let's have a seat and talk about this over an early dinner," she said. "The sauce is just about finished, and I was poaching eggs before you arrived."

Poached eggs. Hollandaise sauce. A glance at the oven showed a tray of bacon inside. I adored breakfast for dinner. If Nana was making my favorite meal when it wasn't my birthday, I absolutely did not want to hear what she was about to tell me. But it was too late. The boxes and the look on her face said it all.

Woodenly, I allowed Nana to lead me to the table. My knees bent enough to take a seat. Nana had lived below me for years. We ate breakfast together every morning. We chatted about life while Nana gardened in the summer or drank hot cocoa and baked together in the winter. She was the person I came to for advice whenever anything went wrong.

"Stop looking like you've been invited to my execution," Nana said. "I'm not moving to France."

"But you *are* moving?" Hearing it confirmed settled my heartbeat a little. Knowing the worst meant I could figure out how to deal with it.

She nodded. "To be honest, this has been a long time coming. It's getting harder and harder to climb the porch steps every day."

"You know I'd help you!"

"Well, that's wonderful," she said. "Because you never need to leave the house, so you're free to do nothing but help me up and down the stairs all the time."

Her words made me flush. "Okay, but what about an elevator or a chair lift?"

"They're expensive and would have to be removed when you eventually sell the house after I pass away."

"Don't talk like that." Then a horrible thought struck me. "Are you sick? I thought the doctors said—"

"Shh. I'm fine, dear. As long as I don't exert myself too much. Michael's place has an elevator. They also have a concierge service to help out with things like bringing deliveries up to the apartment."

"I do that, too," I grumbled.

"You've been a huge help to me," she said. "But I'm ready to let this old house go. I don't have the energy to do the repairs it needs, nor do I want to live in a construction zone."

I choked on my eggs Benedict. When Nana said she planned to move out, that seemed like the worst that could happen. But now...it sounded like I might have to leave, too. "Are you selling the place?"

Michael appeared in the kitchen doorway, plate in hand. He moved around the room, getting himself breakfast/dinner while he spoke. "Now, don't blame your nana, Shannon. This whole thing was my idea."

The "whole thing"? The hollandaise sauce turned to glue in my mouth. There was more? Nana got married and suddenly my whole world turned upside down? Unable to speak, I gulped my coffee while Michael settled himself at the table.

Finally, I said, "What are you talking about? You talked Nana into selling her home?"

"Don't be ridiculous," he said. "I'm not a gold digger, and even if I were, your grandmother is too smart to fall for some hustler."

"We were going to wait for the right time to tell you this," said Nana, "but it seems like the time is now. Don't stay at a job where you're not happy just for the money."

My brow furrowed at her words. "Thanks for the advice, but what does that have to do with anything?"

"We're giving you the house," Nana said.

"I don't need this place," I said, not quite understanding. "I live upstairs."

"Yes, I'm aware of that," she said dryly. "What I mean is, before the wedding, I signed a deed transferring ownership of the entire property to you. Consider it a gift."

My mouth fell open. "But why? How? I love you, but Nana, that's too much."

"No, it's exactly right," Michael said. "Under Massachusetts law, a marriage invalidates any existing wills. We didn't want you to lose out if your grandmother got sick before we had a chance to have our lawyer draw up new documents. Which very nearly happened."

"You were going to inherit the property anyway," Nana said. "But if I died without a new will, the house would've gone to Michael and your mother. Reviewing all our assets will take time. I couldn't risk you losing out on what's rightfully yours."

"It's not rightfully mine. It's your house. You bought it," I said.

"Yes, and you've taken care of me."

"Because I love you."

"And I'm giving you this gift because I love you," she said. "Neither Michael nor your mother needs a two-family house in Boston. Your brother will be taken care of in the updated will. Renting out my unit will give you steady income, which you can use to cover your personal expenses while launching your own business. The place needs some work, but we've set aside money to help you out with that."

"I can't take your money," I said.

"It's not up for discussion," Michael said. "We will be deeply insulted if you don't accept this thank-you. Also, it's finished. The deed can't be undone, and neither can the money transfer into your bank account this morning."

He held out an envelope. With shaking hands, I slit the top and slid a single sheet of paper out. The language was simple: *I, Rose Lynn Hendrickson, do hereby transfer the property located at 253 Beech Street, Revere, Massachusetts, to my granddaughter, Shannon O'Rourke, in consideration of years of love and affection and personal assistance.* The document was signed, dated the day before the wedding, witnessed by Michael, and notarized. In a daze, I looked back and forth from Nana and Michael to the paper multiple times.

Finally, I said, "Mom doesn't know about this, does she?"

"Wouldn't matter if she did," Michael said. "That's a copy. The original has already been filed with the Registry of Deeds."

"Don't worry about your mom," Nana said. "She's getting the bakery, which is worth plenty. She'll probably turn it into some kind of hippie health food store, but thankfully I'll be dead and won't know about it. Along with her shop in Florida, her hands will be plenty full."

Unable to resist, I jumped up and hugged them both. "I can't believe this. Thank you so much."

"You're welcome. I'll be out by the end of the month. You can convert the place to condos and sell this unit, sell the whole thing, or find a tenant. No matter what you choose, you should have enough money to focus on your own game company, if that's what you want." She patted my arm. "And, Shannon, if that's not what you want—you don't have to start your own business. You can find another job or accept the promotion or go backpacking through Europe. You only get one life. Do whatever will make you happy."

Emotion overwhelmed me, so it took a moment before I could respond. "You have no idea what this means to me. I can hardly believe it."

"Believe it," she said. "Now finish your food so you can help us pack."

Always practical. That was my Nana.

* * * *

After leaving Nana's apartment, I went straight for my phone and texted Ryan.

Me: *Hey. You won't believe what just happened. Are you free for a drink?*

Ryan: *How soon can you meet me?*

He named an Irish pub roughly halfway between work and my apartment.

Me: *I can go to you. It's no big deal.*

Ryan: *It's good. They have trivia later.*

Ryan: *I'm meeting Tessa.*

Ryan: *For a date.*

Me: *Cody's sister, Tessa? Excellent!*

Ryan: *Yeah. It's new. We got to talking after the focus group. But I'm hopeful.*

A huge smile split my face in two at the last message. Tessa had things rough with Preston's deadbeat father; she deserved someone who made her happy. As far as I knew, she hadn't dated anyone seriously since the boy was born two years ago. Good for them.

Me: *<3 <3 <3 <3*

Me: *I can be there in 20, as long as there isn't a game.*

Although I'd never been a big baseball fan, shortly after moving to Boston I'd discovered that it behooved me to check the Red Sox's schedule before taking public transit. Fans packed the trains before and after each home game, increasing travel time significantly. Sometimes walking took less time, especially when the Yankees were in town.

Today, however, the schedule favored me: About fifteen minutes later, I sat ensconced in a booth. When he arrived, Ryan threw back a couple of shots while I sipped a whiskey and soda.

"How's Zoe?" I asked.

"She's great, and you know I'll talk about my darling dog all day and night, except for right now. Tell me what happened."

With a grin, I filled him in on the details of my meeting with Jameson and Nana's very surprising gift. His eyes grew rounder by the second. When I got to the end, I asked, "How have things been for you?"

"Eh," he said. "No one seems to know what to say to me. Justin thought all transpeople were drag queens, which concerns me on several levels. But he wasn't a dick about me correcting him."

"Good. If anyone gives you a hard time, take the company to the cleaners."

"That doesn't sound like something management would say," he pointed out.

"You're not going to tell on me," I said. "Besides, I haven't decided whether to accept Jameson's extremely generous offer yet."

Ryan asked, "What's the alternative?"

"Part of me wants to take my savings and make a go of running my own business. The rental income from Nana's place will help. Thing is, I'm not sure I'm ready to go out on my own yet. I don't have much name recognition, and there's only one game ready to sell. I had another in the works, but..." I blinked a few times before waving that thought away with one hand. "Anyway, I could make it work for a little while. I met a lot of distributors at the convention who might help. At the same time, BGG has better contacts than I do. They've got vendor relationships; they can get me into conventions. And I keep coming back to something Jameson said during our talk: I can change the corporate culture from the inside."

"Then why are we sitting here? It sounds like you know what to do."

"Can I really make a difference? Will anything change? I put up with sexual harassment for years. The executive game designer reports to the board, but I wouldn't have hiring or firing authority. It would be easier for me to just put this entire experience behind me and move on."

"You're right," he said. "But easy isn't always better."

"I know. If I go, who will fight for the other non-cishet white dudes? The people of color, the queers, the women."

"Take a step back for a minute," Ryan said. "I appreciate you wanting to fix the company, but what's best for Shannon? What do *you* want to do?"

I stared at my drink for a long time, considering the question. Making games had always been my dream. But making games for adults, not kids. I wanted to make the kind of games my friends and I enjoyed playing, games like *The Haunted Place* or *Speak Easy.* It had taken years of dreaming and waiting before feeling adventurous enough to make that first game. If I took the job Jameson offered, it would mean long hours. Lots of late nights and early mornings, which translated to less time with Nana.

Ever since I started, Jameson had been the first person to get to work in the morning, the last to leave. We frequently received emails from him in the middle of the night. The big boss couldn't show up for work every morning at nine because she needed waffles with her granny on the way in. Would there be time for me to create anything of my own?

Finally, I met Ryan's eyes. The answer was as obvious as his nose ring. "I want to start my own company, create a positive work environment from the ground up instead of cleaning up someone else's mess. And I want you to be my partner."

His eyes lit up. "Do you mean it?"

I nodded. "Yeah, I do. We're stronger as a team. I've got one game ready to distribute and a second...close enough. Meanwhile, you can work on marketing and advertising to get the word out."

"That sounds amazing!"

"Now that Nana's given me the house, I don't have rent or a mortgage payment. I can rent out the entire downstairs. Along with my savings, we should be okay for a while." In time, I could start the search for another roommate, but my poor heart couldn't stand the thought at the moment. One thing at a time. "We can even work out of my apartment in the beginning to save money."

He nodded. "I've got some money saved, too."

"Let's do this. Quiltbag Gaming? Rainbow Gaming?"

"What about Gaming Plus? For the + at the end of LBGT+."

"Perfect," I said. "I love it."

"I can't wait to get started." He raised his glass, and we clinked. "Cheers!"

I smiled at my friend across the table. "Thanks. I've missed you. Now, get out your phone because I am *way* behind on my Zoe pictures."

Chapter 22

"Be yourself. Everybody else is taken. Everyone thinks Oscar Wilde said that. He didn't, but it's still good advice." —Nana

The next morning, I gave my two weeks' notice. Jameson was understandably surprised, but supportive of my decision. Bonus: The company would pay out the weeks of paid time off that I'd accrued but never used over the years. The additional cash made me feel even better about starting Gaming Plus.

That night, my friends came over for some much needed board-gaming. My brain welcomed the distraction to keep me from nursing my heartache over Tyler. An afternoon of cleaning and baking made me feel much better. I didn't have any answers, but at least I got a break from worrying over the questions swirling around my head.

"Tell me about your new game," Gwen said as she settled down at the table with a diet cola. "*Speakeasy?*"

"*Speak Easy*. Two words." Thinking about the new game reminded me of Tyler, which was the last thing I wanted to do. And yet, as avid gamers, I needed Gwen and Cody's perspective at some point.

I went to get the box containing *Speak Easy* out of my office. Before the game went to play testers, it needed at least two hundred fifty words and phrases to be used as passcodes. I'd taken to carrying a stack of note cards in my bag so I could add new ones at any time. People could add their own, and once Holly made the app we could add words at will, but to start, I needed a decent amount of variety. For the initial release, the words and phrases should be largely 1920s-themed, so I was nowhere near my goal.

"It's not ready to be played yet," I said. "But I can show you what I've got and see what you think."

Gwen and Cody joined me at the table, both wearing looks of excitement. Knowing how much they enjoyed my last game made me much more confident about sharing this one. My friends loved me and wanted me to succeed. They weren't going to rip the game apart.

"Essentially, one player is the owner of the speakeasy," I said. "The other players are people who want to come get a drink, but they have to guess the passcode. One person is secretly an undercover cop. If they can stop the other players from guessing the code, no one can get into the club and they all get arrested when the cops arrive. If the speakeasy patrons figure out the code, then they can hide inside and police will drive right by without seeing them."

"Love the theme," Gwen said. "How does the undercover cop stop people from guessing?"

"At the very beginning, after the owner selects the code from one of three drawn cards, and they place it faceup in the middle of the table. The cop is allowed to look before the owner takes the card back. Then he tries to stop everyone else from guessing by asking questions to lead people in the wrong direction."

"Interesting," Cody said. "I'm guessing there's a time limit?"

"Yeah, the low-tech game will come with an egg timer. The app will include a timer, which can be adjusted to change the difficulty."

"Excellent!" Gwen's eyes danced. "So if I'm the cop and I stop everyone from guessing the word, I win?"

"Maybe," I said. "The revelers get one chance to unmask you. If they do, they still win."

"Sounds cool. I like that there's something for everyone to do, even if they don't have a special role," Cody said. "That makes it a little more interesting than *Werewolves*."

"Right. You still have to figure out the passcode. That part is cooperative. And I'm working on some other special roles." This was the time to mention Tyler's involvement, but it hurt too much to think about him. I'd left the role sheet we'd worked on in my room, not even wanting them to see the artwork, as beautiful as it was.

Gwen asked, "How many does it play?"

"Four to ten at the moment," I said. "If the Kickstarter gains enough interest, I may do expansions with additional roles. And I'm also going to make a pure social deduction version. First, I want to get the details of this ironed out, make sure I have enough words, and get started on the app."

"Holly's not doing the app?" Cody asked.

"She'll help once the baby's born. But I know enough about the basics that I can start on my own."

Creating apps frustrated me endlessly, which made working on this one exactly what I needed to take my mind off how much I missed Tyler. I hadn't seen him since the day he moved out. When I texted him to say thank you for the drawings left behind and to apologize for upsetting him, he never replied. The silence hurt.

Cody spoke, breaking into those thoughts. "And it's cool that you'll have income now without needing the nine-to-five job."

"Yeah, I guess." The thought of Nana moving out still made my heart ache, but I knew it would be best for her.

"We realize this is probably a sore subject." Gwen settled into the seat across from me. I refused to look at the empty chair to her left, where Tyler should have been sitting. "But have you thought about what you want to do with Nana's apartment?"

"Going to start charging everyone who asks me that," I replied with a smile. "My brother called me this afternoon to talk about setting up a trust or giving him the lower unit at a 'family rate.' Then Mom called five minutes after he hung up."

Cody laughed and turned to his wife. "Told you so."

"No, it's fine," I said. "I'm sorry. I honestly don't know yet. I'll probably rent it out eventually, but I can get more money by doing repairs first. It's a question of how much I'd have to spend versus how much extra rent I'll get. I'm meeting with a Realtor next week."

Gwen and Cody exchanged a long look. Finally, Cody tilted his head upward, barely, and Gwen broke eye contact.

She said, "We have a proposition for you."

"Oh, yeah? You guys want to move in?" While posting Nana's apartment online and sorting through dozens of applicants to weed out the deadbeats, the scam artists, the racists, and other deplorable candidates didn't appeal to me at all, living above my best friends most certainly did.

She smiled and nodded. "The thing is, we could use the space. Cody and I are thinking about starting a family."

"Oh my goodness, that's amazing! Congratulations! I'm so happy for you!" Jumping up, I raced around the table to hug my friend.

Cody laughed. "Don't get too far ahead of us. We're not there yet. But we were talking about having some additional space. I thought maybe we could take some of the burden off you and do the work on fixing the place up in exchange for a discount on the rent."

"Also, you're two blocks from the beach," Gwen said.

Cody rushed to say, "I mean, we'll pay the current market value. Just not the market value if it were all fixed up. You save money on labor, we save on rent."

It all sounded too good to be true. At the same time, I was smart enough to know a good thing when I saw it. "How soon can you move in?"

By the time we finished talking about the logistics, the game spread out on the table before us, and Holly and Nathan were knocking on the front door. I let them in, happily sharing the news that I wouldn't have to sell or go through another long, drawn-out process of finding acceptable tenants.

"That's awesome!" Holly said. "Now we'll have three babysitters in one building."

I stuck my tongue out at her. "As if I won't be banging down your door to hug that little cutie as soon as she arrives."

As we passed the food around the table, I looked at my amazing group of friends. Maybe life had taken some twists and turns lately, but having everyone here reminded me that some things were still pretty great, too.

We chose our starting positions, took coins from the bank based on our player order, and began to play. Always the most competitive one, Gwen paid to go first. After so many years, Holly and I usually let her have it. Not Nathan and Cody. Gwen's father swore up and down he hadn't let her win a game since she was a little kid, and Gwen backed him up. Cody and Gwen had met as competitors, and their love never dampened the "game hate." They strove to beat each other, trash-talking from the second someone picked a game until we replaced the lid and put the box back on the shelf. Game hate stayed at the table, and their relationship worked for them.

Although their particular brand of love wouldn't work for me, I longed to find someone who got me as completely as they understood and cared about each other.

I wanted what Nana and Michael found together. The easy love and friendship Nathan and Holly shared. I wanted the easy camaraderie and companionship I experienced with Tyler. Not just as roommates, but as friends and partners.

As difficult as it had been for me to realize that I was fine on my own, that I didn't need a partner, it was just as tough to admit that it was also okay to want to be with someone. Freedom to be alone meant freedom to choose not to be alone, too. My life was great, I could live fully and happily without a romantic partner. But a romantic partner would enhance certain aspects of my life, and I wanted one. Not just "a partner," generically. I missed Tyler.

I loved waking up and sharing breakfast with him and Nana and Michael in the mornings when he joined us. I loved hearing him and Nana gardening together on the weekends while I worked in the office. I loved that we liked the same games, and the way he gave up his time to help me talk through a problem when I got stuck. I loved that we watched the same streamers on Twitch, the way he enjoyed baked goods with gusto, the way he always ordered extra takeout for me even when I wasn't home. He fit into my life so seamlessly that the loss of his presence exposed a gaping hole I'd never known existed, and I wanted him back. Not just as a friend and roommate, but as something more.

The time had come to make my move, because I owed it to myself to give us a chance.

Once upon a time, Tyler wanted to be with me. Over the summer, he knew how much I valued our friendship, but I'd hidden my developing attraction. Maybe part of me wanted him to sense it, to feel the change and say something, which was ridiculous. I couldn't fault Tyler for respecting my feelings when I said no rather than continuing to push. Especially not when I faulted other guys for doing exactly the opposite. He couldn't read my mind.

At this point, I didn't have any idea how he felt. He was in a relationship, and maybe he was happy. But he deserved to know the truth. He'd defended Megan against his roommate, like any good boyfriend. He couldn't know I wanted to be with him. I couldn't decide for him whether we would have a future together.

All of a sudden, I needed to talk to him. I could text him or send a video chat, but some messages needed to be delivered in person.

Before I could overthink things any more, I turned to Cody. "Where does Tyler live now?"

"He's been sleeping on our couch."

"He's not staying at Megan's?"

Cody and Gwen exchanged a glance. Finally she said, "I think they've been having some issues."

The wave of relief that hit me at her revelation surely made me a terrible friend, but he was much better off without her. "I need to see him. Do you know if he's home?"

He shrugged. "Want me to find out? I can text him."

"No, that's okay. Thanks." I worried my lower lip between my teeth for a minute, staring at the game board without seeing it. Then I leaned forward and plucked my piece off the board. "You guys finish without me. I've got something I have to do."

* * * *

Boston traffic crawled at the best of times, but now that I had somewhere important to go, it came to a complete standstill. After watching the same traffic light cycle three times without moving an inch, I seriously considered getting out of my car and taking the T to Cambridge.

Unfortunately, the Red Sox were playing one of their final home games of the regular season, so public transit would be a total zoo.

At least the parking gods smiled on me. Once I finally made it to my destination, a massive SUV left a spot right in front of Gwen and Cody's building. Pulling into the giant parking space felt like a victory before even speaking with Tyler. It had to be a good sign.

My heart thundered in my ears as I skipped up the steps and knocked on the door. What if he wasn't there? What if he looked through the peephole and refused to answer after seeing it's me? What if—

The door creaked open.

—he answered the door wearing nothing but a pair of rather tight workout shorts? Hello, Tyler. If possible, my heart beat faster.

"Hi." His voice lacked any emotion whatsoever. He might have been greeting someone passing out ads for a funeral home.

Not the reception I'd hoped for. My stomach dropped into my toes. Even when he moved out, it never occurred to me that our friendship couldn't be salvaged. All I did was try to save him from being with the wrong person. He never even gave me a chance to explain why he needed saving. Just cut me off.

Driving out here had been a huge mistake. Tyler didn't want me. But the little voice that got me out here in the first place spurred me on.

"I'm sorry," I blurted out.

"Go on." He stepped backward, leaving the door open. I followed him into the living room and perched on the edge of the couch. He hovered near the door to the kitchen. "Want something to drink? Water?"

I shook my head, then immediately realized that a long conversation would be easier if I wasn't so parched. Too late. I didn't know how to tell Tyler that my feelings for him had evolved over the past few months. My crush on him grew stronger every day. Too often, I lay in bed at night thinking about him, wishing he weren't in a relationship. With a deep breath, I went over the words I'd practiced so many times on the drive over.

"During the conference, I realized that I'd been developing an attraction for you. We've been friends for so long, it snuck up on me. That's why I was so rude to Liz when she started talking to you. I lied—absolutely, I was jealous. You flirting with another woman bothered me, even though you had no reason to think it would."

"I wasn't flirting—"

"I know. I get it now. But at the time, I thought you were. Everything stemmed from me freaking out. Realizing that I missed out on a good thing when I turned you down really threw me for a loop."

He wrinkled his brow. "But you said you couldn't feel attraction."

"Not without that deeper connection, no. But we have that now. Our friendship has evolved since you moved in with me. Or at least, I thought so."

"Yeah." Finally, I got the hint of a smile. "I thought so, too. Things were good."

I let out a sigh. "What happened? Why did you leave?"

"Two things," he said. "One, I decided to make things work with Megan. Maybe I should have told you, but I didn't think you'd want to hear it, especially with that stupid Pact. You were right; she didn't like us living together. We argued about me never inviting her over; we argued when she showed up uninvited that one night."

Right before stealing my password. But this wasn't the moment to tell him. Not when things were still so uncertain.

"I'm sorry," I said. "Maybe moving in while you were dating her was a mistake after all."

"I don't think so," he said. "Things were great for a while."

"True," I admitted. "You were an amazing roommate. You're kind, you're considerate. You never leave the toilet seat up. And you helped me kick Dennis's ass at *Construct Me*, not to mention all your help with *Speak Easy*. No one else could have done that."

He smiled, flashing those perfect white teeth. "That guy is the absolute worst. Handing his ass to him was my pleasure."

I laughed. "That was one of the greatest moments of my life. I've missed you."

"Are you asking me to move back in? Honestly, I miss you. But Megan would flip, especially after you got her fired."

"She told you about that?"

"Yeah."

"Did she tell you why?"

"I didn't ask," he said. "Since we're not roommates anymore, it didn't matter. But it's another reason I can't move back in. I can't be entirely comfortable knowing how you feel about someone who matters this much to me."

My heart sank as he spoke. I'd driven over here based on the assumption that his feelings for me still existed somewhere between the surface. Now it sounded like I was too late.

All of a sudden, I couldn't figure out how to tell Tyler the one thing that most needed to be said. He was so caught up in Megan's web, everything I said against her only allowed her to tighten her hold. Maybe once he knew how I felt, that I spoke entirely out of love for him, he would accept the truth more easily. This wasn't about me not liking her. It was about him deserving the best.

Words utterly failed me. Everything I wanted to say rang false in my ears.

Oh, well. Actions speak louder than words, right? Without another thought, I launched myself into his arms, and I kissed him.

He stiffened, then pulled back. "What are you doing?"

Oh, no. Definitely not the reaction I wanted. "I told you. Ever since the conference, I find myself attracted to you. More every day."

"Thank you," he said.

Ouch. That didn't sound promising at all. "You're welcome?"

"We have the worst timing." He sighed. "The thing is, like I said, I'm trying to make things work with Megan."

"I know, but I also know you used to have feelings for me. I thought some of that still existed. You needed to know that things had changed, that I want to be with you. Megan's not right for you at all. I am."

"Right," he said. "I get that you only started to find me attractive once I found someone else and now you want to sabotage our relationship. I appreciate you coming over, but you should go."

My ears must be deceiving me. After everything we'd been through? She'd gotten her hooks into him too deeply. Desperation filled my voice. "It's not like that, Tyler. I can't switch it on and off. My feelings have nothing to do with Megan. She would be wrong for you even if I hadn't had this epiphany."

"So you say."

"You really don't want to hear what happened? You want to walk away from this? From everything?"

"From everything? I don't know. Maybe we can still be friends. I'll see you at the store. But I can't be your roommate, and we can't be anything more. It's too late."

What was even happening? I'd played this scene in my head endlessly on the way over, but never once had it gone this badly. "I thought you understood that it takes time for me to develop an attraction to someone. It can't happen based solely on physical appearance."

"I do understand," he said, "but I couldn't wait forever. I've moved on. I'm sorry."

"Wait," I said desperately. "There are things you need to know. About Megan."

He shook his head. "Don't be like that. You're better than this."

Again, he was shutting me down. He didn't care about what I had to tell him. It's true what they say: There are none so blind as those who will not see. Stupid. I'd badly miscalculated. I should have told him the truth about her before mentioning my feelings. That way, he wouldn't have assumed jealousy motivated me. But it was too late now. Willing my legs not to shake, I moved away, needing increased space between us.

"So what happens now?" I asked.

"Now? You go home, I finish my workout. I order dinner and go back to looking for my own place. You work on your games. We lead our own lives. Maybe we'll see each other once in a while, and that's cool. If not, that's cool, too. We're adults. It's time to move on."

My heart broke, but there was nothing left to say. Megan had sucked him in too deep. So I stared at him, letting the seconds tick by. He met my eyes with an unwavering gaze. I listened to the beat of the music emanating from the neighbor's apartment for what felt like an eternity.

Nana once said that some people come into our lives and stay. These people become our friends, our chosen family. Others pass through, teaching us what we need to learn at the time our paths cross. Tyler came into my life when I needed a roommate, a muse. He helped me create a new game I loved, and he pushed me to start my own business.

Now it was time for our paths to diverge. I'd go home, make cupcakes, and cry. Then go to sleep, get up, start working tomorrow, and kick some ass. I'd make more board games. Like he said, we'd move on.

Separately. I wouldn't beg him to listen. I wouldn't ask Gwen or Cody or anyone else to intervene, to tell him the truth. Sooner or later, Megan would show her true colors, and Tyler would leave her. But I wouldn't force him to see the truth. It killed me to know she would hurt him, sooner or later, but he'd made his choice.

Finally, I broke eye contact and turned away.

Epilogue

"Love can be a giant pain in the butt. It's also worth it." —Nana

Two months later…

BoardGameNerd Con had been great, but Northeastern Gamer Con blew it out of the water. For one thing, I'd brought my extremely talented partner along with me, so we didn't have to deal with awkward sexual tension or unresolved jealousy. Even better, my lawyer brother had helped me negotiate a very lucrative distribution agreement with Board Game Giants, Inc. That deal gave Gaming Plus the influx of cash we needed to keep the doors open and paid for us to attend the conference.

Being allowed to present my games here thrilled me to the core, even if no one showed any interest. But on Friday morning, Ryan and I had lovingly unpacked about a hundred copies of *The Haunted Place*. By the time lunch rolled around on Saturday, five copies remained. Although Gwen started out as a travel blogger, as she gained popularity, she occasionally spoke about her life and other areas of interest. She blogged the entire American Board Game Championship a couple of years ago, so the online gaming community knew her. Her post the day *The Haunted Place* went up for preorder got tens of thousands of hits, and we'd received hundreds of orders. Now, two months later, conference goers couldn't wait to pick up their copies. The game had already succeeded beyond my wildest dreams.

Beside me, Ryan chuckled at a video of Zoe and Preston, sent by Tessa. They were taking things slowly, but their relationship seemed to be going well. Luckily, dog and child bonded instantly. Tessa was ecstatic to dog-sit during the conference. I turned to ask Ryan to show me the video again when a tall, dark head caught my attention through the crowd.

"Everything okay?" he asked.

"Hmmm," I said absently.

Of course, everything had to be okay. There wasn't a single reason in the world Tyler would be at this convention. As much as he loved games, he'd only gone to BoardGameNerd Con because I'd won the free passes. I must be hallucinating.

We hadn't spoken since the day he turned me down. A couple of days later, I mailed him a refund check for his security deposit, ready to put the entire non-relationship behind me. Some life lessons hurt worse than others, but I'd learned a lot about staying out of other people's relationships. Tyler deserved so much better than Megan, but he didn't want better. I only hoped he figured out the truth before she destroyed him.

Still, every day, something reminded me of him. Two weeks after he'd moved out, I found a note he'd left near the bottom of my tea canister, reminding me to buy more. A week after that, I found his missing Xbox controller on top of the fridge. I'd left it in Gwen and Cody's new apartment, trusting them to get it back to him.

If Tyler had come to visit them, he'd done it when I wasn't home. But even seeing Cody made my heart ache, as he reminded me of his friend. I wondered what could have been with Tyler if I'd handled things differently.

"Earth to Shannon," Ryan said. "Come in, Shannon."

"Sorry. What?"

"I said, I'm going to lunch. Do you want anything?"

I shook my head. "I'll go out and grab something when you get back."

"Okay. I won't be long."

"Take your time. I'm not hungry yet." With luck, by the time he returned, I'd have seen the owner of the close-cropped black curls I currently strained to glimpse again. Confirmation that at least two black men in the world wore that same haircut might help me get my mind off Tyler. If it didn't, I'd want a very large whiskey with lunch after Ryan came back.

He disappeared into the crowd with a smile and a wave. I watched him go, thinking about how much he'd changed. Still indisputably the same lovable guy, but now he walked with a quiet confidence he hadn't possessed before we started Gaming Plus.

He seemed more comfortable in his own skin. Personally, I enjoyed being able to walk around our office without seeing bikini pictures on screensavers or getting leered at or insulted. Once in a while I wondered how the environment at BGG changed after we left, if Dennis got the promotion after all, but I felt sure I'd made the right decision.

My phone pinged on the table beside me, and I picked it up to find a new email. Nathan and Holly had posted about a dozen new pictures on Tinybeans, an invite-only social media site for displaying photos and videos of your children. At three weeks old, Mariah's smile lit up the screen. Every day, my heart melted at the sight of her. Her laugh shook off the remaining dregs of melancholy that tried to sink its hooks into me when I spotted the guy who reminded me of Tyler.

Whoever it was still hadn't passed by again when Ryan returned carrying a sandwich.

"You didn't have to get your food to go," I said. "You could have taken an hour to eat somewhere else. I can manage on my own for a bit."

"I know you can," he said. "But I spotted something amazeballs, and you should see it."

My ears perked up. "Oh, yeah?"

"Yeah. Some dude over there set up a booth, but he's only selling a single copy of his game."

I deflated. For a split second, I'd been hoping he'd also seen the guy who resembled Tyler and came back to tell me he'd shown up. Stupid. "That's not that weird at this point in the conference. He probably sold out."

Ryan shook his head. "No, he only brought one copy. He's selling it for one kiss, but only to the right buyer."

Okay, that was not the response I expected. "It seems like there should be easier ways to get someone to kiss you."

"Maybe," he said. "Anyway, the game looks cool. Go check it out."

"I'm fine here."

He moved around to where I sat and tugged my wrists, bringing me upright. "Shannon. Go see this. Now. Don't come back for a while."

I sighed. I'd been sitting for several hours, so it would be nice to get up and move around a bit but I didn't feel like going to ogle some guy looking for a kiss. "Fine. But I'm not kissing some random dude to get you a game just because you have a girlfriend now."

"I wouldn't dream of asking you to." He grinned. "Take a left at the *Ticket to Ride* booth. Straight ahead. Can't miss it."

Following Ryan's directions, it didn't take long to find several people crowded around under a big sign that said "LIFE LESSONS." Was one of those lessons not to use kisses as a commodity for obtaining goods and services? I still didn't know why Ryan sent me here, until the crowd parted and the person running the booth appeared.

Tyler.

My breath caught in a gasp. What was he doing here? Selling a game? My Tyler didn't make games. Even when he helped me with *Speak Easy*, he worked on graphics and game execution. To my knowledge, he'd never been interested in making an entire game from scratch.

He looked up and spotted me, a smile spreading across his face. He beckoned me close, and the entire crowd turned. The realization that people stood here, waiting for me to show up, made my face burn. But when I got to Tyler and our eyes locked, everyone else faded away.

"So you fancy yourself a game designer now?" I asked.

"Not quite," he said. "There's only the one copy of my game, and it needs a play tester."

A box sat in the middle of the table, with LIFE LESSONS printed in large black letters on the top. Half a dozen drawings surrounded the text: Gwen and Cody, Holly and Nathan, Nana and Michael.

"Open it," Tyler said.

Lifting the lid, I found a white index card and read it aloud. "'They say never to discuss religion or politics. I say that's hogwash. If I meet someone with the poor taste to hate Justin Trudeau, I want to know right away.' That sounds like something Nana would say."

"Ding ding ding! Nana did say that. You get a point."

"So that's the game? Figure out who said what?" I shuffled through the cards, skimming them. Most of them were about love and relationships, but many of them spoke to me in Nana's voice or Gwen's or one of my other friends. "When did you do this? How?"

"I was working on it over the summer," he said. "Chatting with Nana while you were at work, writing down stuff she said. She loved the idea. It was going to be your Christmas present."

The game-designer half of my brain still didn't quite understand what was going on. "So how do you win?"

He pulled out the last card and held it out to me. It said simply, 'I love you.' When I looked back up into his eyes, finally, I got it.

He said, "I broke up with Megan."

"Good," I said. "Why?"

"Ryan told me everything," he said. "Texted me the picture of her with Dennis, and explained what she did to you."

"So you believed him?" To be honest, it hurt that Tyler would let Ryan tell him all the things I'd tried and failed to say. Why couldn't he have trusted me when it mattered?

"Kind of hard to ignore that picture. I wish you'd made me look at it, forced me to see the truth."

"I tried! You freaked out, took all your stuff, and left."

"I know. I screwed up. It took a lot of guts for you to come to me, tell me how you felt. Especially after I shut you down the first time you tried to warn me about Megan. After you left, I kept thinking about your courage. About how the person who became one of my best friends wouldn't try to wreck my relationship out of spite, despite what Megan told me."

"Thank you." Better late than never.

I'm really sorry," he said. "When I moved in, I thought I was over you. But being around you every day, I realized it wasn't going to happen. You're amazing. You're smart and talented and sweet and everything I'm looking for in a partner."

"Then why couldn't you trust me?"

"You weren't interested. I had Megan in my ear all the time, talking about how she thought you might be secretly dating Ryan."

A sputtering laugh escaped me. "That's ridiculous. Why wouldn't I have told you?"

"I know, I know, it sounds stupid. But she played on all my insecurities. We were going through a rough patch after I helped you win the *Construct Me* tournament; it almost broke us up. After the conference, she apologized and told me how much I meant to her. I committed to making it work since I couldn't have you. She's very good at concealing who she is. I didn't have any idea."

"That she is," I said. "I'm sorry I didn't tell you outright. She threatened Ryan, and I couldn't take a chance that she'd follow through."

"I know. He told me."

"So what now?"

He waved the card again. "I'm in love with you. I'm sorry I didn't listen, I'm sorry I left you in the lurch with the apartment. I want to start over and do things right."

I couldn't believe my ears. "You mean it? You love me? Even though I chose to protect Ryan over you?"

"You're a good friend. I could never hold that against you."

"I wanted to tell you. It killed me to watch you dating her. But early on, I couldn't articulate why I had such a bad feeling about her. It took time before she revealed her true colors." An invisible string drew me toward him, my upper thighs pressing up against the edge of the table. My hand landed on the place where his rested beside the game box. "I've missed you."

"I've missed you, too." He caught my eyes, his mouth widening in a slow, sexy smile that made my heart pound. "I'm willing to move back in if you'll have me. Unless, of course, you've already found a new roommate."

"I haven't, no." I took a deep breath. It was now or never. He'd put himself on the line in Mexico, and I'd shot him down. Sure, he shot me down too, but he took another risk by flying here in the first place. Now it was my turn. "But I'm not looking for one. I'm looking for something more."

"Oh, yeah?"

A person could lose themselves in the depths of his gorgeous brown eyes. I took the plunge. "Yeah. I want to be with you. I realized it at the convention. I never should have waited to tell you."

He tugged on my fingers, pulling my hand to his chest. I leaned forward, lips parted. Tyler met me halfway. His lips were every bit as soft as I remembered from that aborted kiss on the beach, so long ago. This time, fire swept through me at his touch, and I forgot where we were. I ran my fingers over his jawline, imprinting his features on me. My tongue dipped into his mouth, dancing with his in the way I'd wanted for so long. When we finally broke apart, I could hardly breathe.

One thing still bothered me, though. "If you and Megan were having problems, why were you looking for the tie she gave you before Nana's wedding? What made that your lucky tie?"

"It's the one I was wearing the day you agreed to let me move in with you."

My heart swelled until I thought it would burst. All this time, he was waiting, patiently, letting me know he cared without being oppressive or obnoxious about it. "I'm glad I did. I'm so in love with you."

"I love you, too," he said, kissing me again.

Nearby, someone applauded. Dimly, I realized that Ryan must have followed me to the booth to see what happened. No one else would stand by to watch our reunion, or get excited by two people kissing in the middle of a convention. I pulled back, before leaning in for just one more quick kiss. "Do you want to get out of here?"

"I thought you'd never ask," Tyler said. "There's a *Construct Me* tournament starting at one, and I need a partner. Care to join me?"

A sound of pure joy escaped me. "Nothing would make me happier."

ACKNOWLEDGMENTS

Once again, a huge thank-you to my editor, Wendy McCurdy, for giving me the opportunity to write a nerdy board game series. I had a blast. There's so much of me in these books. Thanks also to Norma, Lauren, Alex, and everyone at Kensington for your unending support and willingness to answer random questions all the time.

Thank you to my critique partners: Laura Brown, Marty Mayberry, Kara Reynolds, and Farah Heron. I know that writing so many books so close together meant a lot of leaning on you and more hand-holding than usual, and I appreciate it more than I love board games.

Thank you to all of my Mensa friends for unknowingly lending your names to this project (especially Megan and Dennis). You may have become minor characters in this series, but you're major players in my life. An extra-special thank-you to my darling husband, Andrew. You are my light, my love, the inspiration for this series, and the one person I never want to imagine life without.

Special thanks to everyone who entered my contest to name Ryan's dog, especially Zoe's owner, Heidi Robbins. Your beagle is absolutely the cutest. Thank you to Lara, Padma, and everyone at the YMCA's Child Watch program. This book never would have been finished on time without you.

And as always, thank you to my amazing agent, Michelle Richter. Look! We've got six books together. J

Honorable mentions to the creators of the games mentioned in or borrowed for this story: *Instructures*, *Shadows over Camelot*, *Speakeasy*, *Werewolves*, *Don't Mess with Cthulhu*, *The Thing*, *Donner Dinner Party*, *Secret Hitler*, and *Werewords*.

Printed in the United States
by Baker & Taylor Publisher Services